Antagonize: From the Logs of Daniel Quinn

www.thomasrmanning.com

I0532478

Cover Design: Megan Kennedy www.abuseofreason.com

ISBN: 978-0-9895068-3-0

For my father, who has taken the journey

beyond the final frontier.

I love you dad, and I'll see you again one day.

There's something to consider when you're traveling between alien planets—they have no idea how to cook a human meal. I sat in a bistro, created by the Karthans to facilitate comfort for smugglers and travelers who delivered to their planet, and all the while I stared down at the plate of 'food' and used my fork to poke at the grey looking pasta. The respite was a welcome one though, considering I wanted to lay low and stay hidden from any prying eyes throughout the galaxy.

That's when a distraction in the form of a young alien joined me at my table, his small, oval shaped mouth turned in a wide grin. His skin was pale blue and there were no ears on the sides of his head. Instead a pair of antennae protruded from his thick, blue hair. I knew he wasn't a Karthan because they never showed themselves to you above the surface of their planet.

"Rotu nah-oh," he said to me in a high pitch voice. "Nah-oh ja Daniel Quinn!"

I recognized the language . . . He was a Restran from the planet Tristain. I never traveled there personally, but I spent the past year familiarizing myself with all of the aliens and languages in my ship's database. Twice in my mind I played his words over so I could translate them.

I know you, you are Daniel Quinn!

Confusion would be an understatement. I figured Karth to be the perfect planet to visit. From outer space it appeared desolate and floated within toxic nebulae, making you wonder how the damn thing was habitable. I arrived less than a day ago, transporting chemicals and weapons to their dock, and now I sat waiting for payment. Smuggling jobs were the only kind I accepted. When you use the Starcade to apply for jobs, you risk taking something more extreme, such as sending a message to the buyer's enemy or outright killing someone.

Somehow in my short time here, this Restran found me. Alarms in my head rang out, warning me that potential danger could lie ahead. The Restran just sat there with the goofy grin on his face and tapped two of his four fingers on a computer tablet of some kind.

I did my best to appear hospitable to the young being, but under the table I cocked back the hammer of my revolver.

"Ih na, buu Ihn rinya ri tis karta-oh," I said. *I am, but I'm confused why that excites you.*

"Oh ja rikrik?" *Are you kidding?* The more he spoke my mind translated the words—almost in real time—making it less difficult to understand him. "You're a hero! Is it true that you went to an uncharted planet and saved the lives of the natives?"

I nearly fell out of my chair when he described my time on the planet Dawn. How the hell could he possibly know this, unless he was working with one of the enemies I made on the planet? I slowly gripped the handle of my gun, wrapping my finger against the trigger.

"Who the hell are you and how do you know about this?" My voice broke slightly.

Tress's excitement faltered as he registered my confused, frustrated expression.

Don't dwell on the past. Just worry about the present, I thought. I breathed deep and exhaled slowly in an attempt to relax.

"You know about me, and you've met me, but you still haven't told me what you're doing here or how you found me in the first place."

"I can answer that for you, Captain," a voice said from the entrance. Turning, I found a stocky man gripping the door frame. His forehead glistened and his chest heaved.

Although there were accommodations for humans, the chances of two of us being on Karth at the same time were slim. The man stepped over to my table, favoring his left foot as he did so. My stomach churned like a raging tornado and I felt cornered. I blinked hard, disguising it by rubbing my eyes. When I opened them again my right eye—a bionic one that replaced my biological eye after a skirmish against Sarah King—displayed a series of scans and readings of my surroundings, including the human and Restran. From the outside, the eye appeared real unless I shifted my vision to night or thermal imaging so they didn't know I was scanning them. The human's pulse was racing, his heartbeat dangerously high, but he didn't carry any luggage or even identification. All he had was his clothes. His clean shave and combed hair made his appearance this far out in the galaxy odd. And when I looked at the Restran, a faint energy signature emanated from behind him. A weapon?

"His name is Tress," the man said, his hand gesturing toward the alien beside him. "And my name is Damon Derringer. Tress's planet is within the same solar system as mine, Captain Quinn. I enlisted his services to help locate you. It would seem that I made the right call." He gave the young alien's back a large pat. His hands, however, trembled. The alarms in my head and my uncomfortable stomach—they indicated something was wrong here—and I'd be damned if someone tried to make a fool out of me.

I eased my revolver from its holster, lifted it above the table, and pointed it at Derringer.

"Captain! What are you doing? I'm not here for trouble!" He practically spit out the words as he raised his hands.

"I don't really care who you are," I said with agitated roughness. "The fact that the two of you know who I am makes me nervous, and I don't like being nervous."

"Please, sir—"

"Shut up." I kept my composure calm. If things escalated, I wanted to maintain control. "The last time a strange man joined me at a table, it resulted in a few near-death experiences and he almost enslaved an alien race. So here's what we're going to do.

Get up and get out of my sight before I count to three and pull the trigger."

"Captain!" he yelled as I counted to one. "I know about what happened on Dawn! That's partially why I'm here!"

"Two," I growled. Damon backed away to the door.

"Please, sir! Just let me explain! I am here for your help!"

A high intensity plasma beam burned straight through Damon's midsection and passed within inches of Tress. A smoking black hole was scorched into the wall of the bistro. Damon didn't get a chance to react. One second he lived and pleaded for his life, and the next he fell onto the table, dead.

I never counted to three. I didn't fire my weapon. The target reticle in my eye scanned behind Damon's last position where a hole had been burned through the door.

Tress dropped to the floor squealing as I jumped behind a table for cover. My hands gripped the revolver hard as I kept myself low to avoid the additional shots, but none came. I risked a glance to the side, but no one attempted to fire on me.

Seconds later, energy shields activated and dropped from the window and door frames. We were locked in, and even better, the killer was locked out.

The Karthans don't take well to killing, especially when an off-worlder does it. The planet's surveillance system was advanced by my standards. An electronic security web runs down from the dock to the town, and everything is under the scope of a camera. Whoever shot Damon Derringer, it's likely the Karthans were pursuing him now.

With the blast shields activated, I felt safe enough to stand and take stock of the situation. The weight of Damon's body on the table caused it to topple during the lockdown, and he was now on his back, facing the ceiling. The wound in his chest smoked and smelled like charred meat. It had been cauterized from the plasma. Tress stood beside me and stared at the recently deceased.

"Is he gone?" he asked.

In reply, I shoved him against a wall with my forearm and pushed my gun under his jaw. His hands flailed and smacked my arm and the wall, but I was stronger. His mouth moved erratically and his eyes shifted color to a shade of indigo, which announced his fear.

"Enough! What do you want with me?" I asked. The revolver's chamber spun and charged its plasma round. The weapon was lighter and more compact than my multi-chamber rifle that I destroyed some time ago. I'd spent months building the new one. Well, no, that's a lie. Technically I built it, but my advanced artificial intelligence on the Belle instructed me on how to do it.

"Please," he muttered. "Please, please... don't kill me! We came here to talk to you!"

"Right." I growled. "Talk. Except your buddy down there has a hole blown through him, so the time for talking is over."

"I don't know anything about that! I don't know why he was shot! Please! I don't want to die!" The alien, no older than a teenager, cried out hysterically. The indigo in his eyes glowed brighter and radiated a neon kind of intensity. My conscience overpowered my survival instinct at that point and I eased off Tress.

There was a time when I couldn't hurt a bug, let alone another humanoid, but after the events on the planet I named Dawn, I wasn't sure what kind of person I was anymore. I killed men on that planet and now I had been ready to kill Tress.

Get a grip Daniel, I thought.

A loud humming emanated from behind the bar across the room. A small, square-shaped droid hovered toward our position. At the top of the cube, a bright read beam scanned Damon Derringer.

"Human. Dead," it said in perfect English. Behind the robotic voice and static, I heard another voice with intonations native to the Karthan language. Since Karthans kept to themselves underground, they used service bots and droids to play as hosts to visitors. Rumors suggested that they were short people, half my size, and large around the midsection. I also heard the under city of planet Karth was a thriving utopia, but since they never allowed any aliens access, none of the rumors ever changed to facts.

These droids were controlled by operators and I could only assume depending on the alien species, that each droid was outfitted with a vocal translation module. The droid rotated and scanned the two of us.

"Human. Restran. Elevated heart rates and minor scratches, but no critical injuries detected. Do you require assistance?"

"Just finish my payment so I can get off this rock," I said while moving to a table with a little less Damon on it. The droid lingered but when Tress didn't say anything, it returned to its point of origin behind the bar.

Tress reluctantly joined me at my table, his hands entangled in one another and shoulders hunched. He never took his eyes off of Damon.

"So, you're not going to do anything?" His voice was soft.

I shrugged. "If you don't have any idea what Damon wanted me for, then it's none of my concern."

The words felt foreign as they left my mouth. I was jarred by the murder of another human being who seemed innocent. I wanted to stay off everyone's radar as best I could, but the knowledge he had of me and my past left me wondering what he wanted. Of course, that answer died with him.

"He wanted your help" Tress said. "He said you could save lives . . . that you are a hero."

I laughed. I never thought of myself as a hero. A hero saves lives, sacrifices his needs over others. Was I a hero when I saved Captain Gregory Smithson's life on the Echelon? If I didn't act, Sarah King wouldn't only have taken the ship, but also his life and the artificial intelligence program. But in the end, the captain and I fled. King still got the ship, killed people, and even used my best friend Jason Hobbes as a cyborg experiment.

Was I a hero when I saved the Dawnians? It was my fault they were discovered in the first place. Sarah King and Raymond Erebos had the information on its location, but they would have needed months, maybe years to translate it all. I found it and tried to sell it, and that led them to the most powerful energy source in the galaxy. How did I save the Dawnians? I blew up their processing facility and destroyed their technology which harvested the energy. King and Erebos didn't get it, but now no one could.

Hero was the last title I'd give to myself. If anything, I'm just a guy who gets in over his head and has to make up for it later.

The droid's buzzing sound returned. It hovered toward me.

"Is my payment complete?" I asked.

"We would like to negotiate the terms of your contract, Captain," the voice said.

"No, absolutely not," I replied. "We agreed the price on the contents I delivered—$575,000. I am not lowering it."

"Nor are we. In fact, we would like to double the amount."

My jaw gaped open. With more than a million dollars I could refit the Kestrel Belle, get her engine replaced, strengthen the hull, and more. But the Karthans weren't just offering that money freely. No one ever did, especially not after an establishment was damaged with me in it.

"What are your new terms?"

"The murderer of your fellow human has proven difficult to apprehend. We would like to hire your services."

"Why me?" I asked, interested in the offer, but curious about why they weren't looking elsewhere. Smuggling items was the best use of my mercenary talents. I sorely lacked skill in the bounty hunter department.

"You are the only other human on this planet, which makes you somewhat responsible for this situation. Our security droids have been unsuccessful up to this point and we feel a sentient life form above the ground may benefit our efforts."

"Wait a second, how the hell am I responsible for this? This man came to me. I was here first. It's not my fault he got himself shot."

"Those are our rules Captain," it replied. "Visiting species on our planet are responsible for their own kind."

"Well, all you had to say was *please*," I said with a sarcastic tone. I guess I should be glad Damon died in front of me and not on the other side of the planet. In truth, I could really use the money, but did I really want to go up against Damon's murderer? Was he killed for talking to me? And if so, why? What information did he intend to give me before his death? Did he have sensitive information he intended to give me before his death?

If Damon was murdered for talking to me, that meant I was already involved somehow. All I could do at this point was speculate, but it nagged at me—Did the killer have the same information on me that Damon did? He might have shot me after all, but missed his opportunity when the barriers dropped over the bistro. Right now I was safe, in the sanctuary of a protected building, but what about after?

"What can you tell me about the murderer?" I asked.

"Leondren male," the droid said. "We estimate his height at seven feet tall. Weight unknown. He is currently advancing to the docking gate and carrying a briefcase that likely holds the weapon responsible for the murder of the human."

Leondren. I heard that name before, likely from researching the alien database with Al on the Belle. I couldn't picture them or recall their capabilities, but he was obviously a skilled marksman. He managed to accomplish a precise kill shot from outside the bistro without collateral damage.

"Is it just one Leondren?" I asked.

"Affirmative."

There was considerable danger going after the killer, but it could be worth it for the payout. Money wasn't everything to me, but at the same time it made the starships go around the galaxy.

"Alright, I'll agree to your terms," I said, pushing my thumb to a print scan on the droid. "I'll make an attempt to apprehend this Leondren, but if I find my life at risk I have the option to pull out and receive my original payment."

"Agreed, Captain," the droid said. The entrance's barrier deactivated. I stood and moved forward with my revolver still in hand, the plasma charged and ready to fire. I turned back to Tress, who sat there silently the whole time, his eyes still the same fearful color.

"You stay here. If you're associated with Derringer, then you may be target as well."

His eyes glowed, but he nodded at me.

"Be aware, human Quinn, you are advancing into danger," the droid warned.

"Yeah, don't I always," I muttered.

I ran for the dock. The town looked to be deserted. The buildings were covered in light brown sand and metal barriers covered all the windows and doors. I ran past domed buildings, ones which ended in sharp points, some square and others circular. Each building was designed with the idea of familiarity and comfort to any visiting species. The bistro I dined in, or lack thereof before things got tense, was constructed when the first human scheduled a visit to Karth. The actual surface of the planet was a desert—all sand and rock. There may have been plant life, maybe something reminiscent of cacti on Earth, but none within view. The biggest problem for me was the humid weather and bright sunlight, which left me sweating and panting after about a hundred steps. I'm in pretty good shape, but the heavy atmosphere from the gases surrounding the planet caused my lungs to argue with me. I imagined my lungs saying, 'this is why you should carry an oxygen mask with you'. My body begged me to stop and rest, but I pushed harder.

I saw bodies when I was about halfway to the docks. They weren't humanoid or alien—they were the security droids, all of them scattered on the ground. Claw marks covered their metallic bodies and wires hung from limbs. I couldn't guess how many of them were there. Plasma burns striped the ground, but not the droids. Using my bionic eye I scanned over the area. The plasma fire was consistent with the type of rifle the droids were equipped with. Could the killer seriously tear these machines apart that easily, alone, through those blasts? I continued with caution.

By the time I reached the large, gray walls separating the world from the starships, my clothes were damp with sweat, which also burned my eyes. A crowd of aliens were pounding and screaming on the sealed doors. I couldn't recognize most of the aliens by their appearances. A few of them were half my size with silver spiky hair and long arms hanging down to the ground. A handful of others wore thick white robes that covered their entire bodies, but their bare feet looked soft and round, almost like a suction cup. Their fingers ended in the same shape. I also caught glimpses of a family—two adults and a child, their skin light brown and textured with lines crossing over each other. A Karthan announcement repeated over the loud speaker. The aliens must have been outside the buildings before the security measures had activated. I couldn't translate the entire announcement through all the noise, but it basically said the doors were sealed due to criminal action on the planet.

This was a lost cause. Even using my bionic eye I could detect dozens of different weapon signatures. I dropped to the ground, exhausted from the thick air and frustrated at the sight in front of me. I didn't know what I was supposed to do next.

"They all swarm the gates like insects, don't they?" The deep, raspy voice startled me.

I jumped to my feet and spun to find a . . . well . . . a lion. He looked enough like one, except he stood on two feet like a human would. A radiant brown mane surrounded his head and his flat, wide nose ended in triangular nostrils. We stared at each other and goose bumps crawled up my arms and legs when his humanoid round eyes contracted into slits, the irises colored gold. He produced a sly smile, which showed white teeth formed into sharp points. He wore form fitting armor the color of dull silver. Held at his side was the long, metallic case the Karthan droid mentioned.

"For a Leondren, you speak English well enough," I said I felt my heart beat against my chest a little faster, but I remained outwardly calm. He bowed to me.

"I am humbled by your knowledge of my race."

We both assessed each other. Every second that passed, the crowd at the doors grew louder. My fingers twitched and the hand around my gun tightened its hold. My legs argued for movement, but I forced myself to stay still.

"So . . . are you looking to get off this rock like the rest of the . . . what did you call them . . . insects?"

"I am. My job here has been completed," he replied. His composure was calm, his smile warm and welcome. It made my stomach churn.

"And that job was? Do you mind me asking?"

"I do not," he said. "I am proficient in silencing individuals who step over their bounds." He talked as if he were boasting about his job. The hairs on the back of my neck stood erect. Despite the Karthans hiring me to apprehend him, the Leondren seemed conversational. Why not push the discussion further?

"You're an assassin," I suggested.

"I suppose your kind would give it that title, yes."

His composure, his mane hovering in the soft wind, he looked like he could crush a stone in the palm of his hand. Would I even have time to raise my revolver? I could only assume that the Karthans were sending more security forces this way, so maybe I just needed to keep him busy until then.

"You silence people, even when they're defenseless? Can you justify murder when a man's back is turned?"

"When the price is right, I can justify anything," he said, a soft purr emanating from his throat. His voice was cold, as if he didn't care for anyone. I swallowed hard but tried to look calm.

"What's your name?" I asked him.

"Granak," he replied. "And I already know your name, Daniel Quinn."

That didn't surprise me.

"Well, Granak, what happens next? Your contract here is done. I know you killed Damon Derringer, but what about me? How do I fit into all this?"

To my surprise, Granak laughed.

"I will not be killing you, Daniel Quinn. At least, not yet." He turned toward the crowd and walked away from me.

That was it? Not yet?

I pointed my revolver at his back.

"Granak! You aren't going anywhere. Stop right there or I'll open fire."

He stopped and looked over his shoulder at me, the smile on his face never faltering. He regarded me, then the crowd of aliens at the dock.

"If you miss your mark, Captain, you'll kill one of these helpless insects."

I hesitated. That was all the time he needed. Granak reached into his pocket and pulled out some kind of mechanical sphere. My bionic eye acted instinctively and scanned it. A sonic detonator.

I fired a direct plasma blast, thinking I could hit him before he threw it, but he let go as the shot hit him in the upper back. I watched as the sphere traveled toward the crowd. My breath stuck in my throat. They were all about to die. Maybe there was no hope, but that didn't stop me from screaming at them.

"Everybody down! Detonator!"

The device exploded just before making impact. A violent shockwave erupted from the source of the explosion, hitting me like a shuttlecraft. My eye flashed static, my eardrums blew out, and it felt like all oxygen was forced out of me, my lungs and body burning with the need for air. The ground came up and hit me. I couldn't hear a damn thing except a high pitch ringing, and when I touched my ears I felt blood. I opened my human eye, though blurry, and watched as Granak walked through the aftermath. He stepped on bodies, or what was left of them, as he strode toward his escape, his hulking mass taking his time and surveying his work.

All I could think about was the number of aliens he killed and his careless attitude toward life. I pushed myself up to pursue him, but fell in a dizzy haze before I could take a single step. All I could do was watch as his ship, nothing but a giant blurry spot to me, took off into space.

Meanwhile, a voice in my head kept asking, *What the flux am I supposed to do now?*

TWO

"You have sustained hearing loss, Captain. There will be bruising on various parts of your body from being flung by the explosion and your ankle has been sprained, but otherwise all injuries are minimal."

We were back inside the bistro. I couldn't hear the medical droid speak, obviously, but a screen on its chest flashed the diagnosis to me. I nodded to him as I jammed my fingers in my ears, attempting to clear out a blockage that wasn't there. Inside my head a battle raged between a solid high pitch noise and a constant ringing.

Shortly after the explosion and Granak's escape, Tress came to investigate and found me lying on the ground with blood oozing from my ears. He helped me walk back into town, which I had to admit was impressive, especially considering I threatened his life less than an hour earlier. I later learned that only two other aliens survived, though both were missing appendages, while I got away with a twisted ankle, a few cuts and bruises, and the hearing loss.

Tress didn't understand the concept of hearing loss, and as such he felt it necessary to blabber on about how sorry he was for the position he put me in. The medical droid was kind enough to type out Tress's apology to me, though I wasn't terribly interested. All I could think about was how fluxing stupid I was for landing on this forsaken rock of a planet.

Two disposal droids were bagging Damon's body. The image of him being shot replayed in my head, and as it did I noticed things. Both Tress and Damon came looking for me, but Granak only killed Damon. At first I thought the barriers stopped him from killing Tress, but if that's the case Granak wouldn't have told me his job was completed. Didn't Damon say something about their planets being in the same solar system? If that's true, Damon was marked before he even left his home planet.

If I knew I was going to die, but I had to find someone, how would I pass on my information? Find a partner to deliver the message I couldn't. But Tress didn't know anything, unless he was lying to me. Then I remembered the faint energy signature coming from behind him.

"Tress," I tried to say, but not hearing my own voice was jarring. I must have screamed at him, because he jumped as I spoke. I grabbed his hips and spun him around in a circle, then reached into his waistband and pulled out a metal, rectangular object.

An electronic memory drive. Damon Derringer you smart son of a bitch, I thought.

Tress screamed out something, but I couldn't even read human lips, let alone alien ones. I pointed toward the medical droid and typed on the keyboard.

"This drive can record and contain memories and files. I use something similar to record logs on my ship. Damon must have known someone was following him," I said. Tress's eyes turned pale blue, but I didn't know what that meant. I reminded myself to ask Al what the color combinations within Restrans' eyes meant.

The droids finished the containment process for Damon's corpse. They loaded him onto a large hover bed and the droid closest to me turned and spoke to the medical one.

"Where would you like the body?" The words on the screen said to me.

"Um, come again?" I typed.

"You are the only other human on the planet, Captain. You are granted all rights to the corpse and are required to transport it off Karth."

"Flux." What the hell was I supposed to do with a corpse on my ship? I didn't know this man or where he came from. What were the Karthans going to do about the various remains of aliens around the docking gate? Call their native planets and request a pick up?

"We do not understand your use of language, Captain. If you are unable or unwilling to remove the corpse, we do have the option of vaporizing it."

I nearly said yes just to have it finished, but my conscience took over. This man traveled far to find me, and to leave him on this barren rock would be a disgrace to whatever legacy he may have held back home. But maybe his memory drive would tell me where he came from. Would it be such a bad thing to return his body to his family?

"No," I typed. "I'll take him. Deliver him to the Kestrel Belle, docking platform thirty."

"Yes, Captain. In regards to the Leondren, we are still willing to hold our terms of the contract."

"Forget it," I said. "That lunatic spent no effort killing a dozen aliens at the dock. Just pay me the original fee."

"His attack on our dock escalated our need to capture him," the droid typed. "If you will pursue and apprehend the Leondren, we will not only pay you $3 million Earth dollars, but we will submit favorable Starcade ratings to your account."

"Ratings . . . as in plural?" The Starcade is an intergalactic bulletin board for mercenaries, rogues, and anyone trying to work outside the law. It's a simple system where you apply for a job and, depending on your rating and reputation, you're either hired or you're not. Often times I was looked over because of my low rating. Give me a smuggling or courier job and I had no problems getting it done, but a lot of Starcade jobs required assassinations, signs of violence, and outright murder. I wasn't comfortable with that, and I lost a lot of job opportunities because of it.

If the Karthans were willing to make this new deal, I wouldn't just have a ton of money to spend on the Belle and myself, but my Starcade rating could rise high enough to earn me better jobs with better pay. How could I turn that down?

But I would have to face Granak again. If another face off situation arose, did I have any chance of winning? For all I knew he was halfway across the solar system by now, on his way to a new job and target.

"I agree," I typed. "But I want an advance of my original payment."

The Karthans agreed. Now I had the money I was originally promised, with more on the way provided I take down Granak. If I never saw him again, it would be no different to me. Something in the back of my mind told me we would meet again, though.

An hour passed as my cargo was loaded. The medical droid was able to manufacture a serum compatible with human biology and the ringing in my ears slowly faded, but was replaced by bleeps and bloops of the computer in front of me. I could hear Tress muttering something, too. But my hearing wasn't completely restored, and everything sounded as if it came from across the room.

The Karthans cleaned up the mess Granak left behind while I checked over my weapon and armor, and signed the new contract for the Karthans.

"Captain Quinn," the bistro's service droid announced. "Your cargo has been successfully loaded and your ship has been cleared for departure."

"It's about time," I muttered as I stood. Tress followed suit. Stars above. I didn't even think about him, but obviously I couldn't leave him stranded. I still felt guilt over threatening his life. But maybe I could make it up to him. Damon mentioned Tress lived in the same solar system, so I could drop him off on his home planet on the way.

"Doratu no ja!" I said sternly to him. *Listen to me!* Finding the right words to say in his language took me a while, but I managed to roughly say, "You follow my rules on ship. You lock door to your room if there is trouble. You leave ship if we need to abandon. Understand?"

He nodded his head violently.

"Ta!" *Yes.*

Get a grip Daniel, I thought. *He's a frightened teenage Restran. It's not like he's a cold, ruthless, assassin who seems to befriend you only to betray you later.*

Oh wait, that was my last passenger.

The docking gate was ruined when we approached it. Entire sections of the surrounding wall were missing, cut out in the shape of Granak's sonic shockwave. I walked past it and wondered whether the ground I stepped on was actually dirt or dusted remains of the fallen aliens. Somewhere in dock, a number of ships were now up for grabs without a pilot to captain them. The thought nearly brought me to tears. Being a captain myself, I was affectionate of my ship.

I found her right where I left her; the Kestrel Belle. The model was an antique design—only a handful of Kestrel class cruisers remained afloat in space—but she was nimble and quick. She resembled her namesake, the falcon. The bow ended in a sharp point, which faced downward like a beak, the midsection was elongated and smooth, and the wings curved outward with the slingspace turbines attached at their backs. Her color was supposed to be dull silver, but various sections on the belly and starboard wing were bronze-colored plates that had been fused to the original hull to repair damage.

Two carrier droids that prepared Damon's body hovered down the ramp to my cargo bay.

"Cargo is secure, Captain," the one on the right said with a faint sound of Karthan language still audible behind the droid's voice. "Don't forget our agreement. Deliver the Leondren criminal to us, dead or alive."

"I haven't forgotten," I told them.

When I stepped onto my ship, all the stress and worry of the day slowly evaporated. I was home. The Belle was a three-deck ship. The cargo bay was the size of a miniature warehouse and was the only way to get on or off the ship. Technically there was an escape hatch outside the bridge, but I could never get the fluxing thing open. The ladder at the end of the cargo bay led to the second deck of the ship, which held a very empty and cobwebbed armory. From there you could gain access to the third deck, engineering, and the first deck with the bridge and crew quarters.

I made checking the cargo my first order of business. The Karthans surprised me with the research they conducted on our species. Damon's remains were placed in a crude coffin built with some type of sandstone. Belts and braces latched it firmly in place. The Karthans were a damn mysterious people, but they knew what they were doing and they treated their visitors with respect.

Everything was set. With Tress and me onboard, I pushed up the lever to the bay doors. The mechanisms creaked and moaned as the door closed. The natural lighting and humidity of Karth disappeared, replaced with the Belle's artificial life support systems.

Tress followed me as I climbed the ladder's cold metal rungs. Deck plates clanked as we walked across them into the second deck. From there we climbed the stairs and walked down the corridor towards the bridge. I stopped at the first door on my left and tapped it with my knuckles.

"This here will be where you stay," I said to Tress. As my hearing improved, my Restran language flowed more smoothly than before. "There are a handful of beds. Choose whichever one you want."

The familiar sounds and smells of the Belle made me smile as I left Tress to inspect his new quarters. I walked through the small arch onto the bridge and closed the door. It was the size of a large closet with three chairs and stations. The left station was used for tactical and security purposes like weapons and shields. The right was main operations where maps were reviewed, courses were evaluated, and engineering and other ship statistics were calculated. The center station was for navigation—my station—though the two consoles that surrounded it also connected functionality with tactical and operations. In front of the chair was a silver globe; a navigational sphere or navsphere as I came to call it, which controlled the ship.

I sat. The familiar texture and shape of my chair melded with my body. I cleared my throat.

"Al, you there buddy? Time to wake up," I called out. A number of indicator lights on the right console flashed blue and red, and I heard a deep computerized voice come from the speakers around me.

"Captain, may I remind you that because I am a machine, I do not sleep. The correct term would be 'hibernate' or 'standby'."

Stars above, Al, I thought.

"I am relieved to see that you are not harmed, sir," he continued. "I detected the explosion at the space dock. Before we continue our discussion, I feel I must warn you—"

"Yes, Al," I interrupted. "I know we have a passenger on our ship. Activate passenger protocol immediately."

The protocol was designed to keep Al a secret from any and every passenger I took onboard. He was the most advanced computer intelligence humanity had ever created, and he had been installed on my ship so I could keep him safe. There were people out there like Sarah King who would, and did in fact, kill to acquire this technology. As long as we had passengers, Al and I would only communicate by text unless, like now, I isolated myself on the bridge.

"CAPTAIN," Al typed out on my front console screen. "THAT IS NOT WHAT I MEANT—"

There was a loud knock at the door. I stretched to open it for Tress, who poked his head in with his antennae shifting from side to side.

"Captain Quinn," he said. "Who are you talking to? I heard two voices coming from this room."

Oh flux.

"SIR, THE RESTRAN PASSENGER CAN DETECT ME SPEAKING, EVEN BEYOND THE BRIDGE."

I sighed. I guess passenger protocol wouldn't be needed then. I deactivated it. I considered that Tress's antennae were used as his primary senses, but I never thought they'd be so strong as to hear past a thick metal bulkhead. I introduced him to Al.

"Ra chintu comp?" Tress said. *A living computer?* Al was the one who had been teaching me alien languages for the last year, so I wasn't concerned with him translating the question.

"In a manner of speaking, yes," Al answered back in Restran. "I am an advanced mechanism with the potential to learn and grow as I absorb new information."

Depending on the level of interest Tress showed, this conversation could keep them busy for hours. I took hold of his shoulders and eased him into the communication's chair. I buckled him in and returned to my seat to fire up the thrusters.

"What is your primary function?" Tress asked Al as I flipped a couple of switches to ignite the main engine core. The Belle began to tremble, as if it were anxious to get back into space. The navsphere, silver ball with directional angles and numbers, hovered in front of me, its magnetic charge at maximum. I placed one hand on it as I used the other to grab the thruster lever.

"I serve mankind, more specifically Captain Daniel Quinn, on his various missions throughout the galaxy," Al explained. "I process data, control the Kestrel Belle during autopilot mode, and I am programmed with a subroutine that allows me to provide council to humans in times of strife."

I snorted at that comment, never pegging Al as a psychiatrist. He was a good listener, though, I had to give him that much.

"I must admit I rarely get the chance to converse with other species," Al continued. "If I am correct, your home planet Tristain has similar atmospheric conditions to human worlds, does it not?"

"I, uh, suppose so . . ." Tress said hesitantly. "Are you capable of operating a ship without a human to command you?"

He changed the subject about his home planet. Interesting, I thought.

"I am more than capable of handling ship operations. In fact, I would find it more accurate to say the Captain cannot operate the ship without me."

"Har har," I muttered, though he was telling the truth. Cruisers like this operated best with a handful of crewmates, namely an engineer, a communications officer, tactical officer, and the captain. Al covered three of the four most of the time.

I activated the dorsal thrusters. They fired toward the ground and slowly lifted the Belle into the air. Outside my shield window, the town of Karth shrank away. I spun the navsphere to the left, turning the Belle towards the sky, and then transferred power to the aft thrusters. We launched upward and the dull blue color grew darker and darker until finally we cleared the planet and saw nothing but the vast reaches of space.

The reason I joined the Earth Star Alliance years ago was to explore space and meet new alien cultures. After I was betrayed by Sarah King, my commanding officer, and locked up, I thought space would be my prison. Now I did everything I could to make it my freedom, but those days seemed few and far between when I was given missions like this one.

I set an automated course out of the Karthan solar system and engaged. Once we achieved a safe distance from inhabited planets, I could launch the ship into slingspace, a speed faster than light. I pulled out Damon's memory drive from my pocket.

"Al," I said as soon as there was a break in his conversation with Tress. "I want you to download this and replay all information"

I plugged the drive into an open access port on the console to my right.

"Yes sir," Al said. "Processing . . . There appears to be audio and video files, twenty-four of them to be exact."

"Can you determine which file might have the most pertinent data, anything about a request, or orders, maybe something about danger?"

The room was silent except for Tress and my breathing. I didn't get a chance to learn what planet Damon came from, but I searched for Tristain on my star maps. Sector by sector the computer searched. I set my feet on the console and rested my hands behind my head.

A holographic image of Damon Derringer appeared in front of me and I nearly fell out of my chair. He wore the same suit as when I saw him—he must have recorded this message right before he found me.

"Captain Daniel Quinn, my name is Damon Derringer. I regret to admit that if you're watching this recording, then I am most likely dead. I come to you now under grave circumstances. The planet Terra, my home, has been at war with its sister planet,

Gaia, for 55 years. Millions of people are dying and I am asking you to help save our worlds."

Apparently my plans were going to involve one minor alteration.

THREE

The war between Damon's home planet of Terra and its sister planet Gaia has been waged since before he was born.

"Captain," Damon's recording continued. "In the last two years, our planets decided that too much blood has been spilled, and thus a peace council was formed. Twelve of the highest ranking government officials signed a declaration in pursuit of a cease fire, one that will benefit both worlds and usher in an era of prosperity. But now the council is in danger. As I speak, members are being targeted for assassination, proof of which I obtained at great risk. This memory drive contains all the information you will need, as well as encoded passwords for my database on Terra. You must travel with haste and make contact with Harold Scott, commander of the Sentinels, the Terran security force."

As I watched Damon's hologram speak, I grew increasingly confused. What the hell was I supposed to do about this so called war? My skills in diplomatic relations were nonexistent. Besides, I never visited either planet and, to my knowledge, I didn't know anyone who lived there.

Just turn off the hologram and think nothing more of it, I thought.

Nerves crept into my stomach and up my spine. Memories surfaced, some old, some recent, but they all had one thing in common: Every time helped someone, shit always blew up in my face. My best friend was captured and mutated into a cybernetic freak when I helped my old Captain, Gregory Smithson, escape from the hands of the mutinous Sarah King. And an alien I bonded with, Laraar, was killed by a woman whom I had tried to befriend and show mercy.

Why the hell would I want to be placed between two warring planets? How could that end in any good way? What difference could I make? I considered asking Al to stop processing the information. If I did that, all I had to do was deliver Damon's body home. But how many people could die from this war?

There were never minor casualties in war. The lives lost throughout history can't be summed up by using numbers. I agreed to take Damon's body home. I would already be there anyway, so why not look around? Would it be so bad to take a look around?

Yes, probably, but despite my trepidation I stayed silent and let Al continue the download.

You want to involve yourself because you care, I admitted to myself.

But why do I care? Was I seriously having an internal discussion with my conscience right now?

You care because of all the wrong that's been done to you— Ashley's murder, your failed jobs, the destruction and deaths on

Dawn, Jason Hobbes. You can't change the past, so you look for things you can change in the present and future.

I wanted to think of an argument against what I thought, but I couldn't. The holographic video ended and Damon's digital body dematerialized. I breathed in deep and let it out slow. I didn't have to do this. All I needed to do was chart a new course, somewhere far away, and hide.

Hide, like a coward.

"Al," I said, resolved. "While you're processing the memory drive, I also need access to any records we have on the alien race known as Leondren. One of them was responsible for bombing the docking gate on Karth. We're going to try and hunt him down."

"Acknowledged, sir," Al said. "Although that will not be difficult. There is a Leondren starship precisely 1,875 meters off our starboard bow."

"What?"

"That will not be difficult. There is a Leondren—"

"Al, shut up! I heard what you said the first time!"

I cut the power on the thrusters and scanned the area Al mentioned. There was definitely something out there. I rotated the navsphere gently to bring the Belle into position facing the object, and then turned toward my operations console and zoomed in to the location I had submitted. I never got a chance to see the Leondren vessel up close, but the ship in front of me was the shape of a diamond with three separate wing structures on each side of her. The hull was a dark grey color, but my databanks couldn't register the metal. Sensors indicated the ship was stationed at a higher altitude than the Belle and she was leaning down facing us, like a predator looking to strike.

Granak.

He denied every attempt I made at communication, and scans of his ship revealed weapons fully activated and charged. The time for talk was apparently over. He said his business, successfully intimidated me, and pissed me off at the same time.

"What's happening?" Tress asked as he leaned over my shoulder.

"He's waiting to see what I'm going to do," I replied.

I wanted to attack, to fly in and unload a barrage of plasma, but his ship was superior to mine in weaponry alone and I didn't even compare other systems yet. The Belle was agile, but could I really outmaneuver him if I made the decision to attack? I didn't want to take that chance. My mission was to apprehend him, but I needed to face him on even ground, wherever that may be. I hated to admit it, but the best option was to turn and run.

Live to fight another day, a voice echoed inside my head. It wasn't my voice, but that of Captain Gregory Smithson. He had said that to me after our successful escape from the Echelon.

"Al, do we have the coordinates for Terra?" I almost whispered as if Granak could hear me. I doubt he was going to let me escape, so we needed to be quick and precise.

"Affirmative, Captain. The course is entered into navigation."

I reached to the slingspace primer, pushed it forward, and waited. The only way I could engage the ship faster than light was to keep my thrusters at half power, but if I did that Granak would have no problem advancing and taking us out. I silently hoped that his ship wouldn't detect my engines' increasing energy so I could turn and launch us instantly once the core fully charged.

"All right then," I breathed. I wiped my sweaty hands on my pants and placed them back on the navsphere. It trembled against the cool metallic device. "Tress, make sure you're buckled up."

I took my own advice and strapped myself securely into my seat. I breathed deep in an attempt to calm my nerves. Power levels rose and the soft hum of the Belle grew louder. Granak's ship kept stationary. I imagined the human eyes of his feline face staring right at me, his mouth formed in an open smile with those sharp pointed teeth.

The slingspace engine core blinked green.

"Hard starboard," I whispered.

I thrust my hand to the right. The sphere effortlessly spun, turning the ship. That's when Tress started mumbling something.

"Look out! Look out!" I translated too late.

The display screen in front of him flashed red. Granak had fired his weapons.

"Flux! Al, engage slingspace!"

I expected to see the stars around me shift and fade away as my ship launched, but instead the Belle flew off course. The bridge violently shook and the straps around my shoulders dug into me as I jerked forward.

"Captain, impact on the dorsal midsection. Slingspace has been deactivated."

Granak knew exactly where to hit me. I grabbed the navsphere and activated the main thrusters. The Belle groaned but responded and we shot forward.

"Al, keep an eye on Granak and prepare to drop the aft weapons."

"Acknowledged. Leondren ship closing in at 300 meters. Mines are set and ready to deploy."

Granak's ship easily matched our speed as it fired another round. The disruptor fire missed but was close enough to make me hold my breath in anticipation of a hit. I took evasive maneuvers, turning left and right, diving down and shooting up. Every time I turned the Belle, I released one of the mines in the hopes that Granak wouldn't see it coming. I couldn't hear the explosions, but I felt the Belle shudder, the floor clanging. His weapons were locking on to the mines and destroying them shortly after I ejected them.

"We are dead!" Tress shouted from behind me.

"No we're not," I replied, though I wasn't completely sure of that answer.

That's when I remembered the marksmanship Granak displayed on Karth. He hit Damon in one shot, but after multiple attempts he either missed the Belle entirely or grazed her hull. He was toying with me. Just like back on the planet surface, he had no intention of killing me, but to what end? Was he going to give chase and fire at me until my power reserves drained out? Our two ships danced in the darkness of space. I lost track of how much time passed. Tress whimpered behind me, terrified.

"Al, divert power to the port thrusters and prepare to fire forward plasma guns," I said, tired of the battle being one-sided.

"Sir, that is not—"

"Just do it, Al!"

When the adjustments were completed, I cut power to the main thrusters and activated the port side. In the blink of an eye, the Belle spun 180 degrees and we faced Granak's ship.

"Fire!" I screamed. Two beams of pure green plasma erupted from my ship. A barrier of energy stopped the plasma from directly hitting his ship.

"Impact to vessel's forward shields, Captain," Al reported.

Flux. I returned all power to main thrusters and shot past Granak. He had more weapons and more defensive systems, but I turned toward him again and fired my plasma at his stern. Each hit met the same barrier as my first. I gritted my teeth. Anger fueled me, the same anger I used when I nearly shot Damon Derringer.

"Captain. This is futile. We will exhaust our plasma banks long before the Leondren's shields fail. I recommend a full course correction back to Karth."

Al wanted me to tuck my tail between my legs and run. That's what I tried to do in the first place, but Granak had other ideas. He wanted me to attack him.

He wanted me to attack him, I thought in a moment of clarity. *He's trying to cripple my ship . . . and I'm helping him.*

My slingspace drive was out of commission and the main thruster control felt sluggish the more I pushed the ship. If I continued my attack I would be a sitting duck, completely defenseless.

"Stars above, Al," I said out loud. "You're right. I'm sorry. Set course back to Karth. Maybe we can get the bastard to follow us back."

If I didn't know any better, I thought I heard Tress sigh.

That's when Granak resumed his attack. His ship turned toward us, the exact same tactic I used against him earlier, and unloaded multiple disruptor blasts. Every one hit my ship. The lights on the bridge flashed red, a sign that hull integrity was dropping. In any other circumstance that would have scared the shit out of me; a hull breech on a ship this old could tear her apart. But before I could react, the computer station in front of me exploded and showered me with sparks and smoke.

Tress screamed; the sound came out of him like the combination of a loud whistle and the screech of an earth elephant. I threw up my hands and turned my head to guard from the damaged console and I saw his eyes shimmer deep, neon indigo. He was more terrified than when I threatened his life and I didn't blame him. I told him we weren't going to die, but the onslaught of weapons fire convinced me of that inevitability. In those last few seconds, I regretted bringing him onboard.

"Tress," I said. "I'm so sorry."

I closed my eyes and waited for the Belle to shudder, to split apart and suck me into the void of space, but the attacks stopped. The Belle didn't break apart like I thought she might. When I opened my eyes, Granak's ship was right in front of me, on the other side of the shield window. He won and I lost, and this felt like his way of gloating. After a minute or so, the ship turned and thrust out of sight. A ripple effect from his ship traveling faster than light caused the Belle to drift backward. I unbuckled my harness and stood carefully. The left side of the blackened main console still smoked. The right side seemed intact as well as the navsphere, but when I attempted to turn the ship nothing happened. The thrusters were offline.

"Al," I said, hoping to hear an answer from him, but it didn't come. I called his name a handful more times, but heard nothing.

For the last five years, the only companion I truly had was Al. He was an artificial intelligence, sure, but he was the only voice I consistently heard. When he was first installed on the Belle, he spoke like nothing more than a standard computer, assisting me with operations on the ship. But he was designed to evolve, and after years of traveling together, he began to show signs of emotion and sentience. He joked with me, insulted me, and I him. Man and machine became the closest of friends. He used his vast database to teach me about the worlds and races we met in space, and I taught him how to behave more like a human.

Now Al's mainframe had been damaged in the attack. I wanted to scream, to throw or punch something. Al was literally a one-of-a-kind A.I. I didn't have access to replacement parts, nor did I have the technological prowess to repair him. And what if he couldn't be repaired? What if I had lost him forever?

"Tress, are you okay?"

"Yes," he said with a hard grunt.

"Okay. Stay buckled in your chair," I told him as I moved back toward communications. I leaned over his chair to input commands and activate the ship's damage report.

Main power was online, but fluctuating rapidly. Life support was offline in various parts of the ship, namely the crew quarters, cargo bay, and engineering. There was damage to the outer hull of the ship, but no breach. Thrusters were nearly drained of their power, and the slingspace drive was damaged.

Great, only a few minor problems, I thought. Granak knew exactly where and how to hit enough to cripple but not destroy my ship.

There was only one sure way to repair the Belle. I always considered it to be a last resort, but at this point I had no other options. With the slingspace drive damaged, we couldn't travel faster than light and reach Terra.

I almost left Tress, who stared at the console in front of him. But as I looked closer his eyes were focused on something unseen and his eyes glowed the same indigo color I saw before. My thoughts were so focused on everything that happened to me and little on what happened to him, but his youth and inexperience couldn't have prepared him for everything that

42

happened today. I put a firm hand on his shoulder and leaned down to him.

"We're alive, Tress," I said in Restran. "Do me a favor and look over these controls and screens. I know you won't recognize the language, but come and find me if anything looks wrong."

He said nothing but nodded his head, and I clasped him once more on the shoulder before I walked down the corridor toward my quarters. The light above me flashed on and off, creating a disorienting effect on my eyes. When I reached my door the power fluctuations stopped it from fully opening. I had to grab onto the frame and pull hard to fit through. The room was cold and my lungs worked harder to breathe as the life support from the corridor slowly traveled into my room. It was a mess; the mattress had fallen off its frame, and the tall wood dresser had fallen forward. All its drawers stuck out and clothes were everywhere.

At the far wall was my secret compartment, one of the fun features of the Kestrel class captain's quarters. Inside were a number of items, the most important being a vial of golden liquid known as empyreus, which could absorb into most material objects, including metal, vegetation, and even human skin. Once done, empyreus could repair, recharge, or heal that item or person. I had little left, having used it on my engines in the past to maximize their power output. Now I could only hope that it would be enough to get my ship working again, including Al. I input a key code into a specific section of the wall and the door opened with a groan.

Fortunately the compartment was well sealed and secured. Even with the damage Granak caused, the three items hadn't budged from their holding places. My tactical suit, created from a rubber-like material, hung from the wall on the left side. The alloy was soft but allowed for a moderate amount of buffer where weapon fire was concerned. In the middle, an ancient samurai sword, a katana, with a hilt of red leather and gleaming steel, was mounted against the wall. Although the blade was clean, occasionally I swore I saw blood running from the tip to the hilt; the blood of a friend.

Finally, the vial of empyreus sat in a protective box on the right. I grabbed it. Only a couple tablespoons remained. I had choices to make and priorities to set. Main power needed to be restored, first and foremost. After that, the engines needed to be repaired so I could reactivate the thrusters. Whatever empyreus was left would be saved to try to fix Al. As a machine, he didn't technically have emotions, but I still hoped he would forgive me for using the liquid on the ship first.

The Belle's main power grid was in engineering, so most of my time would be spent down there. I returned to the bridge, my lungs appreciative of the fully-powered life-support. Tress fidgeted with the collar of his shirt and his legs were bouncing up and down, but his eye color returned to normal and he seemed to be looking over the various controls of the station. I tried to remind myself that he was my responsibility being on my ship.

"Anything out of the ordinary?" I asked him.

"Honestly, I do not know," he said, unsure of himself. I leaned over and pointed to an indicator light of solid green.

"See that? That color means the communications array is functioning normally." That surprised me. "And if we turned this knob here . . . we can scan out for any transmissions or messages in our area, but so far it looks like we're alone. You're doing great, Tress."

He looked up at me and smiled. When I saw his eyes gleam silver, I knew my words helped him calm down. I gave him my best reassuring smile, which wasn't very good, admittedly. I sat across from him at the tactical station and pulled up a blueprint of the Belle.

All life support bulkhead doors were closed, which they were supposed to be if one of the ship's sections lost power. Tress and I would eventually need power in our quarters to rest, but we would have to wait a while longer for that.

I tried to find a suitable supply of life-support to divert to engineering, but the only sustainable sections were the bridge, armory, and corridors. There wasn't enough in the armory to power engineering fully, and our lives depended on the oxygen supplied to the bridge. The only other breathable environments on the ship were the corridors. I ran a couple of simulations, diverting power from them into engineering. Time would be short, but it would be enough to reach the power grid.

"Come over here, Tress," I said and input the necessary command codes to divert the power. The buckle clicked open and the seat squeaked as he stood.

"I need your help. I need you to turn this switch." I pointed to it and mimicked the motion of turning it clockwise. "Once you do that, you'll need to communicate through the ship's audio network and tell me how much time I have before life support fails. Press this button here," I said while showing him the round blue button near the center of the console. "Hold it down to speak and keep an eye on the percentage bar. When it reads five percent, let me know." I keyed in the number and symbol so he would know what to look for.

"Okay," he said softly.

"Tress," I replied. "This is important. Without you, I can't do this. I need to know you're going to be okay."

I wanted him to feel helpful, to show him he was needed. In times of struggle a man, or in this case alien, needs to be given direction, needs to be led. I just wish there was someone here to lead me right now.

"I can do it," he said, his voice louder and more confident. I smiled.

"Good."

I walked to the third deck, caressing the bulkhead with my hand as if I were telling my ship she would be okay. I climbed down the stairs and walked in front of the door to engineering. I had no idea what kind of damage was waiting for me on the other side. I took a deep breath and pressed the communication's button on a control pad.

"Tress, whenever you're ready." I watched above the door where an indicator light flashed red, telling me the life support was offline. Gears along the second floor corridor ground and closed. Once the door shut, all power between the bridge and me would be off. I don't know why, but I felt like a rat trapped in a cage. I didn't train Tress to divert the power back to the other decks, so I was literally stuck down here until I could initialize main power at the source.

The light turned green and the doors opened, somewhat. After passing a foot away from each other, the doors jammed, but there was enough space to squeeze through and enough room to see the mess.

Conduits, wiring, and glass shards littered the floor. From what I could tell, half the light fixtures in the room exploded during the attack. The lights that still worked flickered off and on, causing a disorienting effect on my vision.

Engineering was the only other room that competed in size with the cargo bay, mostly because it housed two large turbines that powered my thrusters and slingspace. I stepped over debris on the floor and leaned over the banister. The engines both looked to be in good condition, but the conduits that connected them to the main power grid were lying on the floor.

"Stars above," I cursed. If I reactivated main power before the conduits were connected, there would be an enormous backfire of energy above the turbines.

I spent nearly an hour dragging the conduits and lifting them against the bannister. I wiped the sweat off my forehead and jumped atop the engines. I leaned forward and grabbed the edges of the conduits, and pulled them up with me one at a time, connecting the turbine with the power grid. Once I felt the connection was secure, I dropped a small amount of empyreus on the connecting points. The glowing liquid absorbed into the metal and began the fusion process. I repeated the same step with the other turbine, nearly pulling a muscle in my back while lifting the second conduit. Once everything was done, the engines looked as good as new, and I could finally energize the main power supply.

The main operating station was across the room. Glass cracked beneath my feet as I approached the breaker box. I double checked to make sure none of the wires were disconnected. Empyreus was a powerful agent, able to fuse and power, but it couldn't create something from nothing. It couldn't build new pathways, only strengthen existing ones. My bionic eye wasn't always so easy to use. After its installation, I couldn't use the damn thing without sharp pain radiating through my head. But then Laraar, a friend from the Dawnian race, used the empyreus on it. The electronic components fused together with my optical connections, or what I had left of them after my eye was taken. Now it worked flawlessly.

As soon as the liquid absorbed, sparks shot out and multiple humming sounds of different tones emanated through the room. The flickering lights turned solid, the computer displays turned on and registered the ship's operations and statistics. Finally, a sound like thunder boomed and made me jump. I turned to see the turbines spinning.

The Belle was alive once more, and I couldn't help but smile. I left just enough liquid to use on my bridge console and hopefully repair Al. There was still a lot of physical repair work and clean up, but at least I could move the ship. I didn't want to be found adrift by a ship 'salvager'.

With main power on, life support flowed throughout the ship and all doors opened. I squeezed back through the engineering entrance and climbed to the bridge where Tress anxiously waited.

"You did great," I told him, patting him on the shoulder.

Over the next half hour, Tress acted well in his role as shipmate. On my back under the main console, I studied the computer boards and wiring carefully, making sure all connections were in place. Copper wiring had melted away in a couple spots, but Tress retrieved new wiring from the cargo bay. From what he told me, the bay was just as much a mess, if not more, than engineering, but Damon's coffin remained intact and secured. The Karthans were a talented bunch, no doubt about it.

Once I finished repairs, I had a couple of options. I could return to Karth, but they might terminate my contract when they learned I failed to apprehend Granak. Also, fixing the Belle wasn't going to be quick. Broken lights and messy floors were the least of my problems. Some computer terminals still didn't work, and the hull had been weakened during the attack. There was risk in my other option, too, which was traveling straight to Terra. If the outer hull was damaged too much, traveling faster than light would shake the Belle apart.

Should I get stuck on Karth with potentially little to no payment, or travel to Terra and possibly die on route? Decisions.

I knew the Belle could hold her own in slingspace. I'd have to travel directly to Terra, but once there I should be able to arrange for a repair crew. But first thing's first. I finished the connections under the console, satisfied that it should come online, and Al with it. I stood, brushed myself off, and let loose the remainder of the empyreus. As I watched it drop, I felt guilty for using it so quickly. The alien species I called the Dawnians were out there learning how to live without the stuff. I didn't want to take it for granted, but what else could I do?

The computer console lit up instantly, the star map blinked our location and navigation held the course previously set to Terra.

"Al," I said. "Al, can you hear me buddy?"

Nothing. I waited a few minutes, thinking maybe his system required a reboot.

"Al? It's Daniel. Can you hear me?"

He didn't answer.

I slammed my hand on the console. The pain only added to the fear and despair; I might never talk to Al again. I slammed my hand again and again, each time increasing speed until the throbbing pain was all I felt. I wanted to storm through the ship and tear things apart, and might have done so if it wasn't already a mess. Did I lose my computer, no, my friend forever? I checked all the connections again and studied the motherboard that was comprised of Al's chips and circuitry while nursing my bruising hand. The circuits looked fine, better than fine. I refused to admit that Al was gone. Instead, I promised that once my mission was completed, I would use the money to find a way back to Earth, or to at least communicate with my father. If I could find him, then, as Al's creator, he would know what to do.

I closed my eyes, taking all the emotion I felt over Al's disappearance and pushing it into an imaginary door. I closed it, shoving hard against the latch as they fought to unleash upon my consciousness. Once the door was closed, I opened my eyes, told Tress to buckle up, and I engaged the slingspace engines.

FIVE

Never before have I been so terrified on my own ship. The Kestrel Belle was my home, but numerous loose items flew around the ship, clanging against the walls, floors, and ceilings. More than once I thought the noises were the hull splitting open, preparing to suck us out into oblivion. My knuckles were white and after every deep breath I held it in just as long.

I heard Tress mumbling behind me. He was easily more scared than I was, but I have to give him respect; not once did he throw up.

"Tress," I said, thinking of a way to keep ourselves distracted from the stress and terror. "Tell me about yourself. You and Damon are from the same solar system, right? So that means there are three planets that are inhabitable?"

"Yes," he said, his voice more high pitched than normal. "We had not achieved space flight until after humans discovered their planets, otherwise we may have colonized them."

"How did your kind feel about the new neighbors? Were you resentful that we took the planets next to you?"

"I was taught that humans were our friends," Tress said, the tension in his voice dissipating. "For many years we bartered with humanity, shared our technologies. What would you call it? A business ship?"

"I think you mean partnership," I said, stifling a laugh. I turned my head to look at him and I found him staring out the window to the stars we flew by. Something troubled him and since he really didn't have anywhere to escape to, I pressed the issue. "The last time I asked you about your home planet you quickly changed the subject on me, and now that I mentioned it again, you seem like you're in some kind of daze. There's more to this story I don't know about, isn't there?"

Tress shrugged, which wasn't an answer, but he still gave me something. Maybe I had to show him some trust to get some in return.

"It's been a long time since I last saw Earth, close to six years now. I had just graduated from the Earth Star Alliance Academy and received my first post in outer space. My life kind of went to hell after that, but that's another story. Maybe I can tell it to you sometime."

I sat there and waited. If he kept quiet, I would continue with the story and tell him about my horrific time spent on the Echelon after I was framed for killing my girlfriend and bride-to-be, Ashley Pierce. I didn't want to, simply because of the painful memories it raises, but if Tress and I were going to be on the Belle together, we needed to trust one another. To my surprise, he told me his story.

The entire planet of Tristain was evacuated. With no warning whatsoever, no alien invasion alerts or planetary disaster signals, the government of Tress's planet ordered everyone world-wide to board their ships and leave. Emergency transport shuttles were rerouted to Tristain in order to help with the evacuation. On one of these shuttles was Damon Derringer. That's how the two of them met.

"Damon hoped that if he found you and convinced you to help him, that maybe you could help me find out why I was forced to leave my planet." His eyes were closed, but I imagined a deep shade of blue underneath his thick, leather-like eyelids. "My parents stayed behind, as did some of the other elders, but the rest of us were scattered into the stars."

"I'm sorry Tress," I said, my mind blank for any other response. I, myself had been isolated from my own kind for years, but humanity was still together on their inhabited planets and space stations. I couldn't even imagine what we would do if Earth was forced to evacuate, the billions of people sent out in different corners of the galaxy.

I looked over at my navigational display and keyed in the coordinates for the solar system known as Gamma 32. Terra and Gaia were about an hour away from each other, assuming you traveled at the speed of light. Tristain was farther away, about two additional hours, but the Belle would be flying close enough by it that we could make a pass-over. I altered the plotted course marginally.

"We'll swing by your planet and take a look, but my priority is to get to Terra. Once we unload Damon and find out what's going on, we'll investigate your problem further, okay?"

Tress's mood changed instantly. He opened his eyes, which shifted color to bright white.

"Thank you Daniel!"

The two of us spent the next two days making minor repairs to the ship. Tress was curious enough about how the Belle operated, so I figured why not put him to work? We cleaned the rooms that were tossed in the battle with Granak, the cargo bay being the most demanding. I didn't have any active cargo deliveries, but I still kept a supply of boxes and crates in case they were needed. We even managed to fix the engineering door. Afterwards I taught Tress some of the controls on the bridge. I kept him away from the communications, since he only knew a few English words up to that point, but he got the hang of the weapon systems quickly.

I knew that our time together was short and our first meeting didn't go so well, but I felt a sense of trust for Tress. He was eager to learn, and he looked up to me like I was some kind of icon for him. No one ever looked up to me like he did and I couldn't help but feel good about it. I suppose he could be doing this to gain my trust only to betray me later, but based on his actions, the way he moved and spoke, I didn't think that was possible. I've been proven wrong before though.

During his weapon's training, I taught him some of the English words associated with the weapons, like plasma, missiles, mines, and shields. If we ended up in another skirmish,

I didn't want to have to evade enemy weapons while trying to translate my orders.

The lack of Al's presence certainly caused a hole in my life. I kept expecting him to respond to my comments with attempted jokes or sarcasm. I never had to correct myself because Al always did it for me, so if I accidentally misspoke to Tress, I waited for Al to chime in, only to not be there. Despite this, having Tress on board was a welcome presence. I rarely had passengers on the Belle, and when I did they always had ulterior motives, like the assassin Cessa. Her job was to shadow me and make sure I did my job, but during our time she showed me a side of herself that was broken, that I was led to believe I could fix. Then I realized she played me the entire time, waiting for the right moment to take advantage.

I almost felt more like a Captain now than ever, with Tress acting as a member of my crew. The second morning, the day we would arrive at Gamma 32, I woke up to a status report. Tress was too excited to let me know he checked over all the ship levels and operations, one's that he knew of anyway.

Food was scarce. I kept a supply of rations on the ship, but living off those wasn't entirely satisfying. We managed to nourish ourselves with some grain and fruit. It wasn't bad, but the first thing I wanted to do when I arrived at Terra was get some meat, preferably a cheeseburger.

When the Belle passed into the solar system I turned up the communications signal. I needed to get a message to Terra and let them know we're coming, but it couldn't reach out far enough. I kept Tress focusing on the sensors just in case any ship, namely Granak's, moved to intercept us. Every time I thought of my Leondren adversary my nerves trembled, but my blood boiled. His love of toying with people and his utter lack of morals irritated me to no end. It didn't help that a lot of money was riding on his capture.

We were a few minutes from visual range of Tristain. Tress stood behind me, leaning over my shoulder to get a good view of it. A small dot outside the shield window grew bigger over time. I pulled back the slingspace lever and we dropped back to thruster power, the Belle groaned and clanked as we slowed.

"Sorry girl," I muttered to her. I just need one more jump after this, and then we'll take care of you."

Tress pointed excitedly as we saw the entirety of his home planet. White clouds covered a lush green surface. I was admiring the view when a red light blinked on my console.

"Tress," I said, checking the sensors twice. "Does your planet have a militarized defense grid?"

He didn't answer me, but looking at his face, his mouth was pursed and forehead scrunched up. I took that as a no. I tried scanning through the grid to detect life signs or power emissions from the surface, but some kind of deflector blocked me. I couldn't tell what was going on down there.

"We never used any devices like that in the past," Tress said after a couple minutes of silence. "Something is not right. I hope my family is okay."

There was nothing more I could do. With a defense system activated I wouldn't be able to pass through without proper authorization, and I had none. I felt guilty as I turned the navsphere away from Restran, but I promised Tress that we would figure out a way to get on the planet.

He left the bridge after that and didn't return during the rest of our journey. I spent the few hours alone on the bridge, going over Damon's data. There was so much. With Al he could have analyzed all of it and given me the most important details, but without him all I could do was look piece by piece.

The peace council was founded by six members of each planet's government. A security force called the Sentinels was tasked with protecting them as they made multiple attempts to call off the war that plagued them for years. Apparently Damon was the lead advisor to the council, handling all of their correspondence and information. Now someone was trying to put an end to the prospects of peace. Someone wanted the war to continue. Killing off members of a peace council seemed to be a great way to do just that.

The two planets, during the time of colonization, were terraformed differently. Terra had an abundance of metals and other elements that allowed it to evolve into a technological marvel. Cities spanned the globe and they exceled at industrial manufacturing. On the other hand, Gaia was rich with vegetation and plants with medicinal properties. Humans were colonized there to build a thriving utopia of farming and horticulture.

Two planets, both with vastly different ecosystems; I imagine they were built this way to strengthen each other. With Terra sharing its technology, and Gaia its herbs and market of fruit, vegetables, and other delicacies, this solar system would have been close to a paradise for humanity.

Instead of sharing, these two planets degraded into selling their exclusive items. Fights broke out among them. I read testimonies of raids being performed on each other to steal equipment, until finally Terra and Gaia declared war on each other in an attempt to control everything.

Somehow I was supposed to help put an end to this. The thought nearly made me laugh out loud. I didn't want to dishonor Damon Derringer, but what was he thinking when he came to find me? I wish I knew. In some ways I wish I never raised my gun to him. Maybe with an additional few seconds, I could have gotten more answers.

No. The past is the past and I often have trouble realizing that. I turned my eyes away from the articles and rubbed my eyes, trying to coax the soreness to go away. When was the last time I slept? I leaned back in my chair and put my feet up on the console. Every time I did this, Al would make a comment about my feet unintentionally hitting a button and causing a malfunction. Normally I would tell him to shut up, but now all I wanted was to hear his voice, to tell me to put my feet down like some kind of robotic parent.

My mind drifted towards thoughts of Earth and how my family was doing. I tried not to think of them, or else my eyes water and a dive into a deep depression of loneliness, but sitting there in silence I couldn't help myself. Plus, with Al damaged, there was a good chance the only person who could repair him was his creator, my father Alexander Quinn. By now he was probably hiding somewhere on Earth, staying quiet so he doesn't arouse suspicion from the Earth Star Alliance. It's funny how one man can set out to change the world, only for his experiment to cause chaos because others see it as a way to gain more power and influence.

After I escaped from the Echelon and the clutches of Sarah King, I never knew what happened on Earth. My father's best friend and my former captain, Gregory Smithson, told me my family would be safe, but I wouldn't be able to count on my hand the number of times I wanted to fly the Belle back to Earth. The only thing that stopped me was King. After she framed me for murder, the news would have traveled to the entire fleet, and now I was a wanted man within the distance of my birthplace.

I disengaged the slingspace and the Belle trembled. She was a damn good ship to me. Now I had to take care of her, otherwise the next time we jumped into slingspace she would spit me out like rotten meat. I searched through the Derringer records until I found the frequency to contact the Sentinels on Terra.

The power on the communications console cut out momentarily, until my fist hit it. It lit back up and transmitted the signal I sent out.

"Unknown vessel," a man grunted out as if his mouth was stuffed with food. "This is Terran Orbital Command. Transmit access codes for clearance to land. Any hesitation on your part will result in the destruction of your vessel and crew."

Flux. No warning whatsoever? These Terrans were strict, though I suppose I understood given the extremity of their circumstances. I quickly sent the codes through. The Belle was in no condition to dodge cannon fire."

After a couple of minutes of what I guessed was a verification process for the codes, another man came on the line.

"This is Commander Harold Scott of Sentinel command. Identify yourself."

"This is Captain Daniel Quinn of the Kestrel Belle," I replied. "I'm requesting permission to dock."

"Quinn?" He said, sounding perplexed. "Do you have Damon Derringer with you?"

Had Scott been expecting me? I assumed I'd be getting the usual interrogation when landing on a planet for the first time. What's your business on the planet? What cargo do you currently hold? What's your ship's registry number?

"Um, in a manner of speaking," I said. "Damon Derringer is dead."

Silence. At first I thought the line went dead or my power cut out, but all other lights were on and there didn't seem to be any disruption across the line.

"Access granted," Scott said. "Proceed to docking tower B-4, but I highly recommend you alter your course. I see your ship on sensors and it –"

The signal definitely went dead that time, but it wasn't my console. Sensors detected some kind of dampening field that we passed through, which was odd. Dampening fields are used to cut out outward or inbound communication, but it's usually when someone wants to jam your signal intentionally.

A knot tied in my stomach and I checked the radar for Granak, thinking that maybe he followed me here, but instead of one red blip on the radar, I counted a dozen. All of them were straight ahead.

"Tress," I jumped out of my seat and opened the bridge door, calling out for Tress. Sound carried well through the corridor and he would've had heard me. By the time he joined me on the bridge, I could see flashed of blue and green among the white stars ahead.

"What is that?" He asked.

"Trouble," I said. "The war between Terra and Gaia is happening, right now, directly ahead."

SIX

Stars above, I thought as we neared a battle zone of starships. Smaller crafts shot out from bigger ones and engaged in what looked like a fireworks show. Ships exploded and spread fire and debris among the stars. How many lives were being lost right in front of me? It was one thing to be told that Terra and Gaia were at war with each other, but to see it in plain sight was nothing less than horrible.

"Is there a way around this?" Tress whispered. I nodded, unable to speak. We had to give the zone a wide berth to stay clear of weapon fire, and I didn't want to fly through that mess. I cleared my throat and blinked a couple times to find my resolve.

"Tress, sit at the tactical station. Remember how I showed you? Power up the deflector shield just in case."

I waited for the hum of the shield activating, but nothing came. Tress turned up the dial multiple times to no avail. Shields were offline.

Don't bang your head against the console . . . Don't bang your head against the console . . .

We just had to stay far enough away from the battle and we'd be fine. Unless, of course, one of the ships mistook me for the enemy; in that case one well-placed missile or plasma burst would obliterate my ship and the two of us. No worries, right? I grabbed the navsphere and twisted it starboard. As the ship turned, I found myself glued to the battle. One of the larger ships took on heavy fire and pieces of the hull broke apart in various sections. Flames shot out from the bow, traveling all the way to the stern until the hull expanded like a balloon and exploded.

No thoughts formed other than numbers; thousands, maybe tens of thousands of people could fit on a ship that size, and all their voices were suddenly silenced in the darkness. The battle fanned out and ships altered their maneuvers, a couple moving close to my position. I quickly shifted my course to increase distance between us.

I hummed, not a song I knew of, but just a melody I was creating at that moment. I never realized how much music could affect a person's mood until I made first contact with the Dawnian race, who literally spoke in musical intonations. Their voices had the ability to manipulate emotional responses within a person. I noticed for the last year I tended to hum to myself during difficult situations. Sometimes it helped, and sometimes not.

I concentrated on its melody as I took the Belle past the battle. Weapon fire from both sides continued and two smaller ships rammed each other, resulting in another explosion. A couple rogue missiles came toward the ship, and I eased the navsphere forward and dropped the ship below them.

A couple of times I glanced back to see if Tress was still there, and he was, but was so silent I couldn't hear him breathe. He couldn't look away from the battle, from the death.

Something changed. One minute the bridge was silent and the next a distress signal sounded throughout the room. Whatever ship emitted the dampening field must have either been damaged or destroyed. I hit the button that allowed the message to play over the speakers.

"Can anyone hear me? This is medical freighter Zolo, requesting assistance. A Gaian attacker is pursuing us. Our energy levels are weakening and shields are almost out. Please, we have no weapon capability." The voice was shaken, soft, and female. Her words stuttered. I pushed the sensors to their limit, scanning for the source of the message. There, about two thousand meters away, a ship was flying towards Terra with a second ship following it, firing its weapons.

The Belle wasn't in any condition to pursue, but the thought of more people in danger, especially defenseless people, nagged at me. I checked the radar for any additional ships that were moving to intercept.

None.

Damaged or not, I couldn't keep the Belle from danger and allow more people to die. I set course toward the two ships and turned the navsphere.

"Tress, at the tactical station there is a green gauge on the top right corner. Tell me how full it is."

I kept my eye on the enemy ship as Tress moved behind me.

"Under half," he said.

There was enough power for a few plasma rounds, but I had to make them count. The Belle closed in on the attacking ship, which continued to lay into the Zolo with its weapons. I used my bionic eye to zoom in toward the source of the weapon fire. Port and starboard there were two disruptor emitters. Each had to charge for a few seconds before it could fire.

One blast. One, two, three, four, five, and then a second blast, I thought, counting out the durations between the two emitters.

I opened a sensor display of the enemy ship, a rounded edge saucer with two small wings, and touched the two sections of the ship from where the weapons fired. Red circles zoomed in on the area until the word 'LOCKED' appeared on screen.

The three of us advanced toward planet Terra, and the sight distracted me. I assumed the planet would bear some resemblance to Earth, but the entire sphere was colored a variety of gray and white. There were some blues and greens, but sparse and spread out. Terra could have easily been a giant metal ball if it wasn't for the few shades of color.

The Zolo entered into the atmosphere, which gave the attacker a perfect chance to hit them and overload their hull armor. The ship would burn up in seconds. I had to make my move now. I allowed the first blast to fire and hoped the Zolo survived.

"One, two, three, FIRE!" I shouted and jammed in the trigger on my weapon's console. Green plasma erupted from the beak of the Belle toward the enemy ship. Time seemed to stop as I waited and watched to see if I landed a hit. The enemy ship, either unknowing or uncaring about my weapons, fired their second attack, but my plasma hit them as their weapons fired. An explosion of green and red tore through the ship as it spun out of control. Small human-shaped figures were sucked out through its hull. One of them, a man, floated past my window, half his body scorched and his eyes wide open and lifeless.

"Stars above," I whispered. This wasn't my war, and by looking at the carnage around me, I had no idea how Terra and Gaia even agreed to peace talks. Even by saving a medical ship from being destroyed, I killed a number of men and women to do it.

I kept on course for Terra as the communicator on the bridge spurted out static, and then the woman's voice came back online.

"This is the Zolo, whoever saved us, you have our thanks."

In war, there are winners and losers. People die and that's a fact, but what keeps a person from going insane is knowing why they fight. I didn't like to kill. Even when it came between me and an adversary, killing was the last option on the table. But what mattered more than that was my honor. I didn't want to kill those people. In fact, I hoped the only damage sustained was to their weapon systems. But if I had let them go, they would have destroyed a medical ship filled with doctors and personnel who usually had no allegiance in war. From the brief training I had at the academy, medical staff will treat and care for anyone who needs it. In a way the enemy ship acted like a bully, and I can't stand bullies.

The Belle traveled toward the planet, following the coordinates given by the docking tower. I didn't have full autopilot control with Al out of commission, but I tried my best to survey the planet. With the sun now set, the Terran city glowed in vast magnificence. Sensors detected a handful of ships higher in the sky in defense positions, in case any Gaian forces got close enough. Even taller skyscrapers had orbital cannons built on their roofs. Below the skyline, squares of lights danced around the buildings—vehicles I guessed. As far as the eye can see, skyscrapers towered over the surface. I passed a large park, filled with trees and a lake. The view looked a lot like, well it's been a while since I celebrated it, but it looked like Christmas.

I turned the Belle starboard and an indicator on the console's map showed the B-4 tower. It was a tall, square building with long glass platforms attached to various sides and levels. Each one had a shining number on it and I circled the building looking for B-4. I found it near the top of the building, as well as five small figures waiting. A welcoming party. Would one of them be Reynold Scott? I brought down the Kestrel Belle, easing her with thrusters at quarter power, and landed her on the platform. As soon as the docking clamps locked onto the landing gear, I shut down all thruster and engine power.

"Good girl," I said and then turned to Tress. "Follow me."

We walked to my quarters, where I opened the secret, which I guess wasn't so secret now with Tress standing next to me. There wasn't time to dillydally and I would be taking all of the equipment with my anyway. First, I pulled out my tactical suit.

"Listen." I pulled off my shirt and pants and replaced them with the armor. "I need you to stay with the Belle."

"What?" Tress said with a minor gasp. His next words were a mixture of Restran and English. "Itu . . . stay . . . ponta jiji . . . planet." I stepped towards him and put my hands on his shoulders.

"Tress, calm down. Take a deep breath . . . or whatever you do to relax yourself. He tilted his head back and moved his arms in circular motions. Once finished, he seemed calmer.

"Daniel," he said, fully in Restran. "My people suffer and have no home. Humans are at war. And you ask I stay on your ship?"

It's true I was basically confining him to the ship, a prison which blocked out everything happening outside, whether it was the crisis between Terra and Gaia, or his home planet. But being on a new planet like this, I didn't know anyone and had no clue whom to trust. Tress was the closest thing I had to a friend and ally right now.

"The Belle's in bad shape, Tress. And right now, more than anything, she needs repairs. I need someone to stay behind and look after her, someone I trust. I'm not telling you this because I don't want you with me. To be honest, I could use your help with whatever waits for me outside, but you need to be here for my ship, to make sure she gets the care and attention she deserves. Can you please do this for me?"

Tress stood silent. I couldn't read his expression, though his eyes were wide and his mouth hung open. Either he was still insulted that I didn't want him coming with me, or he was shocked that I asked him to take care of my ship. He finally straightened with his hands to his sides and answered in a tone more serious than I have ever heard him use.

"Yes, sir! You can count on me!"

I admit I grinned. The kid was growing on me.

The suit was always a little tight after putting it on. I took a couple of minutes to stretch, then reached for the sword. I hesitated a moment, looking at the shining steel blade, and closed my eyes tight to prevent any unwanted images.

Just grab the damn thing . . .

There was something about swords and knives—basically anything sharp—that gave me nightmares. Ashley was found stabbed in my quarters on the Echelon. Laraar had been impaled from behind by this very blade. But the more I studied it, the more I used my fear as a means of curiosity. With Al's help, I'd begun training with the blade, learning how it moved and felt. I was no master, but now after a year of training, I had a good grasp of the concepts. I took the sword in my hand, swung it around, and then attached the sword to a magnetic strip I installed on the back of my armor, and the sword clung to it securely.

"Okay," I said, more to myself than to Tress. "I'm ready."

We walked toward the cargo bay. Tress hopped along, excited that he was an honorary member of the crew overseeing the repairs. I kept wondering what waited for me outside the ship. Would I unload Damon's body and be done? Maybe I didn't even have to leave the ship, and we could have it repaired and leave. But what about the people of Terra and Gaia, and this peace council that was apparently in danger? I still didn't know what I could do to help, but if there was a chance, any chance at all, shouldn't I take it? How many lives could be spared if this war ended?

For a moment, I stood in front of Damon's coffin. His last act alive was finding me, looking to me for help. All I did was aim my weapon and threaten him. I felt like I owed him something, to ensure he didn't die in vain. I pulled hard on the control lever beside the doors. The large bay door opened with a loud groan.

Five people walked around the ship and greeted me as I stepped off the Belle. The first man had a narrow face, skin sunken in with deep set brown eyes. His hair was a mix of salt and pepper color, and he looked like man who hadn't slept in days. He also looked to be in charge.

"Captain Daniel Quinn?" he asked and extended his hand. His handshake was firm and I nodded. "I'm Commander Scott of

Sentinel Command. These are my lieutenants. Charles Orson and Kenneth Strong."

I nodded to each of the men and shook their hands. Behind them were the last people in Scott's party. They wore dark blue jumpsuits and held a hovering stretcher. Medical personnel, I guessed. I brought them onboard and took them to Damon's coffin.

"Damn you, Damon," Scott muttered. "He was a good man."

Tress joined the group and I introduced them all.

"Commander, my apologies for your loss," I said. "I need a repair team to take care of my ship. I can have all specifications and blueprints made available for them, but the sooner the better. Tress will oversee the repairs. Can you make that happen?"

Scott narrowed his eyes and gazed at me sidelong. I shut my mouth and allowed him a moment of closure with his fallen comrade. After a minute or two of silence, he stepped back and beckoned the medical personnel to take the coffin. He then walked to me and pulled a radio from his belt.

"Repair crew is needed on platform B-4. Cruiser is in need of repairs, looks like an old Kestrel model." I nodded in confirmation. "Get up here and see what you can do. Make sure a Restran translator accompanies you."

"Acknowledged," a voice replied.

Scott eyed me up and down and shrugged his shoulders. By the look of his scowl, I'd say he wasn't too impressed with what

Damon's search brought back. He noticed the sword hilt sticking out above my shoulder.

"A sword? That seems like an odd weapon choice."

"It gets the job done," I said.

"I guess we'll find out," he answered and walked off the Belle. His associates followed him. I turned to Tress before leaving.

"Take care of my ship. If you need anything, just let the translator know once he gets here."

"Okay," he said, holding out his hand. The memory drive Damon brought to Karth was in his palm. "Just in case you need this." I took it from him and gave him a pat on the shoulder, then I caught up to Scott and his men.

"So what can you tell me?" I asked him. "You obviously know a little about me, but I'm in the dark about the situation."

"You may want to get caught up fast," he said. "Damon named you his successor in his will."

I tripped on one of the platform's plates and nearly fell on my face, but caught myself. Maybe I was imagining things, but one of Scott's men laughed.

"That has to be a cruel joke, right? What the hell do I know about his position?"

"Good question, one I would like to know myself." His voice was hard, his mouth formed in a scowl, and he walked at such a brisk pace I had to take large steps to keep up. He obviously wasn't happy, but I had to wonder whether it was just because he lost a friend, or if Damon naming me in his will struck Scott as odd. If they were friends, maybe Scott assumed he would be named successor. I decided not to press the subject.

"I look at you, Captain, and I don't see much. For now I'll entertain your presence, but make one move I don't like and I'll have you shipped off planet before you can blink."

Gulp.

"Um, understood," I said. "So since I'm the advisor now, what exactly does that mean? What did Damon do?"

"This isn't something we should be talking about in the open, Captain."

"Oh, right." My nerves were crawling over me like a mess of Tirnden ants, and those things are nasty. I just wanted some answers, but with the battle in space and who knows what on the surface, maybe discussions were best left until we found a private place to talk. Still, I couldn't help push the issue a little further. "At least tell me this—Damon advised this supposed peace council, right? He told me someone is trying to kill them."

He stopped and looked at me.

"Not trying. Accomplished."

"What are you talking about?" I asked.

"Three members of the peace council were found dead this morning."

SEVEN

Past a large glass door was a large hallway with gold and silver chandeliers that illuminated the area and reflected off grey marble walls. Scott wasn't in a talkative mood, but I didn't care much at the moment. All I could think about were the horrible outcomes of this unfolding situation.

Back on Karth, it was easy to second guess Damon's mission. All I had to do was say no, which wouldn't have been hard because he was already dead. I could have taken my half a million dollars and flown away, just me and Al. No Tress, no attack on my ship, and I would've been none the wiser.

Now I stood on Terra, and in less than a couple hours, I had seen up close and personal the terrible things happening, the war between two worlds, the death of thousands of people. And now peaceful members of the council, high ranking officials of both Terra and Gaia, were being murdered.

Maybe I could've walked away on Karth, but could I turn my back now? Obviously Damon knew something about me that could help change the course of events. I didn't know what it was and neither did Commander Scott, but if there was any chance, no matter how small, I felt obligated to at least try.

We followed the hall until we reached a wide lobby. It contained no desks, chairs, or windows, only two sets of elevators and a door far to the right of the wall. We stopped at the elevator and waited for the medical team to catch up, then Scott pressed the down button.

"The first thing we'll do is go to headquarters. General Ambrose will want to meet you. Together we need to figure out what your role here will be." Scott's tone gave me little reason to be excited.

I should have agreed with him, but I was tired of people telling me what I should or shouldn't do. Yes, it was my choice to come to Terra, but that didn't mean I would be ordered around. Damon saw fit to bestow his job on me, and I would do it as I saw fit.

"No," I said, without looking at him for a change. "First you are going to take me to the murder site and then I'll meet your boss."

"Excuse me?"

"If I'm acting advisor to the council, then they're my first priority. I want to know what is happening here. You will take me to the site, and on our way you will fill me in on everything you know."

Scott's eyebrows shot up. I forced myself not to look at him, but out of my peripheral I saw him nodding as if impressed by my stern commands. A humming sound grew louder until the light above the elevator door blinked. A wave of confidence passed through me as the doors opened. When I trained at the academy on Earth, I graduated in the field of security. The ESA command assigned me to the Echelon as a Tier 2 security officer, which handled all day to day activities on the Echelon. That meant I wasn't completely useless on Terra. My training included surveillance and examination of crime scenes. That couldn't have been Damon's reason for finding me, though. I seriously doubted my skills could compete with the Sentinels on Terra. Scott himself looked like he'd been through hell and back when it came to protecting this city.

Before we could enter the elevator, the humming stopped. The lights above us shut down one by one, cascading into a power failure that left us in the dark.

"What the hell?" one of the lieutenants cursed.

"Commander Scott to ground command. Jones, what's going on? We just lost power up here."

No response.

By now my bionic eye had activated night vision and I could see well enough. The medical team was looking in various directions. Commander Scott stood with his eyes closed and his radio to his mouth. He tried twice more to contact the ground floor, but failed.

"Can we return to the landing pad?" I asked.

"No. The doors seal if there's been any kind of security breach, and this counts as one."

"You don't have manual override?" I asked.

"Not from here. The switch has to be activated from the main level. That's how the tower was designed. We didn't need visitors, authorized or not, coming and going and making attempts to alter or operate equipment."

Fantastic.

Scott smacked his radio a couple times before he sighed and clipped it back on his belt. "We'll take the stairs," he told the medical team. "Remain here and we'll try to get the power back on."

We moved to the doorway and the soldiers took positions in front and behind of Scott, their weapons lifted and flashlights under their muzzles turned on. I wondered whether they expected trouble, or if that was their only means of illumination. Orson pushed on the handle and cracked the door open as Strong peaked through, investigating the stairwell.

"Well, at least there's some good news in all this," I said.

"And what's that?" Scott replied.

"At least we're going down the stairs and not up. Downhill is always easier!"

He didn't appreciate my humor, just shook his head and turned back toward his men.

"Let's move, one man in front of the other. Quinn, you stay between Strong and Orson."

We descended, and after about a hundred floors we were all breathing harder. We took a break halfway down and I leaned on the rail, sweat falling down my face and dripping from my chin. I watched the drop fall with my bionic eye, until it detected movement below. I switched to the thermo vision and a number of heat signatures moved up the stairs. Five, I thought.

"Lights out," I whispered. "Now!"

Scott moved to argue, but I threw my hand up and pointed down.

"There's movement down there. Five men climbing."

"It's probably the rest of my men," Scott said. I switched back to night vision and tried to get a good look at them. They wore black just like Scott, but they were covered in it. Their faces were painted black and protective helmets covered their heads. I focused on their weapons and detected some kind of carbine with a long scope and a launcher. I compared it to the shorter, more curved rifle Scott and his men carried.

"They're not friendly. Get your lights out," I said again, gritting my teeth. This power outage wasn't an accident. The men listened to me and soon we were submerged in darkness.

"How the hell are you able to see them?" he asked me.

"Let's save the explanations for later." The men moving toward us were twenty-five floors below us but were moving quickly. Their hands gripped their rifles, which were raised at the ready. I explained this to Scott, who was squinting down towards them. I had to give the advancing force credit, if it weren't for my bionic eye, I wouldn't have seen them or heard them; they moved with flawless grace.

"Everyone down and back against the wall," Scott whispered and his men followed his command. "We'll need to take these bastards by surprise. Get out flashbangs."

They reached into their cargo pants and pulled out four baseball-sized grenades. Orson handed me one.

"Here's the plan. Quinn, when they are two floors below us, we're all going to toss our grenades across the room. Count to three and shut your eyes as hard as you can. Understood?"

Whoever they were, they must have been using some kind of night vision to climb so quickly. I withdrew my revolver and turned the power down, setting it to stun. When they reached the second floor below us, I tapped Scott on the shoulder.

"Now!" he said, barely above a whisper. We all threw our grenades and counted.

One, two, three. I shut my left eye and put my hand over my bionic. I heard one of them shout "Grenade!" just as it went off.

The blast was bright enough that some of the light passed through the gaps in my fingers. Below us the men screamed and we took that as our cue to attack. We leapt down the stairs and I aimed my gun for the first attacker I spotted. Orson and Strong ran ahead, meeting them close quarters. I fired one round and hit my target in the chest. He fell back, but not down.

"Flux, they have armor!" I wanted to smack myself for not focusing on their outfit more with my bionic eye. I increased my gun's plasma settings when a bright blue ball shot from one of the grenade launchers, passed by Orson, hit the wall, and melted a hole through it. Orson screamed. His arm was burnt badly. What the hell kind of weapons were these?

We weren't going to win in a fire fight with these men. Orson had the right idea, though. Another attacker shot a ball of blue fire but missed, the smell of the fumes intoxicating as another hole was burned through the wall. Still, with the damage this weapon was causing, I didn't want it to land anywhere else, or on anyone else. Orson kept writhing in pain, but Strong got to him and pulled him back. Scott fired his own weapon at the attackers. Its bursts echoed through the stairway as his face was illuminated by yellow sparks from his muzzle. A barrage of bullets smacked into one of the attackers, the impacts sounding like hard taps against the armor. I fired my revolver again and hit another man the shoulder. He grunted and grabbed his injury, now smoking, but shouted to the man behind him and nodded in my direction.

Uh oh.

With just a second to react, I didn't have time to think of the best course of action. But only two options were presented to me—get melted by a blue ball of death or fall a hundred feet. Between the two, I chose the ridiculous one.

I backed toward the wall and pushed off from it, jumping over the railing like some kind of action hero. In truth, the distance wasn't that far, maybe ten feet across. But there was still a moment when I was suspended in air and the only thing between me and the floor was . . . nothing. I was already in the air by the time the attacker lifted his weapon. I reached back and pulled the sword, swinging it down as I landed. The blade cut right through the weapon and a broken piece clanked to the floor. I jammed the sword's hilt into the face of the man to my right, breaking his nose. He fell. I thrust my left hand forward and punched the jaw of the man on the left, who doubled back from the impact. I used the opening to shove my foot into his midsection and he fell into the man behind him, altering the aim of his rifle. He pulled the trigger and the blue blast melted the stairs across from us, only a couple of feet from where Strong had pulled Orson.

I fired two plasma rounds into both guards, the power level strong enough to incapacitate them. Then I sighed with relief, shocked I took down three men by myself in such an enclosed space. Back in the academy I had combat training, but years later I didn't know how much I had retained. Adrenaline can do that to a person—bring that knowledge forward so you don't have to think about it. Of course I didn't realize there was still another guard behind me.

"Quinn! Down!" I didn't look to see who said it or why. I obeyed and fell to the ground, jamming my back against a step's corner in the process. Still, that was far better than being consumed by the blue blast that passed over me. A round of rifle fire shot through the stairwell and after a moment, the final guard fell to the floor. I didn't move for a couple minutes. My chest heaved and salty sweat burned my eyes. Two men grunted and gasped, one of them Orson and the other the guard with the broken nose. The other four enemies were either unconscious or dead; I didn't know what Scott's weapons were designed for, stun or kill.

Commander Scott walked over to me. His flashlight was back on and provided a small source of light. He offered his hand, which I grabbed and he pulled me to my feet.

"Not bad, Quinn," he said, then addressed his men. "Orson, you okay?"

"It looks like a second degree burn on his upper arm," Strong answered. . Orson was tough. His clothing had burned away and his skin appeared deep pink and raw.

"Okay," Scott said. The two men down the stairs didn't move, and of the three above us, only one was mobile and he was easing himself against the wall while holding his nose to stop the bleeding. I looked at the sword. No blood. The corner of my mouth turned up and I reattached it to the magnetic strip.

"Orson and Strong, stay here and wait for back up. Keep your weapons on this guy," Scott ordered while pointing to the enemy. "Quinn and I are going to rush down to the lobby and get the power back on, and I'll send medics up to you."

"What if there are more attackers?" I asked. He smiled.

"Then I guess we won't send medics up here, will we?"

Good point.

We stepped over the two men and I noticed a tablet protruding from one of their pockets. I pulled it out and investigated it as we trekked our way down.

"Gaian spies, most likely," Scott muttered as we skipped every other step to hurry. "How the hell did they get on my planet and where the hell did they get that kind of weaponry?"

"I'm guessing Gaians don't normally have that advanced technology?"

"Not as far as I know, but the proof is upstairs."

With weaponry like that I was surprised the war still raged. Those rifles were lethal. I flicked through the pages on the tablet, trying to look for anything that could help us. I saw nothing of consequence, except one page toward the end.

"Stars above. Scott, take a look at this."

I had already stopped in my tracks, and Scott had to jump up a few steps. The page was a receipt for a signed assassination transaction, to kill us. At the top it read Starcade Business Receipt.

The Starcade was an intergalactic bulletin board. If you needed a job done outside the law, that's where you went. My job with the Karthans was performed through the Starcade. Someone not only wanted us killed, but they were willing to pay a lot of money to have the job completed.

EIGHT

Commander Scott and I emerged in a dimly lit hallway on the first floor. The only illumination came from a door cracked open on the left side. Commotion echoed through the halls, originating from around the right corner. Scott stood against the wall and peaked over, and then I saw the weight lift off his shoulders.

"It's my men," he said to me. "This is Scott!" he yelled.

"Sir!" Multiple people shouted and ran toward us. The lead soldier was a tall and well-built man with auburn hair. He stopped in front of Scott and, with his index and middle finger extended across his heart, saluted him.

"Commander. What the hell happened?"

Scott briefed him about the attempted ambush. Four additional men ran past us when the officer, whose name I learned was Tallet, ordered them to investigate and provide assistance to Orson and Strong.

"I don't understand," Tallet said. "I posted two men at the base of the stairwell when the power went out. Lee and Jones should have been here."

We found them outside the cracked door, their necks broken. Scott leaned over each of them and whispered in their ears. He stood and screamed out loud, kicking the wall and smashing his weapon against it. The soldiers with us did nothing to stop him, so I chose not to either, and made a note to never get this man angry if I could help it.

After he calmed down, we returned to the main lobby where engineers wearing white hazardous material suits were hard at work on the circuit breakers behind a large, glass desk. At first I stopped, thinking their outfits meant the air was dangerous, but I suppose it was a cautionary procedure. There were men without face masks walking around freely.

"What the hell happened?" Scott asked through his teeth. "How did those men get in this building?"

The engineer on the right turned around, his suit swooshing. His eyes were wide, as if he stared at a monster, as opposed to the Sentinel's commanding officer.

"Yes sir, um . . . it appears that they overloaded the power couplings from the generator. They used this device. Quite genius really." He held up a flat rectangular black box with no wires or connection ports.

"Genius," Scott muttered. "Why don't you go down the hall and tell the two dead Sentinels outside how genius it is?"

The engineer froze. Everyone in the room held their heads low, as if they all felt guilt from allowing the death of their comrades. Those attackers were skilled, and the only reason we had the upper hand was thanks to my bionic eye. Commander Scott was convinced they were Gaian assassins, but I wasn't so sure. Why the need for the Starcade and payment? From what I saw, Terra and Gaia wanted to kill each other for free.

"Commander, sir," Tallet said softly as he approached Scott. "She's here, sir. She's outside."

At the name of *her*, the anger surrounding Scott melted and his shoulders slouched.

"Get the power back on. Now," he said. "Get Damon down here and let's get these doors open."

Damon didn't mention family in his reports. Was it a wife or sister? Guilt tightened my stomach. I swayed and pressed my fingers into my abdomen, trying to calm the uncomfortable feeling. The engineers worked hard, even more so after Scott yelled at one of them. I felt a thud below my feet and heard a low hum. Light-by-light, the electricity surged once more through the building. The front doors opened and a plethora of people stepped into the lobby—some of them medical personnel, some holding cameras and microphones. One particular person caught my attention—a young woman with a soft face, high cheekbones, and eyes the color of a warm, golden sun. Her eyes were red and a path of tears led down her face.

She was too young to be Damon's wife. Possibly his sister, but I was willing to bet this was his daughter. I felt even worse for taking her father away from her.

It's not your fault Daniel, I thought. *Granak did this.*

She caught Commander Scott's gaze and walked toward us. Lieutenant Tallet handled the press, but I found myself staring at the young woman. She wore black pants that hugged her legs and a khaki jacket covering an ivory colored blouse. The somersaults in my stomach evolved into a small tornado.

"Hello, Autumn," Scott said, opening his arms to her. As they embraced, she nearly lost her composure again.

"My dad," she said in a voice light, but strained. "Is he…?"

"He's here, love." I blinked at Scott's sudden change of personality. The hard, grizzled Sentinel had turned into a sympathizing, nurturing man in a matter of minutes.

"This is Daniel Quinn," he said, waving his hand toward me. "He brought your father."

I felt caught in that moment. I wanted to tell her everything would be okay, though that was a lie. I knew what it felt like to have someone you love taken from you unexpectedly. A memory of Ashley passed through my mind, her body on my bed, stab wounds in her stomach. I flinched and shook my head.

"I'm sorry," I said, though she might not have heard me.

The elevator chimed and when the doors opened, the medical team I met on the roof walked out, pulling Damon's stretcher with them. Autumn placed a hand on the coffin. As I watched her cry, I thought about the moment when her father died and looked away.

"You all right, Quinn?" Scott asked, his voice returning to its previous sternness.

"I'm fine," I said quickly.

"You sure? This crime scene you want to see is graphic, a little much for anyone with a light stomach. If you can't stay composed around a grieving young woman, maybe taking you wouldn't be the best idea."

"Don't worry. I've seen my fair share of disturbing images."

One of Scott's eyebrows shot up. He surveyed the scene around him. The press was being addressed. Autumn was with her father's body, and Orson and Strong were escorted around the corner, Orson's arm wrapped up. Scott waved at them and Strong joined us.

"Situation?" Scott asked.

"Mack, Darling, and Iris are handling the prisoner," Strong replied. "Orson is okay, the nurse gave him something for the pain."

"I want you back at headquarters immediately," Scott said. "Two of our own men died today, not to mention Damon and the council members. Find out how they infiltrated this building. Report to me as soon as you can. Quinn, you're coming with me."

Strong saluted his superior officer and moved off, taking control and giving orders to the soldiers. Scott and I walked toward the tower's exit—a giant glass door that could have easily fit one of the Belle's wings. The two panels spread open as we passed through the low illumination of the tower building to a dark, moonlit night—though I didn't recall scanning any moons surrounding the planet when I approached.

A number of vehicles ranging from hover cycles to large armored trucks were scattered in the road. Beyond that, screams, cheers, and a number of different voices filled the air. Signs were held in the air and even with my bionic eye I couldn't count the amount of people.

We Need the War, one sign read.

Death to Gaia, read another.

Control Everything or Nothing at All!

Stars above. I expected indifferences and maybe hesitation toward the peace council, but I was speechless at the sight of hundreds of people screaming in support of the war. A bright yellow stream of energy blocked the civilians from crossing into the tower's parking area. The attackers could have easily camouflaged themselves in this crowd, though I had no idea how they got past the beam.

Scott led us to a sleek vehicle—all curves and no wheels. The roof and hood were dark red, while the rest was black. As we approached, the car scanned Scott, welcomed him, and opened the door. When I reached the passenger side, it scanned me, but blinked red.

"Unauthorized civilian at passenger location," a female voice said.

"Override on my authorization, Scott, Reynold J."

The door opened and I slid into the soft, comfortable seat. The vehicle started and we lifted into the air, above the police and medical units, above the angry citizens, and took off into the night. From the docking tower to the Trenton Hall building, the ride was smooth and the glow of the city passed by us in a stream of lights. Scott remained silent, his eyebrows creased together.

"So what I can't figure out," I said, trying to break the silence, "is how the hell Damon found me, and why he chose me to come here."

He shrugged.

"I keep asking myself this question," I continued. "I never met the man, never visited either of these planets, but he wanted me here."

No response from Scott, again. Either he was a man of few words, or he didn't like me very much. I figured it would be best to shut up for the rest of the ride, which didn't end up taking very long. We followed traffic patterns in the sky, identified by aerial beacons until we reached our destination.

Trenton Hall was hard to miss. It stood alone, surrounded by a field of grass and sidewalks. Its most noticeable aspect was a large red shield that covered the structure like a bubble. I leaned forward and noticed a group of people surrounding the base of the shield. My eyes darted from the shield to Scott, who didn't slow down at all as we approached. I grasped my seat and clenched my teeth together, thinking we might crash into it, but we passed through without any trouble.

"It keeps unauthorized personnel from entering the crime scene," Scott said when he saw my expression. As we landed, I got a better view of the crowd behind the bubble. The sight was the same as the docking tower; men and women of all ages held signs and screamed profanities about peace with Gaia.

"How the hell are you even in peace talks? Everyone here wants the war to continue."

We got out of the vehicle.

"A lot of people don't want peace. Our planets have lived so long beside each other fighting, killing, conspiring, that it's the only way of life these people know anymore."

"So how the hell did your governments agree to form a peace council in the first place?" I asked.

"People don't realize what it costs in finances and manpower to keep this war going. They've just gotten used to it for so long that the possibility of peace is terrifying to them. I can't say I blame them for feeling that way. The truth of the matter is, too many people are dying, and too much money is spent toward advancing our military. Before you know it, Terra will be one of the most technologically advanced planets in human civilization, but there won't be any humans to use it. We'll all be blown to bits by each other."

I could only imagine. Two planets at war with no end in sight until the destruction of one another. It reminded me of something Derrick Kenton once told me. He was the bartender of one of the premier human space stations in the galaxy, Galaxy One Alpha. He said that humanity didn't evolve toward space travel because of discovery or exploration. We moved into space because we had already smothered the Earth with wars and economic turmoil. People with different beliefs and ways of living just couldn't understand each other, which then led to arguments and eventually, bloodshed.

We were quiet after that. We walked through a swiveling door into the Hall's lobby, a grand room with four square columns. To my right, there were chairs and couches for relaxing. Across from that was an area filled with books. The other two sections were more recreational with exercise equipment and table games.

We walked past an empty lobby desk and turned left at a T-shaped intersection.

"You can hear a pin drop in this place . . . did you evacuate the entire complex?" I asked.

"I wouldn't exactly call it an evacuation," Scott said. "Once residents found out that two men and a woman were brutally murdered, they all checked out early."

"Are we the only ones here?"

"No. Some of my men are still investigating other rooms. It hasn't been determined whether the killer had been living here or simply walked in and did his business before leaving."

"What about the other council members? Where are they now?"

"We moved them to various secure locations," he said.

"Various? You split them up?"

"We had to," he continued. "We were lucky that only three were killed this time. Maybe the killer thought they were all gathered together. Who knows? We have very little information right now. For all I know, the Gaians are the ones who set this up."

"Or the Terrans, judging by that mob outside," I said.

Scott sighed deeply.

"Yes . . . I suppose it could have been one of us as well. Here we are."

We stopped in front of an antique door. The wood was dark brown with small variations of white and carvings of Celtic knots interweaving throughout one another. Scott nudged me aside and placed what looked to be a keycard on a rectangular tray beside the door. A green light blinked and the door unlocked. I slowly pushed it open.

Body parts were scattered everywhere; scraps and patches of clothing were still attached to some, but most were bare. Arms ripped out of their sockets dangled from the couch and bed. Legs were twisted in shapes they weren't meant to make. I couldn't see anything that was a head or chest, but there were piles of blood and gore that could easily be a body part turned inside out.

"You didn't clear the bodies?" I asked him, nearly choking on bile.

Scott pulled out a tablet and keyed a code. Before I knew it, every body part vanished. I blinked and stepped back.

"We cleared them a few days ago, but we have the ability to scan a crime scene down to every detail, including odors, exactly as it originated."

"Flux, that's brilliant," I said. It really was. The smell actually burned—a mixture of sweat, blood, and death.

I activated the theoretical analysis function of my bionic eye. It scanned over everything. The front door hadn't been touched except for the doorknob. The walls and windows were sealed shut. None of the furniture in the living area had been used. However, I did find a couple of hair samples on the carpet floor. Unfortunately, the technology that made my eye work wasn't advanced enough to determine whether the hair was alien, human, or other. I pointed it out to Scott in hopes that his team could identify it.

The room itself was the size of a small cottage—separate rooms for the sleeping area, living room, and kitchen. From the front door, you could branch out to any of the areas from the main hallway. My first focal point, indicated by the amount of energy readings from my eye, was the bedroom, which told a revealing story. The bed's size was immense, larger than what I would consider a king size. The same Celtic knots on the door were strewn over the woodwork of the headboard. It contained lipstick stains, sweat, and a couple of other human-type fluids. On the side of the bed that faced the wall sat a shirt, slacks, and a dark purple dress. Except for being a little wrinkled, they looked fine. Another scan revealed various pieces of soft, feather-like cloth that had been shredded and spread throughout the room. I checked the kitchen and the utensils on the counter, but this side of the room looked undisturbed. I disengaged my eye to its normal operation.

"I'm surprised you aren't more horrified by this," Scott said softly. "So, what did you find?"

I shrugged. "This fluffy stuff." I held up the torn piece. "What is it?"

He took it and moved it between his fingers. "It's a robe. Every room in this complex has one."

I took a deep breath and tried to clear my thoughts. "You said three people were murdered. Who were they?"

"Two men from Terra—Patrick Keegan and Paul Winters. Then the woman—she's Ilayna Porter of Gaia. This was Patrick's room. Paul was next door while Ilayna had a room upstairs."

"I assume the corpse with the shreds of clothing is Paul?" I asked. Scott nodded. I tried to picture the scene around me as it happened—the shredded clothes, the bare bodies, the fluids, all the while trying to recover the memories of training as a security officer at the academy.

"Did you realize that Ilayna and Patrick were more than just friends?" Scott nodded to me, his eyes intense and watching my every move.

For some reason, this felt more like an audition than an additional investigation. Was he looking to see what I could do? What if he wasn't satisfied—would he toss me back to the dock and let me be on my way?

If he wanted to play games with me, then so be it. I hesitated coming here in the first place, but felt I owed it to Damon to return him home. But he also knew something. Something about me that could help put a stop to the horror I witnessed. The fact that mercenaries attacked us minutes after I arrived told me the killers were anxious.

I looked over the data one more time, formulated my words carefully, and told Scott my theory.

"The night before the murder, Ilayna and Patrick were intimate; having their own personal peace treaty, you might say. Things heat up, finish, and cool down. Afterward, there's a knock at the door."

"Paul?" Scott asked. I shook my head.

"No, not Paul, but someone they knew just as well, maybe better." I pointed to the door and its peephole at eye level. "The council had to be cautious. Whoever answered the door threw on his or her robe and checked to see who was there. It would have been someone they trusted, because they opened the door. There's also the fact that whoever this is got past security without any problems."

"My security team saw nothing out of the ordinary last night, and they patrolled these halls every twenty minutes," Scott said matter-of-factly.

"Then either the killer was a skilled space ninja or there's some dirt in your Sentinel staff."

Scott flinched at that. He didn't like to hear that his own team might have been involved. I continued.

"I detected no fractures, pressure points, or DNA readings of any kind. The only fingerprints on the door are on the knob. So this person entered the room and the rest was history. Patrick and Ilayna were murdered. I assume that Paul heard the commotion from his room next door and came to investigate."

"Anything else?" he asked.

"Whoever they are, it would have taken a lot of hate and even more strength to rip these three apart like this. I don't think any human could have done this."

"My team considered the same thing. There are some local technologies capable of this, but nothing easily transported. We don't really get many aliens on Terra, due to a lot of those extremist-type people who like to do nasty things to inhuman creatures. Hell, we have enough trouble not killing other humans, let alone not killing aliens."

"You can always find an alien willing to do something or go somewhere as long as his price is met . . ."

"What?" Scott asked as he placed his hands against his belt.

I explained the situation that led me here, my run in with Granak on Karth, and the murder of Damon Derringer. The whole while, I thought about the droids on Karth, how they were torn apart much like the people here. In fact, the carnage was eerily similar.

"So, you think this Leondren mercenary killed them?" Scott asked.

That's exactly what I was thinking. He was more than strong enough to rip the council apart, but I couldn't believe that he personally knew any of the council members. If I was Patrick and I checked my peephole and saw Granak, I'd have locked the door and backed away.

"I don't know," I said. "Granak certainly had the strength to do something like this, but I don't think he had the time or security access. You said these murders occurred a couple of days ago?"

"Aye. Three days ago to be exact."

"The timing is narrow since I met Granak on Karth. After he disabled my ship, he turned and jumped away. But would that have left him enough time to get to Terra, bypass Sentinel security, murder three people, and vanish?"

"Either way, he has some part to play in this shithole of a situation." Scott ran his hand through his hair and released a sigh. "The question is—what the hell do we do now? Do we send the council members home? Do we stop the treaty?"

"I wouldn't do that," I said. "Stopping the peace treaty is exactly what the killer or killers want. I wouldn't send them home, either. Whoever did this, did their homework. They know who the council is and where they're from, otherwise how would they have gained such easy access in the first place?"

Scott nodded in agreement.

"I think you and I are on the same page—Patrick and Ilayna knew their killer. Paul may have known him, too, so we'll start there. I already have my guys screening friends, family, and anyone they had contact with over the last couple of weeks. It's going to be a big list, but it's the best we have. I'll also make sure this hair sample from the carpet gets processed; might as well give it a shot."

"Agreed," I said. "And don't count out Granak either. Someone or something ripped these bodies apart. Keep a sharp eye on spaceports and any unauthorized landing areas you know of. If he isn't here yet, he will be soon. I don't know the specifics of his involvement, but he's probably getting paid by the killers to be a sharp piece of metal in our sides. The way he talked on Karth . . . his job completed, his attack on my ship—there's more here than we realize."

We left the room and walked back to the vehicle. The mob was still there. Their voices cried out for the war to go on, for the Gaians to meet their end. I felt sad for them. Habits are usually hard to break, and these people had the hardest habit of all—the need to feel rage and death. If only they knew it would most likely lead to their own destruction. Humanity always had trouble unifying, even centuries ago. There was always someone who needed to be better than the other, or a group of people willing to fight and kill because of a disagreement. I couldn't help but suspect that the people outside the shield would get their wish. They would have their war and, in the end, both sides would lose—just like Earth. All our natural resources sucked dry, the human population smothering each other to a point of desperation.

Saving these council members was all that mattered now. I had questioned Damon Derringer's choice to find me and ask for help, and to be honest, I still did. For some reason he thought I was the guy to help, that one person who could make a difference. But could I? It wouldn't be the first time I tried to save a planet, but this time I would try to save two.

Something else nagged at me. The carnage was similar to the droids on Karth, but not identical. The droids had numerous claw marks over their metal bodies, but I didn't detect any scratches on the human body parts. At the same time, Granak was involved somehow; otherwise he wouldn't have come after Damon and attacked my ship.

The Terrans and Gaians were no doubt blaming this on each other, which would only add fuel to the fire that was their war. Someone wanted this to happen, wanted them to make accusations. Someone wanted to make sure this peace treaty didn't take place, and from the look and sounds of the mob outside, it could have been any number of people.

NINE

Scott called in to headquarters, letting them know we were bringing samples to analyze. I found myself dozing off a couple of times on the way, though the images of the digital corpses were enough to jolt me awake every couple of minutes.

"Listen, Quinn," Scott said. "I want to apologize. I wasn't sure whether I could trust you or not, and I worried that you would only slow me down. I never said thank you for saving us in the stairwell."

"It's okay," I said through a yawn. "I know what you must be thinking. Damon travels across solar systems just to find a beaten down mercenary; what the hell was he thinking?"

"Maybe we'll both understand it someday. Anyway, I regret my cold shoulder toward you. It just felt like a cruel joke, and this is a bad time for Terra. People are dying right under me, and I'm failing to protect them."

I watched Scott as we continued through the city. His gaze was intense, nostrils flared, as if he was about to explode. He held a tight grip on the wheel, grinding his gloves against it. You couldn't cut the tension on his side of the vehicle with the strongest plasma cutter.

"Almost ten years ago," Scott continued, "I was in charge of a trade agreement between a group of Gaian farmers and Terran scientists. Back then, half of us at least had an understanding that we needed each other to prosper. The two groups met, both with an armed escort. The trade was going smoothly at first, but sometimes when you hold onto so much hate, even if it's superficial, you act recklessly. My men started antagonizing the Gaian soldiers and eventually words turned into action. Four people died that day because I couldn't control my men. I failed as the superior officer. Now we're in the middle of the most important peace treaty in our history, and I can't protect the council tasked with saving our worlds. And two of my own men are dead."

I felt bad for him. Living with guilt for ten years must have taken a toll. No wonder he was cold with me during our first meeting. But as I listened to him confide in me, I hoped it would build respect between us, enough so that he could trust me, and I him. Had he talked to anyone else about this? Being in a position like his, who knew how much time he had for friends? But that's why you need them—to trust and bear some of your life's weight. Sometimes the hardest step is the first one, and if Scott and I were going to work together to solve this, we had to cross that road together.

"Over a year ago," I said, "I saved an alien species from being enslaved, but in order to save them, I had to destroy their only source of energy. They had grown dependent on the power and I took that away from them. It would be like knocking humanity back into the Stone Age. I understand that had I not acted, their entire race would have been extinguished or enslaved by a couple of evil assholes, but that doesn't change the way I feel. It was a no-win situation and even though the aliens are safe, that doesn't mean they'll survive."

"Hmm," Scott said. We veered left and then right after a mile or two. "I guess we all have to come face to face with a no-win situation don't we?"

"The point is," I continued, "that I think I did the right thing, and I'm sure you did all you could when your officers acted against your orders. You're doing all you can now to protect the council, but you can't protect everyone, Scott. You might be in charge of hundreds of men, but you yourself are only one man. Don't let the hatred and rage consume you. I know what that's like. I've lost control before and it's damn scary, the things you can be capable of."

"Isn't that the truth? I just hope General Ambrose isn't too pissed about what happened at the tower." Scott chuckled. We smiled softly to each other, not really a release of our tension, but more of an understanding between the two of us. I liked Commander Scott. His presence and personality kept me level-headed in this flux-storm of a situation we were in.

"So this General Ambrose . . . what's he like?" I asked.

"I don't envy him the position he's in, responsible for the peace between planets, trying to organize the fleets into not only a cease-fire, but a merger should the council succeed. But he's tough, and he will do anything to make sure things get done.

He's a strict son of a bitch. The man knows what he wants and will do anything to make sure it gets done."

"How does it work? You're in charge of interplanetary security and he handles everything off-world?"

"In a manner of speaking, he's the government's military and defense advisor," Scott said. "I haven't seen him much lately because he's been on Gaia trying to work with their security officers. The council can try to create the peace all they want, but if they don't have guards that will uphold and protect that goal, then it's a waste of time."

"Agreed. So what's the plan now?" I asked him.

"Once we're back at headquarters, you will look at the data we've collected and find something we couldn't. With any luck, the boys have also solved how the mercenaries killed the power in the docking tower."

"After we're done with that, I want to see the council members."

"I don't think that's a good idea," Scott said.

"Damon Randolph, for whatever reason, appointed me as his replacement. That means I get access to them, no matter what anyone thinks. If I'm going to help protect them and figure out why my name is involved in this, I must get to know the council."

"Damn you for making a good point," he grumbled as we rounded a tall, circular building and came within view of the security headquarters.

In comparison to all the state-of-the-art skyscrapers surrounding us, the security HQ was noticeably plain. It was a four story, square building with a steel grid wall around the perimeter. A number of weapon turrets were placed on the four corners of the roof and all turned towards us as we entered the compound. Two spotlights from gate-towers illuminated the vehicle, then powered down when it recognized Commander Scott. As he flew us to the ground, I expected the floors to drum, but realized I was only thinking of the Belle. Less than a day and I already missed her.

"Welcome to Terran Sentinel HQ, Quinn." I retrieved my sword, which had been placed in the back seat of Scott's vehicle, and we walked into the compound through a large steel door, which opened as we approached. Inside, men and women jogged back and forth. Phones rang, people shouted, and keyboards clacked. A large, curved metal desk separated Scott and me from the rest of the floor. A bulky man in a skin tight uniform watched as we approached. I couldn't help but wonder if he requested a uniform that tight, or if they just didn't make any in his size. He didn't look to be the sort I should piss off.

"Stern," Scott called out. "Anything to report?"

"Yes, sir," Stern replied, saluting with an open hand over his chest. "Rose and Barton found the Gaian mercenaries using surveillance footage around the docking tower. It looks like they traveled through the crowd toward the side entrance, where some kind of device was used to bypass the security field."

I wondered where these mercenaries got their weaponry, with devices that bypass high tech security, shut down electronics throughout the whole building, and melt flesh and metal. Between the Terrans and Gaians, it seemed to me that Terra was more advanced technologically, unless the Gaians were using a third party to acquire their weapons. It would make sense, considering they were using the Starcade for business transactions.

"Try and find out how the Gaian bastards are getting hold of their technology," Scott said, "and open up a secure communications line to the council. Also, have forensics analyze these hair samples and compare them to any previous findings."

"Yes, sir," Stern said, taking the samples from him.

We passed the main desk and walked through a security gate. The alarm went off for both of us, drawing the looks of everyone in the room. Scott walked over to the side where Stern met us, and he held up a scanning device of some kind, a small shaft with an analysis module on top, its read beam traveling over Scott's body after he removed his weapons. Stern waved him through and moved to scan me. I removed the sword and my revolver, but even after that, Stern's device bleeped.

"What else are you carrying?"

"Probably my eye." I pointed to it. He held the beam up close to it and pressed a couple of commands on his module.

"Bionic?" he asked. "That must have been painful."

You have no idea . . .

"What else? I'm detecting two more signatures on you."

Two? For a moment I stood there, confused, until I remembered the ring around my neck. The inset where a diamond used to be had been replaced by a small micro-memory drive from Al's mainframe. It allowed for data uploads and downloads as well as shortwave teleportation, though I used that last one sparingly. Al always reminded me how slim of a chance I had at rematerializing in one piece. Not to mention, with Al damaged or lost, the teleporter wouldn't work.

The second signature I hoped to keep secret—the memory drive Damon planted on Tess, the one that held all his information. I reached back into my pocket and pulled it out, then held it and my necklace up for Stern to inspect.

"Satisfied?" I asked. He looked hesitant, his eyes darting back and forth to the drives. He opened his mouth to say something, but Scott intervened.

"Is he clear, Stern? We have work to do." For a moment, I thought Stern would insist on studying the drives and my nerves intensified, but he looked back to Scott, nodded, and resumed his original position. Scott waved me over and we entered the main floor of the building. Desks and tables were arranged like spokes in a wheel that led to the middle of the room, which had a round holographic map of the entire planet. Commander Scott led me around the room, where a few dozen officers were hard at work, some looking over holographic displays of the city, others typing furiously on their keyboards. We stopped when we reached the far end of the room where a door had Scott's name on it.

His office was a technological marvel, at least from my point of view. A glass panel was attached to the right wall, holographic maps and markers covering its surface. No computer terminals or items covered the desk that stood in the middle of the room. Instead a glowing keyboard and screen were infused into the desk itself. The surface *was* the computer. Large glowing letters read 'standby' in the middle of the desk.

"Alright." Scott took off his holster and hung it across his chair, then activated his computer. "Let's make sure we're both on the same page." He used a holographic keyboard to bring up a list of the council. Most of them were middle-aged to elderly. Patrick and Ilayna were very attractive. Light brown hair was combed over Patrick's head while Ilayna's sandy colored hair fell to her neck. Their eyes, brown and blue respectively, gazed with gentleness. Their smiles were warm and looked full of life.

Not anymore.

"About six to seven months ago, both planets launched a full scale battalion. Their mission was to exterminate the other side and take control of both planets. But as the death toll rose, our governments soon came to regret their decision. Too many people lost their lives. We've all known war for so long and they felt it was time to change, to try something different so our people could live and prosper. Against many people's wishes, from homeless to high government, the council was formed.

Twelve people were chosen to discuss terms of a ceasefire, and soon the era of peace was looking more and more likely. Over that time, armies and factions still attempted to attack each other, all in hopes that the council would realize how futile their attempt was, but the longer the council held onto hope and continued to talk peace, more people began to warm to the idea.

"You've seen the crowds, the hatred and want for more bloodshed, but what you haven't seen yet is the thousands who cry out for peace, who want their loved ones to come home alive, not in a box like Damon Derringer."

I heard most of this already from the files Damon gave me, but I wanted to hear it again from someone else, just to confirm what I already knew, or to possibly learn something Damon neglected to mention.

"Tell me more about Damon," I said.

Scott leaned back in his chair and crossed his arms. "He was an honorable man, always did his job. He volunteered to be the council's advisor, to see to their needs and record all their notes and meeting discussions. The job wasn't safe, of course. He received death threats constantly, but he took them with a grain of salt, never worrying too much over it. 'Peace is what these planets need,' he always said."

If Damon had waved off previous death threats against him, what caused him to flee his home planet this time? My mind focused on Granak and his hunt for him, but did that originate here on Terra, or was he hired during Damon's flight to Karth?

Something spooked him, or he found something he wasn't supposed to.

"When was the last time you spoke to him?" I asked.

"I saw him off-planet. I escorted him to the space shuttle and watched him fly away."

"What did he say? What did you know about his mission?"

"I knew little," Scott said, his eyes focusing downward. "He called me and told me he needed to leave the planet. I asked why, and he said only three things before he stepped onto the shuttle. He said his mission would ensure the safety of the peace between our worlds, and that he would return with a young man named Daniel Quinn. Lastly, he told me to look after his daughter."

I hadn't really thought about Autumn since I met her outside the docking tower, but the sound of her name summoned a clear image of her. Emotions cascaded, a mixture of guilt and something else . . . almost like warmth. How was she coping with her father's death? I knew that it was only a matter of time before I needed to talk to her. She might have known something about Damon that Scott didn't.

My stomach churned and the warmth faded as my mind changed course. Scott was the last person to see Damon before he left, and he didn't have knowledge of where he was going, only that he wanted to find me. Damon didn't trust anyone, not even his friends. Did he believe what I had been suspecting? Was the murder of the council an inside job?

Advanced weaponry, bypassing security measures, and, worst of all, Patrick and Ilayna opening their door to the killer; it all led to the conclusion that if someone on the Sentinel team wasn't the actual murderer, then someone else helped that person commit the crime. I wanted to bring my thoughts to Scott's attention, but Damon's few words with him made me hesitate. Did he think Commander Reynold Scott could be a potential suspect?

Is that why he needed me? Did he need someone to trust on the outside, someone without ties to Terra or Gaia? If that's true, how was I supposed to trust anyone?

Don't forget, Damon did tell Scott to look after his daughter. Would he really ask him that if he knew Scott was a traitor?

"Commander," a voice called, which sounded like Stern. "The council is prepared to speak with you."

"Acknowledged, Ensign. Patch us through."

A wave of static emerged from the office's sound system and a green check mark appeared over the council members' names and faces on the screen, except for the recently deceased. Trent, Burns, Finn, Larson, Smith, Greene, Maxwell, Rider, and Townsend were the last names of the council members. Any time they talked, a wavelength bar under their profile picture shifted.

"Commander Scott," said Greene, a woman who looked to be in her late fifties. "Do you have any information about the murders?"

"Councilor Greene, I, unfortunately do not have any further details, though we are still investigating the matter with all haste."

"We need this matter solved, Commander," said Burns, though her tone was deeper and more raspy. "We need to reconvene as soon as possible to continue peace talks."

"No kidding," I said out loud, but meant for it to be said internal. I clenched my eyes shut as I heard my own voice.

"Who is that?" many of the council members asked.

"Ladies and gentlemen of the council," Scott said, his narrow eyes glaring at me. "I regret to inform you that advisor Damon Derringer is dead."

I heard gasps, and multiple wavelength bars sharply spiked.

"In his stead, acting advisor Daniel Quinn has been brought up to speed on current events, and he is here with me now to assist you in whatever way possible."

"What did you mean Daniel Quinn, when you muttered the phrase, 'no kidding'?" The stern male voice originated from Trent.

"I'm just surprised that you all want to continue the peace talks. Three of your council were brutally murdered, Damon was chased halfway across the galaxy and killed, and the first thing on your minds is to continue? You're not scared of what could happen, that you might die trying to accomplish a task that no one seems to want?"

"Mr. Quinn," a throaty voice said, coming from Mr. Maxwell. "Do you know what my father and grandfather died for? Nothing. Absolutely nothing. Both served as soldiers on starships, and both were killed in skirmishes between Terra and Gaia. Their goal? To control what wasn't rightfully theirs. There were twelve of us, nine now, yet if we die, we do so with an honorable purpose: the uniting of our two worlds, and to stop soldiers and citizens from dying meaningless deaths. Do you understand sacrifice Mr. Quinn? If you did, then you would understand why we wish to continue."

I heard murmurs from the rest of the group, and the corner of my mouth curled upward. Giving up is easy when the odds are stacked against you, but when people are willing to stand up and give their lives for what they believe in, it creates a spark of hope.

"Thank you, Councilor," I said. "I hope I don't fail you, any of you. Here's what we know so far. It's looking more likely that the killer, or an accomplice, was close to the council, specifically Patrick and Ilayna. What we need from you is to think hard about the types of people you've been in contact with, someone who had access to you at all times. If anyone knows more about Patrick Keegan, friends or even enemies he had, now would be a good time to come forward with this information."

I shifted my weight from my left leg to my right and waited for an answer, but I heard only white noise. Either the council didn't know anything, which was unlikely, or they weren't comfortable sharing the information over this communication channel. I assumed the line would be secured before we made contact, but did their fear drive their hesitation? Scott and I looked at each other, and though I didn't know what he was thinking, I couldn't shake the feeling that these murders looked more and more like an inside job.

"Think on it," I said after a minute of silence. "And please let me know if there's anything I can do for you."

"We would like to discuss a remembrance for Damon," Trent said. "We could all gather together and share his memory with each other, so that his death is secured in our honored halls."

"I don't really think bringing you all together is a good idea," I said.

"In case you forgot, Mr. Quinn," Maxwell spoke again, "our lives are not important as much as the idea of peace and prosperity."

You kind of need to be alive to make the peace, I thought.

"We'll figure something out to honor Damon," Scott chimed in. "For now, we will let you rest. Please contact us directly if you think of anything that could help us."

The council said their thanks and goodbyes, and then Scott deactivated the communicator. He stared at me, which made me more uncomfortable than I already was, if that was even possible.

"Are you thinking what I'm thinking?" he asked. I shrugged. "Trent and Maxwell were adamant about holding a ceremony for Damon, a perfect opportunity to get the council together."

"Well, they seemed kind of self-righteous to me," I said. "I'm not really surprised if this council is as tight knit as I think it is."

"Sure, sure." Scott waved of his hand, then stood up and turned toward his window, which overlooked a backdrop of shimmering skyscrapers and vehicles so far away they looked like Earth fireflies traveling in perfect formations. "Imagine though, if the killer was closer to this than we thought. He moved so easily through our security and the council because he was closer than any of us."

My eyebrows shot up. "You think one of the council members is the killer? Trent or Maxwell?"

"It's a ridiculous assumption, but I find it hard to believe someone infiltrated the hotel without us knowing about it."

Scott grasped for any kind of explanation. I wanted to throw out another possibility, but held my tongue—what if one of the Sentinels were somehow involved? They were the only security team with exclusive access to the council. I made a mental side note to take a closer look at the security group. For now Scott would be better left in the dark. With his distress over the murders, including Damon's, the last thing I needed was to lose any potential trust we gained today. Besides, if he was as capable a commander as I perceived him to be, he'd be looking at his own men already.

The desk blinked green twice and the voice of Stern, who seemed more like a secretary than a soldier, came back on the line.

"Commander Scott. General Ambrose requests a priority channel with you immediately."

"Put him through," Scott said.

I stood up, motioning for the door, but Scott put his hand forward and lowered it, gesturing me to sit down. He placed his index finger across his lip as a deep, rich bass voice spoke.

"Reynold, what the hell is happening on my planet?"

"Sir?"

"I heard about the attack at the tower, and who the hell is this Quinn that landed?"

"Two men have been killed, sir, but we're all hard at work to determine how they gained access. Captain Daniel Quinn arrived a few hours ago at the request of Damon Derringer himself. He saved my life, sir, and the lives of my team. He's helping us with the investigation of the council murders."

"Hmph," Ambrose grunted. "Keep an eye on this man, Reynold. For all we know he's the one who killed Damon just to get access." A shiver crawled up my spine at the accusation. I wanted to say something, but Scott held up his hand again in silence. "I'll be returning from Gaia in two days, and I'll want a situation report on everything that's happened. And I want to meet this Quinn fellow."

"Yes, sir, I'll have everything ready for you. Scott out."

I breathed in and let out more of a yawn than a sigh. Scott did the same, rubbed his eyes, and blinked a couple times.

"It's the middle of the night, Quinn. I think we would both benefit from a few hours' sleep."

"What about all the data? And the prisoner you captured?"

"Everything is a priority where the safety of the council is concerned, but we need to be awake and aware of what's happening around us. We need to recharge our batteries, so to speak. Do you require accommodations?"

I shook my head. "My ship will do fine. I want to make sure my associate is doing well, and I'll look over some data before we get started in the morning."

"I'll have someone give you a ride back to the docking tower, but here . . . take this." He pulled a small sheet of glass, no bigger than a business card from under his desk, and handed it to me. When I grabbed it, numbers and buttons appeared on it. "It's a communicator, just in case I need to get in touch with you while you're on your ship."

He made a call back to Stern and then extended his hand to me. "Good meeting you, Quinn, and good work today. Go ahead back to the lobby and I'll have someone pick you up in the morning, say 0800 hours?"

I shook his hand and stood up, but something nagged at me, something Ambrose said.

"Commander, Ambrose asked you to keep an eye on me, believing I could be a suspect. How is it you haven't voiced a similar concern?"

"I haven't voiced it, but that doesn't mean I haven't considered it," he replied with a coy grin. "Your ship is grounded, and you are within constant supervision of the Sentinels. You do know the phrase, 'keep your friends close and your enemies closer,' don't you?"

TEN

Throughout the night I woke up with the images of Damon's murder and the council members' corpses replaying in my dreams. In total, I maybe slept a couple hours, *after* Tress interrogated me about everything I saw and did after I left him.

Like a shambling corpse and with a pounding headache, I dragged myself into the kitchen, my arms flailing useless at my sides. Tress, of course, was already awake and lunged for the cabinet to grab a ration for me. I dropped onto a seat, which squeaked against my weight.

"Niru danta Prata!" Tress said. A thick fog traveled in circles within my head, and I found it hard to concentrate on Tress's words. After two glasses of water and the ration, which consisted of beans, rice, and dried fruit, my head cleared a little bit and I found it easier to translate Tress's language again. *Good morning, Captain*, he said.

"What time is it?" I asked.

"The sun has appeared over the horizon," he said. "I heard you throughout the night, thrashing in your sleep. Are you all right, Captain?"

"Let's see, I watched a man get murdered, my ship and artificial intelligence broke, I got to see a couple of disgusting digital corpses, and I've been put in a position not only to help stop Terra and Gaia from destroying each other, but it's also been hinted that I'm a suspect."

I told him all this last night before I slept, but it felt good to vent it again. In that time, only more and more questions were ahead of me. Who killed the council? Who hired the mercenaries to attack Scott's team and me? How did Granak fit in with this situation—an alien in the middle of a human conflict?

After the small and unsatisfying breakfast, I spent an hour jogging up and down the corridors, something I tried to make a habit to keep my body and mind healthy. Although I normally sprinted to keep up my heart rate, the pain bouncing in my head kept my pace slow. Once done, I returned to my quarters, allowed myself a quick shower, and changed into loose clothes— soft black pants and a white sleeveless shirt. Then I moved to the cargo bay, where I opened the door to let in the fresh air.

Being docked in the middle of a city meant the air wouldn't be clean, but as it blew into the ship, I felt the cool refreshing wind against my face and found myself smiling. I took a few minutes to stretch out my body, and with my eyes closed, I breathed in deep. I smelled two distinct scents—a dark roast and a sweet, floral smell. I opened my eyes and found Autumn Derringer standing outside my ship with two cups in her hands. At the time, I held one of my legs behind me in a stretch, and when I saw her, I nearly tottered onto my face.

"Uh, hi," I said as I descended the ramp to welcome her. The closer I got, the more butterflies circled in my stomach.

The speaker above me crackled.

"Captain! Proximity alert!" Tress yelled out.

Great, Tress, only a minute too late, I thought.

"Thank you, Tress. Standby."

Autumn's eyebrows shot up when I spoke to Tress in his language.

"I'm sorry," she said. "I hope I'm not interrupting. I just felt like I never properly thanked you for bringing my father home."

Her red eyes were emphasized by the small bags under them. She wore a dark blue coat that ended at her thighs, and denim pants. I tried to keep my eyes on hers and not wander, even with her conservative clothing, but it was difficult. She handed me a cup of steaming liquid and I took it with a smile, which should have been a "thank you," but my voice failed. After a sip, the drink heated my mouth and assaulted it with flavors of mocha. Warmth traveled down to my stomach.

"Wow, that's delicious," I said, finally able to form words. "Thank you."

"You're welcome," she said. I focused on her infectious smile. The two of us stared at each other for what felt like a lifetime.

Daniel, please reactivate your brain, I thought as I motioned for her to come aboard.

She stepped onto the ramp and into the cargo bay, looking around at the struts, catwalks, and empty cargo boxes.

"So . . . this is the cargo bay," I said, giving myself a mental facepalm as I said it. She probably knew this was a cargo bay. Or did she? There's no reason to believe she had any experience with ships before. My mind raced around the question of her ship knowledge until finally she smiled and answered for me.

"I think I was ten years old the last time I stood on a ship. She looks very impressive."

"She's kept me alive, which I think sums it up," I said while memories of the ship played through my mind. For once, I could actually enjoy the memories rather than hide from them.

Autumn followed me on a short tour. Talking to her was a lot easier when the topic was something I had experience in. I showed her the public areas of the ship, staying away from engineering and the armory, though the armory was more like an empty closet. I did show her the crew quarters where I introduced her to Tress.

When he saw her, his posture shot up straight like an arrow and his hands clamped to his sides. He looked her in the eye, but with a quick turn of his head, stared at the wall across from him. Did he do this because he didn't know Autumn, or because she was a woman? Either way, Autumn didn't seem to mind.

"It's nice to meet you, Tress," she said in English, and I translated. "I met a few Restrans maybe five or six years ago, but never learned the language."

"Hira do no, miku renda."

"He said he's sorry for your loss, and it's nice to meet you, too." He didn't actually say the second part, but I added it in.

We ended our tour in the kitchen where we sat across from each other. I finished my drink by the time we climbed the corridor to the top floor, but Autumn nursed hers.

Being on the Belle gave me more confidence and I felt more comfortable with her, enough that I could ask her a couple questions. But I wanted to tread lightly and not upset her with recent events.

"So did you come all this way just to bring me a drink and thank me? Because you could have sent me a communication."

"But then I wouldn't have been able to bring you a coffee," she said. "You already look better than you did before I gave it to you."

I did feel better. The liquid had warmed me and the caffeine helped to block the pain that had been rolling around in my head. She dropped her gaze to the table and rotated her cup, all while I sat with my hands folded together.

"In truth," she said, softer than before, "I wanted to ask you, if you don't mind, about my father's death."

So much for treading lightly. I thought how best to tell her about it before I spoke. I didn't want her to be sad for him, something not easily done.

"He died without pain," I said. "He didn't suffer in any way. He died doing his job, which makes his death an honorable one.

Tears formed in her eyes. She wiped them away before they had the chance to fall, and she took a deep breath, nodding her head.

"He knew," she said. "When he left the planet, the way he said goodbye, the strong hug he gave me that seemed to last forever. I think he knew, and I think I did, too."

I gave her a moment to compose herself. Then I told her the full story, how he found Tress and asked for his help to find me, how Granak shot him dead, and everything afterwards that led me to Terra. I left out the part where I threatened to shoot Damon myself.

"So," she said after I finished the story, which she took rather well. She nodded her head with narrow eyes and tried to make sense of it all. "This Leondren murdered my father to keep you from coming here?"

I nodded. "He didn't want your father passing on his data, but Damon outsmarted him by hiding his memory drive with Tress, who never had any clue what he had."

"But now you're here, so will Granak be coming?"

"I'm willing to bet he's already on the planet, or at least in this solar system. Commander Scott is keeping heavy surveillance on all the docks, but Granak is ruthless and cunning. If he wants to be here, he'll find a way."

"And what about you, Daniel Quinn?" she asked, her voice lower, the sound smooth like silk. I shivered with goose bumps when she said my name.

"Me?"

"What kind of person are you? Why are you doing all this?"

Good question, one I asked myself every day since I left Karth. Technically, the paying job was to locate Granak, but I found myself on Terra ignoring that job . . . no, not ignoring. I still felt confident that he would turn up sooner or later. Still, a part of me wished Damon never found me so I could selfishly get on with my life and try to find safer jobs to earn money. But there were a lot of reasons I involved myself on this planet, such as curiosity to know how Damon learned about me and what role he intended for me to play. Either way, whether I considered the hunt for Granak or saving the council, I wanted to think that I was the kind of person who couldn't turn away when someone was in need, and in this case there were about a billion someones. Sitting here looking at Autumn and her grief, I wanted nothing more than to give her vengeance for her father's death.

So, was I in this for the mystery, money, or justice? Could I choose all of the above?

"I . . ." My voice cracked and I hesitated. The last thing I wanted to do was insult her father's memory. "Your father risked his life to find me. For some reason he believed I could make a difference and I watched him die with that belief. I want to know why he chose me, what makes me so special, and, in doing so, I hope to find some way to track down his murderer and stop Terra and Gaia from killing each other."

Autumn nodded, her face expressionless.

"So, how do we find out what my father was up to?"

"We?" I asked. She shrugged, lifted the cup to her lips, and finished her drink.

"Like you said, he came looking for you, so you're a part of this. But he's my father, and I believed in peace just as much as he did, so I'm a part of this. I won't just sit by as the council is being murdered and the treaty falls apart."

"Okay then," I said while forcing myself not to smile at the prospect of working with her. "So what's the first step?"

She laughed.

"You're the Captain . . . Captain. You tell me what we should do."

She had a point, but I had no clue where to go from here. I drummed my fingers on the table and Autumn watched, amused, her hands folded under her chin and eyes wide.

What did I need more than anything right now? More information. But as far as I knew, Commander Scott had none until we could question the Gaian prisoner. General Ambrose, whoever he was, wouldn't be back on Terra for another day or two.

And then I realized the answer was right in front of me. Damon knew he was going to die, and even his daughter felt it. Who better to learn about Damon and his job than his own daughter?

"I told you about the memory drive, but the information on there was more educational than revealing. Did your father keep any other records?"

"He did have a computer in his office, which he kept locked even from me. We could start there."

"That sounds good," I said while looking at my console to check the time. "But someone from Commander Scott's team will be picking me up in half an hour. We should wait for them, shouldn't we?"

"Oh, Captain," Autumn said. "Do you always go by the book? I thought mercenaries were supposed to be unpredictable."

I narrowed my eyes.

"Tress," I called. "I'm heading out. Keep an eye on the repair team when they get here."

"Yes, Sir," he said, emerging in the corridor. "They have just arrived and are at the door."

"I'll let them in on our way out."

Autumn and I descended the ship toward the cargo bay. I stopped at my quarters to grab my gun and sword. Autumn's eyes flicked to the sword every couple of minutes, but she didn't say anything. When we reached the bay, I threw down the lever to open the door. Three men in full silver suits stepped aboard. Each carried a backpack and duffel bag with equipment pushing outside the seal of the bags. I couldn't tell what the team looked like because each wore a tinted helmet with headlights.

"Welcome aboard," I said to each of them, though I felt apprehensive knowing how easily the mercenaries got into the building to attack us. I couldn't see who these people were, so how could I trust they were an actual repair team?

"Do you gentlemen have any kind of identification, or would you be willing to remove your helmets? I'm not fond of letting strangers on my ship."

The man in front turned to regard me. He took a step forward and put his hand on my shoulder. "Son, we're going to take good care of her. We are here under orders from Commander Reynold Scott himself." The associate to his right took out a card of some kind and held it up to me. Scott's picture and what I guessed was his signature covered it. I wanted to question them further, but my instincts told me these men were the real deal. Was it the way the front man spoke to me with a soft, reassuring tone?

"My associate, Tress, will be overlooking the repairs. Please focus your attention on the engine room, weapons systems, and bulkheads." The engineer's hand stayed on my shoulder a few more seconds before he and his team continued. Tress walked out to greet them.

Strange, they didn't send a translator, I thought.

"Greta! No tu rajat?" The lead engineer said.

Oh, that's why . . .

"Well, shall we?" Autumn asked, stepping off the cargo bay ramp. She walked toward the elevators without waiting for me to answer. I caught up with her.

"Listen, Autumn, about this 'we' stuff . . . I'm not sure you understand the danger you will be putting—"

"Daniel," she said.

"What?"

"Shut up."

ELEVEN

Damon Derringer's home was on the outskirts of the city. I thought the whole planet was covered in a metropolis of buildings, but the long green fields and forests proved me wrong. Autumn spent the trip asking me a lot of personal questions, some of which were uncomfortable. How did you get involved in space travel, how did you get your ship, why are you a mercenary? Others were more complicated than she realized.

Fortunately, she enjoyed answering questions as much as asking them. I managed to turn the tide toward her and asked how she knew Commander Scott.

"My father and Reynold have been friends for years," she said softly, her energy depleted by the memories of her father.

Way to go Daniel, you don't want to talk about sensitive memories but you made her do it, I thought.

"Scott was like an uncle to me. He always kept candy or figurines in his office when dad brought me by to visit. It feels strange when I visit him now, all grown up."

"I'll bet," is all I managed to say. I looked around the office, expecting to see a lone figurine somewhere, forgotten after all these years, but saw nothing.

"Captain," she said.

"Please, you can call me Daniel."

"Okay . . . Daniel. I'm not sure I understand everything that's happening. I know my father died off-planet. I know that whatever he left for, it's connected to the council murders, but what I don't understand is why he transferred his advisor access and information to you when he could have given me all of it."

"Join the club," I said. "I know as much, maybe even less, than you do. But . . . I think we both know that Damon expected to die, and maybe that's why he didn't transfer it all to you. He didn't want someone to come after you and kill you, too."

She nodded, her eyes glossing over. Autumn seemed like a strong and energetic woman, but her father's death cracked at her optimistic shell. Knowing that her father was in danger prepared her for the news, but still, it's not easy to get over a loved one.

"So," she said. "What's with that sword you carry around?"

I wondered when she would ask that question. I stepped around all her previous questions, so I forced myself to answer at least one honestly.

"I found out a while ago that sometimes a close-quarters weapon can be just as useful, if not more so, than a gun. Guns are easy. You just point and shoot, but with the sword I need the skill and agility to use it, and you have to take a lot more into consideration when using it against another human being."

"You sound like you're a master at it," she said playfully.

"Far from it." *Far from the skill its original owner wielded.* "One of my last missions went sour. A renegade captain and her men attacked an alien race. One of the attackers was a swordswoman. She killed someone I cared about, but when the tides turned and we won, I kept her sword."

"I'm sorry," she said. "Keeping the sword with you must bring back painful memories."

"In a way, but at the same time I should know my enemy, and learn all I can about combat. One day, I'm sure she'll be looking to get her sword back."

My pocket bleeped and vibrated. I pulled out the glass communicator Scott gave me. A picture of him was on the screen with his number scrolling below. I touched my finger to the glass and the picture changed to read "active call".

"Quinn? My men just called and told me you weren't at your ship. Care to explain what you're doing?"

"Scott, Autumn and I are taking a look around Damon's home to find anything new."

"I recommend against that," Scott said with a rasp behind his voice. "My men and I have been through his house a number of times. Any useful information will already be stored on the Sentinel database."

I looked over at Autumn, who turned toward me with her eyes wide and eyebrows raised. She nodded in an exaggerated manner, as if telling me, "Yeah, that's right. What are you going to do about it?"

"I understand, Scott," I said while looking at her. "But being that I'm the advisor to the council now, I want to personally investigate as much evidence as I can, and if that means using a fine tooth comb over everything, then so be it."

"You realize that being advisor to the council means you should be focusing on . . . *the council,* right?"

Autumn pointed her finger and shook it at me, as if reprimanding me along with Scott.

"Yes, I understand. But I need to understand what the job entails, and what better way to start than with the home of the previous advisor? Give me an hour to look around, and I'll return to HQ. Okay?"

"Agreed, but don't dawdle. There should be a group of Sentinels securing the perimeter of the house. Just show them the communicator and they'll let you through."

Scott cut off communication.

"Are you trying to get me in more trouble?" I asked Autumn, stifling a laugh. "For someone you see as an uncle to you, you sure know how to mock him."

"That doesn't mean I never pissed him off, or don't know how to push his buttons . . . or yours apparently."

Heat rushed to my face and I turned away, trying to ignore her giggling. I had to admit, though, she did a good job of rebuilding the shell around her father's death, which was admirable. Autumn didn't seem like the kind of woman who sat around and let others do things for her. Maybe it was a result of being the daughter of someone in politics. Who knows? I just hoped that she didn't get herself killed chasing after the council's murderer with me. Too many people died around me already.

The vehicle descended into the forest as the trees grew sparser. A cement road below us led to a valley, trimmed neat and altered to make a large circle. In the middle of the circle was a large home, dull red with three sides ending in a point like triangles meshed together, just like an ancient Earth pyramid. The cement road surrounded the house in its own circle, veering off at the sides through large gardens of flowers. In front of the house, the cement expanded into a driveway where three cars resembling Commander Scott's were parked. My bionic eye zoomed into the vehicle windows, but I saw no one. In fact, there were no life signs around the house at all.

"Strange," I muttered. "The Sentinels are here, but where?"

"Scott said they were securing the perimeter. Maybe they're in the forest keeping an eye on things?"

"Maybe, but he also said we would need their approval to go inside, which means they should be close enough that they can intercept us."

"They are Sentinels. Maybe they're just good at hiding," Autumn said.

I nodded, but felt like I'd just swallowed ice water; my gut didn't agree with her assumption. She landed the vehicle and we both got out. Sharp wind pressed against my body and made me shiver. I shook it off and walked to the Sentinel vehicles. The hoods were cold and the seats didn't have any indentations from the bodies sitting in them.

"These haven't been used in a while," I said. Autumn stepped beside me as her hair flew with the wind. I turned in a circle and analyzed the ground around me, but found no sign of footprints. I looked toward the forest and zoomed in. No activity except for the swaying of branches.

After I grabbed my sword and pulled out my revolver, we walked toward the front door. My eye picked up small traces of splintered wood at the base of the entrance and the door itself was cracked open. I held out my hand toward Autumn, nudging her behind me.

"What are you doing?" she asked.

"Shh. Someone's been here, or still might be here. Just follow my lead."

I knelt and pressed my body against the front wall of the house, next to the door. In the slim opening I detected no movement, but I could already tell the place was trashed. A chair had been knocked over a few feet from the door, and the wind from an open window threw papers throughout the room.

"Hey!" Autumn shouted and my heart felt like it jumped into my throat. "Get out of my father's house!"

No one responded and there didn't seem to be any movement, at least that I could see or hear. I turned and glared at Autumn, who shrugged her shoulders and held her hands out flat.

"What? At least we know nobody is home."

"Don't be so sure," I whispered, and then I lifted my leg and swung it out, hitting the door and sending it flying open. Less than a second later, a blue ball of heat soared past my face. I heard Autumn gasp as I jerked my body into the doorframe toward the blast's origin and fired off a couple rounds of plasma. My eye picked up two humanoid figures at the end of a long hallway. Their weapons faced my position.

"Move!" I said and fell against the house as another fireball blew out the doorframe. Autumn and I ran around the side of the house, my eye in constant surveillance mode, looking for other humanoids. As we rounded the corner, I found the window that was open. The wind pushed an ivory curtain away from it, which gave me a good vantage point. I fired a couple blind rounds into the house, but continued to run.

"This way, come on," Autumn said, turning into a small opening between the front and back of the house. The path led to stairs descending into the ground. Autumn jumped down the few steps and pulled out a key, then opened the door. We both ran into darkness and eased the door shut. The wood of the floor above creaked as a people ran over us.

"Where did they go?" a man asked.

"They moved from the door to the window. Go to the back and make sure they didn't get through that way. You two, get outside and search the perimeter."

More footsteps. Shouts from inside and out. They were searching for us.

"They're going to find us down here," I whispered. I heard a click back where we came in and then Autumn's hand touched my back.

"You'd be surprised how many people overlook this door. If they just run around the house without paying attention, they will mistake the alcove for nothing more than a protruding corner of the house."

We kept still while the guards searched the premises. While I should have been paying attention to what they were saying and doing, I couldn't take my focus off of Autumn's hand on my back. I expected her to take it off after she found me in the dark, but it didn't move. The touch was soft, her fingers barely spread apart.

After a few minutes, what felt like countless thumping heartbeats and a lot of sweating, the men reconvened in the house above us. Some of the footsteps were louder than others, and some sounded like heavy metal boots or something similarly heavy. The voice that spoke was muffled through the floorboards, but understandable.

"They're not here. They must have run into the forest."

I thought I heard something—the sound of soft rumbling followed by sharp gasps, or whispers, or was it sniffing? Why would someone be sniffing?

"*He* is still here," a deep voice said with a sharp growl behind his breath. I nearly dropped my gun, but held onto it. "I can smell him . . . and someone else . . . a female. "

"Oh, flux," I whispered. Autumn stepped closer and moved her hand to my shoulder.

"What is it?" she asked.

I couldn't find any words. Standing above us wasn't just mercenaries or men with advanced guns. Above us stood the creature responsible for Damon Derringer's murder, and possibly the murder of three councilmen.

Granak was on Terra.

TWELVE

"Listen to me," I said as softly as possible. "You need to get out of here. Go get in the car and get back to Sentinel HQ. Tell Scott what's going on. Granak is here already."

"My father's killer?" she asked, louder than she should have, but there wasn't any additional movement above us.

"It doesn't matter." Though I couldn't see her, my bionic eye's night vision showed her face; lips parted and eyes widened in a heightened sense of anxiety. "He's too strong for either of us. We need help. Get to the car and get out of here."

"What about you?"

"Listen, the questions need to stop. If you trust me in any way, I need you to turn around, unlatch the door, and run as fast as you can. No more questions."

Nothing happened. She stood there, her arms at her sides, her face frozen in front of me. Then she backed away, slowly, and turned around. I heard the click again and readied my revolver. Autumn pushed the door open and for just an instant, I saw her back and her hair flying in the air.

"Did you hear that?" one of the men shouted. I pointed my weapon upward at their voices and waited. I closed my eyes and pictured Autumn's face, her smile. I can't remember the last time I felt butterflies in my stomach like I did with her. There have been other women in my life since Ashley's death, and some of them were very attractive, but my shield was always up against them. With Autumn, I felt my shield lowering by itself. Why? Did I feel guilty about her father's death and in reaction felt like I owed her something? In that moment, all I wanted to do was protect her.

"I see movement!" someone above me shouted.

I opened fire. Green plasma illuminated the large room around me in flickers and I heard at least one man scream. I kept unloading weapon fire above me, the blasts puncturing small holes in the wood. A large, hairy fist with claws broke through the floor. It retracted and Granak's face was in sight. Time froze in that moment and I relived the memories of him killing Damon, blowing up the docking gate on Karth, and crippling my ship. The butterflies in my stomach were replaced with ugly bats. I swallowed hard and imagined pushing the nerves down.

Protect Autumn, I thought.

"Hi Granak," I forced myself to say pleasantly just before I fired a plasma round, but he had already taken cover and I missed. Before anyone could retaliate, I ran outside, jerked left, and looked back toward the front of the house. I didn't see Autumn, but a soldier rounded the corner. I opened fire on him. One of the blasts hit him in the stomach and he fell.

"QUINN!" Granak's voice surged like thunder. I advanced toward the front of the house and fired another blind shot into the window as I passed it. The wall blew out behind me and I turned, expecting one of the weapons to be the cause, only to see Granak, who had just run through a fluxing wall.

He wore the same outfit from Karth, and his barred teeth and claws sent chills throughout my body. One of the men ran out in front of him, his weapon focused on me. Something about his uniform was familiar, but I couldn't take my eyes off the Leondren.

"Don't move!" the man said, positioning himself between us. I didn't know what their relationship was, but I knew it was complicated when Granak grabbed the man's head, lifted him off the ground, and threw him back into the house.

I raised my sword.

"You are resilient, Quinn. I knew you would still come, even after I nearly destroyed you."

"Haven't you heard? There's a nice bounty on your head. I thought I'd come to collect," I forced myself to say. I couldn't show fear. I couldn't let him know he could get into my head.

"Brave one, but foolish," he said. He bent his legs, extended his claws, and actually pounced.

He missed my head by less than an inch, but I rolled out of the way and wildly swung the sword. I missed. Outside in the open, Granak would be too fast for me. I stood and ran into the house through the gap he created. A large, brown table had been split down the center and the floor was littered with holes with black scorch marks from my weapon.

A large thud shook the floor and I turned with the sword outstretched. The blade scraped against the armor on Granak's chest and sheared through hair on his arm. I followed with my revolver and shot him in the chest. The blast sent him back a couple of steps, but he didn't fall. I retreated further into the house as Granak let out a blood-curdling roar. One of the guards lay motionless on the floor and I jumped over him. A large stairway led up to a second level and I leapt toward it and climbed. One of Granak's arms shattered the banister beside me. Any closer and I would have been missing a piece of my midsection.

I reached the top and spun around to face Granak, who remained at the bottom.

"I have the high ground," I breathed and pointed my sword and revolver at him. "Come toward me and I'll unleash my full battery at you."

He laughed. To say my confidence dropped drastically would be an understatement.

"With me, there is no high ground." He lunged. I dodged, but there wasn't enough room to evade his swing. His claws struck my arm, tearing the armor and igniting a burning pain. I smacked into a wall. Granak snarled. I fired a barrage of plasma at him, but he leapt into one of the nearby rooms. Hot, wet blood seeped down my left arm, but I didn't have time to look at the wound. I could still lift and swing the sword, so it probably wasn't too bad.

The house was silent. Two of the soldiers were downstairs and I didn't know where the third one was. Did he go after Autumn? Did she get away? I wanted to find out, but I had bigger problems somewhere upstairs with me.

Was Granak recovering, or just trying to freak me out by lying in wait? I knew walls wouldn't be a problem for him and I kept watching the one across from me, waiting for him to tear it down and go for the kill.

Could I use that to my advantage in some way? Granak, like any predator, counted on fear, and the element of surprise to catch his prey. I wasn't faster than him, but agile enough that I managed to escape his grasp thus far. If one thing could anger a predator, it would be knowing his prey didn't fear him. I shoved my revolver in my holster and grasped the hilt of my sword with both hands. Blood from my wound dripped down my sleeve and onto the bottom of the steel blade.

Blood on the sword . . . just like Laraar's blood . . . no . . . not now! I needed all the strength and focus I could muster and hoped I wouldn't regret my next words.

"Here kitty, kitty!" I shouted, followed by kissing sounds. If he could antagonize me, then I would do the same to him.

My words apparently hit a nerve. He crashed through the wall in front of me, snarling with his claws outstretched. I couldn't dodge this time, but I didn't need to. As he flew toward me, I went limp and dropped to the ground. Granak soared over me and into the wall. I took my chance. I thrust the sword and it

144

hit him in the chest, piercing his armor and flesh. He let out a noise, not quite a roar or growl, but something more agonizing. He fell onto his hands and knees and my whole body trembled as I lay under him.

He didn't attack me or attempt to bite off my head, but he brought his right foot forward, then his left. Stars above, he was getting up, even after being impaled. I gripped the hilt and expected him to pull the sword out of himself, but instead he pressed his hand against mine, palming them together. He squeezed hard and pain surged through my hands. As he stood, I went with him, and the strain in my hands and wrists only aggravated the pain in my left arm.

Granak had me. My plan worked, but his body was too strong. Not even a sword through his gut stopped him. All he had to do was wrap his large hand around my head and twist, or throw me like a rag doll like he did with the soldier downstairs.

But he didn't, at least not fast enough. As he straightened and stared at me, someone ran up the stairs.

"Don't even think about hurting him," a female voice said. Autumn. She stood near the top of the steps and pointed one of the soldier's blue fireball guns at Granak.

"Foolish girl," Granak said, breathing hard, though not as hard as me. "Daniel Quinn, you are unlike the rest of these pitiful meat-things." He pushed against me, the sword following along as he removed it from his midsection. The blade came out crimson. "Your time to die has yet to pass. Until then, enjoy the show."

Granak tossed me aside and I landed hard. The wind knocked out of me and my arm caught between me and the floor. I heard a crash and the splintering of wood. Granak escaped, though escape didn't seem to be the appropriate word. It took a moment to assess my condition, and though I had some pain in my arm and legs, nothing seemed broken. I sat up against the wall and heaved in a few breaths. Autumn ran to me.

"Are you okay?"

"Fine," I said. 'Enjoy the show,' Granak had said, and his words played over and over in my mind as I thought back to the events that led me to this point.

Autumn walked to the hole in the wall and leaned over to check for Granak or enemy soldiers.

"Did you get in touch with the Sentinels?" I asked.

"No," she said. "I was running toward the car and one of the men ran after me. By the time I took him down, I heard that . . . thing, that Leondren growling or whatever."

"You heard the growling and you ran back toward the house instead of away from it?"

She shrugged. Her hair hung over the front of her face, obscuring her eyes. I used my bionic eye to scan for any sign of injuries over the rest of her body, but found none.

"Daniel, about the guards . . . should I call Reynold directly?"

"No," I spat out. "Don't call anyone, not yet."

She helped me up and we walked back down the stairs in search of the fallen guards. The sudden calm was eerie, as if a hundred men were about to burst from the outskirts of the forest and rush us. But as far as I knew, everyone with Granak had been dealt with. The one inside the house, who Granak threw like a rag doll, was face down with no pulse. I turned him over and confirmed what I thought I saw when I fired on the guard outside. Their familiar outfits were Sentinel outfits.

Damon's location, the attack on the docking tower, and Granak on Terra all led to one conclusion—The Sentinels were compromised. I suspected it before, but the last thing I wanted to do was voice my concern to them. How far up did it go? Autumn sighed beside me as she looked down on the fallen man.

"I didn't call when I saw the Sentinel uniform. Daniel, you told me not to call Reynold. You don't actually think he's a suspect, do you?"

"Autumn, I don't want to believe it, but someone in the high ranks had to be involved. They had to have knowledge of your father's trip to Karth, and they probably allowed the mercenaries access to the docking tower where they attacked us. Scott himself told me he considered me a suspect, which would make me a scapegoat in all this."

She stood there, not really moving or reacting. Her eyes glistened slightly, but her gaze was focused on something inside her mind more than the surrounding area. I didn't want to suspect

Scott, but everything up to this point was too fluxing convenient for the opposition.

"Listen, it's just a hypothesis. We don't know anything yet, but until we find out more we need to be cautious, okay?" She nodded. "Good."

Enjoy the show, he said.

Damon's assassination was public—no stealth or secrecy involved—which then led to Granak blowing up the gate on Karth. The three councilmen were maimed, their body parts scattered around their room. All the pieces of the puzzle were itching at my mind, as if trying to tell me something.

Enjoy the show.

Autumn grabbed a medical kit from one of the rooms to clean my cuts and stop the bleeding. Once she was satisfied with her work, we moved through the house, careful in case more Sentinels were still here or on the way. The place was trashed. Not only were desks, shelves, and other furniture tossed, but unnecessary items were thrown about, like paper weights and picture frames. For what reason?

"What do you think they were looking for?" Autumn asked with her arms folded, as if fighting off a chill.

Enjoy the show, I thought once more, and then it hit me.

"Nothing. I don't think they were after anything at all. Where does your father keep his computers?"

She led me further down the hallway to a large room. Bookshelves lined one wall, though most of the books were now scattered on the floor. Autumn stepped over the debris toward a dark brown desk, where she picked up a black laptop off the floor. The machine didn't appear to be damaged.

"Turn it on and see if there's been any attempt at accessing the files."

While I waited for her to boot up the computer, I rechecked the house and yard for any additional security. I stopped in front of the Sentinel I'd shot outside. His face didn't look hardened or evil like some kind of faceless enemy. Somewhere behind those motionless eyes there used to be a life, possibly a family. What made him do this? Turn on his own planet and people? I killed him with little thought or consideration. My life had been in danger, but I cringed at how easy it was to aim and fire my revolver at him.

I hated death and I never killed a man if I could do something different to change the situation. Events over the last year hardened me and made me realize that sometimes there wasn't a choice. But even in the darkest times, I could convince myself that killing wasn't the answer.

Paranoia can be a nasty enemy or a useful ally, but it's not an excuse for pointing a gun at a man, like I did with Tress and Damon. But this wasn't paranoia and I had to remind myself more than once about that. This wasn't about paranoia or anger. This was survival. Him or me. If I didn't kill him, he would have killed me. I forced that thought over the confusion and regret from killing him, and stood without looking at the body again.

Still, for all the regret behind my actions, I felt like underneath it all I was a violent man, something I didn't want to be true.

When I turned around, Autumn stood with the computer in her arms, cradling it like a precious keepsake. I must have zoned out longer than I thought.

"Are you okay?" she asked.

I chose to ignore the question and nodded at the computer.

"Any tampering that you can tell?"

She shook her head. "I'm not a computer genius, but as far as I can tell the computer hasn't been used in over a week."

That didn't surprise me at all.

"Come on," I said, putting my hand behind her back and easing her forward. "We need to get out of here."

I found out what happened to the third guard when we reached Autumn's car. His body hung over the window frame of the passenger door, the window itself shattered. I stopped and my eyebrows shot up, then I looked back at Autumn who had the beginnings of a small grin.

"What? I told you I knew Reynold for a long time. You don't think he taught me self-defense?"

THIRTEEN

Terra was an enormous world filled with technological marvels, at least according to Autumn's description of it. The skyline, no matter where you turned, held vibrant lights and colors, and each building was shaped in unique, innovative ways. We drove past a skyscraper that curved from bottom to top and another shaped like a circle, which we flew through. No structure looked outdated or empty. I felt the urge to get lost in the maze of the streets and experience the thrill of something new, but all I could do was focus on the mission at hand, and try to close the door on the explorer inside me.

I didn't think it was safe for Autumn to return home, especially now that Granak and the Sentinels saw her at her father's house. Likewise, I felt returning to Sentinel HQ was out of the question, now that a traitor within the organization seemed likely. I instructed Autumn to take us back to Trenton Hall, where the council members were murdered. I felt confident Granak or whomever he worked for wouldn't be there.

Every couple of minutes I looked at the communicator in my hand. I told Scott I would return within an hour, and that time had passed. He would be calling me or, worst-case scenario, he would find out what happened at Damon's home and to the three Sentinels there. Autumn didn't kill the third, which meant he was alive and free to report us.

The shield surrounding Trenton Hall was gone when we arrived, and from the sky, I saw a large number of people coming and going from the entrance.

"They cleaned that mess up quick," I said.

"Every day without customers is thousands of dollars lost," Autumn said. "We might be light years away from Earth, but no matter what planet you're on, if it has humans, it's all about the money.

"When Terra and Gaia weren't at each other's throats, things were better. The trade industry kept people working and without need. Gaia got our technology to help them farm and process their stock, and in return Terra would get a percentage of their goods. Now with the war, all trade has been cut off. There are some people who still believe in peace and they do what they can to help, but it draws the attention of those who embrace war."

I found it hard to believe anyone would be willing to help their enemy, but then I thought about the medical ship—a crew who almost sacrificed themselves just to provide support to their neighboring planet. As a reward, they were chased down and nearly destroyed.

We landed and walked into Trenton without any trouble or questions. The quietness of the lobby I heard yesterday was gone, replaced with the buzz of social interaction. My eye detected a handful of guards—not Sentinels, but most likely internal security. Once we reached the hall of the murder scene, we ran into our first and only Sentinel.

"Let me handle this," Autumn whispered, and grabbed the communicator from my hand.

"Hey—" I started to protest, but she ran ahead of me toward the guard.

"Curtis!" Autumn waved her hand like she was saying hi to an old friend. Then the two of them embraced and my suspicions were confirmed. But at the same time, their embrace struck a chord in me, something uncomfortable.

"Daniel, this is Curtis," she said after I caught up to her. Curtis's jaw and cheekbones were almost as hardened as the helmet he wore. Blonde hair stuck out from under the sides of his helmet. The corner of his mouth turned up for a second, but quickly disappeared as he tried to maintain a professional posture.

"Ms. Derringer," he said. *Definitely trying to look professional.* "I'm sorry, but this section is closed to all civilians."

"That's okay," she said, typing something into the communicator and showing it to him. "Captain Daniel Quinn has clearance."

My eyebrows shot up at the same time that Curtis's did. I didn't know the communicator could bring up credentials, but I'd only been here a day. There were a lot of things I didn't know yet and as long as my lack of knowledge wouldn't get anyone killed, I was okay with that.

"I still have to radio in that you're here," Curtis said.

"Fine, just let us through," Autumn said, her response forced. He opened the door and we stepped inside. When the door closed, I hurried to the counter and opened Damon's laptop.

"We don't have a lot of time, not if Scott finds out what happened at your father's house. He'll have questions."

I took the memory drive from my belt and inserted it into the side of Damon's laptop. A loading bar appeared on the screen, followed by a box asking for a password.

"Does this mean anything to you?" I turned the screen toward Autumn.

"Hmm," she said, putting her fingernail between her teeth. "I'm guessing Dad didn't give you a password before he died?"

I shook my head.

"Okay then." She leaned over and typed on the keyboard. Strands of hair hung forward, covering part of her face. I couldn't help but stare at her.

Her eyes shifted toward me and her hands froze. "What are you staring at?"

I turned my head quick as heat rushed to my face. In my peripheral, I thought I saw her grin.

"Well, Captain," she said. "It looks like our team-up wasn't mere coincidence."

"What do you mean?"

She turned the laptop back around and numerous folders opened with files, photos, and appointment calendars. I recognized some of it from the data I looked at on the Belle, but a lot of it was new information. The mutual information of the drive and the computer reminded me of the memory module Al used. That small device saved my life on more than one occasion, but it could only work if Al was active. Damn, I missed him, even though he technically wasn't a "him."

Focus, I thought. *Worry about Al later.*

"The password was my birthday," she told me. "I guess he hoped that you would accept his request and come here, and if he died, find me." I caught the start of a tear, but Autumn quickly blinked it away. "So, what are we looking for, anyway?"

"Think about everything that happened. Your father left Terra and knew someone was following him. He knew he might die. Granak shows up and kills him and then he disables my ship so I can't make it to Terra, except I do. Then we're ambushed in the stairwell of the docking tower, and worst of all we find Granak hasn't only landed on Terra, but he is working with the Sentinels.

"Clearly there's someone behind all this, someone above Granak. He's like me, a mercenary who works for the highest bidder. That same bidder hired the soldiers in the docking tower to attack us."

"And you think it's Reynold," she said, her arms crossed.

"I don't know for sure, Autumn. I mean, yes, he was on those stairs with us, getting shot at, but that could have been to sell the point that he was a target, not the ringleader."

"I just don't buy it," she said. "You've known him for a day, haven't you? I've known him my entire life. This is just the result of Terra and Gaia targeting each other."

Her loyalty towards Scott was admirable, and the passion that she spoke with made me want to believe her, so why didn't I? Scott was a soldier, past his prime from the looks of him. Was that the reason I didn't trust him? The vague wrinkles on his face, the grey hair, and though he was ridden with guilt over his past, he held an outstanding amount of confidence. In a way, he reminded me of another old man I had met, and only now I realized it.

Was I set on accusing Reynold Scott because he reminded me of Raymond Erebos? Both of them were leaders in their own right. Erebos wasn't a soldier, as far as I knew, but if he commanded one of his followers to jump out of an airlock, they would without hesitation. Erebos was the reason, the person responsible for my journey to Dawn, alongside his assassin, Cessa. He threatened me, nearly had me killed. I haven't seen him since the battle on Dawn, but did my anxiety of knowing he was still out there pass subconsciously towards Scott?

But if Scott didn't do it, then who hired all the soldiers? Could it have been this General Ambrose? Whoever he was, he spent a lot of time traveling from Terra to Gaia and overseeing the transition into peace, assuming the council succeeded in creating a treaty between worlds. But if he was traveling, how could he organize everything?

I rubbed at my temples. Stress acted like a pendulum inside my skull. The files on the computer looked like business receipts and meeting journals. I skimmed them as fast as I could. There wasn't enough time for me to look over everything, but then the word "Starcade" caught my attention.

There were multiple Starcade transactions, all for enormous sums of money. Personnel transfers. Bulk orders of equipment. These all looked identical to the mercenary receipt I grabbed off of the man in the docking tower. This must have been what Damon found. The routing and account numbers meant little to me, but to Damon, an educated man of the council and everything surrounding them, he must have figured out who they belonged to.

"So what do you think?" Autumn asked quietly.

"I think I need the man or woman responsible for all of this to come out and just scream, 'Hey! It's me! I'm the one you're looking for!'" I meant it, but Autumn laughed at the comment, which lifted my spirits.

"Let's get out of here. There are some account numbers I want to look up. I think your father stumbled upon transaction reports paid for by the killer."

"Nice job, Captain!"

The information wasn't groundbreaking, but it proved her father found something and tried to make it right.

"What I don't get is why all the public violence," she said as we walked back to the door, a crease between her eyebrows. "If this person hired someone to go in and assassinate the council, wouldn't that be enough to stop the treaty?"

"But they didn't assassinate the council. They were literally torn limb from limb, like some kind of sadistic work of art. They didn't care how public the news was."

Something clicked inside me—the thought of assassins, violence, and everything happening around us. I thought about the public outcry for war, the battle in the stars. All of it, merged with the receipts, unlocked the answers. I ran into the coffee table and cursed as I stood and knocked over the chair.

"Flux me, they do care."

"Come again?" she asked.

"They do care how public the news is," I said as I tried to rub the pain away in my leg. "Whoever is doing this, they want people to know about it. They want people to know the council was brutally murdered. They wanted to cause a scene at the docking tower. Think of your father's house, destroyed and turned inside out, but nothing stolen; his computer was even intact, nothing missing from the files as far as you know, right?"

"Right," she said, nodding.

"I'm willing to bet someone is going to pay to have your father's house featured on news segments and reports. People will know that his home was ransacked. This isn't just about stopping the peace treaty. Everything done up to this point is fueling the tension, building up to a boiling point."

Autumn stared at a blank spot on the wall, her eyes turning left and right as if she were putting her thoughts in front of her. When her mouth parted and her eyes widened, I knew she figured it out.

"This isn't just to stop peace, but to ensure the war," she said.

"That's it. Whoever is behind all this, they're antagonizing the people into calling for war. They're going to cause chaos until both planets are ready to destroy each other. That's why the attackers in the stairwell were dressed like Gaians."

"Which means there's more to come. Terra hasn't launched a full scale war yet," Autumn said, pacing around the room.

"We have to find out whose account number is in your father's files, then go from there. We should also look at his calendar and see if there are any campaigns that were scheduled to take place. I'm betting the next set of events will be public, proof to the people that war is imminent and necessary. Then we have to contact the council and warn them."

"There's a parade . . . a week from now, I think," Autumn said.

That was it. If the council intended to continue with this parade, I'd bet my ship there would be an attack.

A floorboard behind us creaked. I turned and something whizzed past me. Autumn's body fell to the floor. I tried to draw my weapon, but Curtis aimed his gun at me and fired. The impact wasn't painful, but more like a pinch from my midsection to head.

The sedative worked its way too fast, and I dropped shortly after she did.

As my mind blackened, I could see all the cogs move and take shape, the prospect of war on Terra's doorstep, maybe even Gaia's. Damon's death, my trip here, Al's damaged mainframe, and the survival of the council members; none of it would matter if someone didn't take action against the bloodshed.

FOURTEEN

Jail cells. Brigs. Imprisonment. I knew the words as well as I knew how to fly my ship. The fact that I kept ending up in cells spoke to how careless I was in life. So I wasn't surprised when I woke up on a less-than-soft cot to find myself surrounded by a red shield similar to the ones that blocked the hotel after the council murders. Autumn wasn't here and only one other person stood outside the shield—a Sentinel guard.

"Where am I? Where's Autumn?" I asked. I faced his back and when I spoke, he didn't turn around. Either the shield was sound proof, or he was ignoring me. I didn't have to wait long to find out. Moments later, Commander Scott entered the room, a deep scowl on his face and his hand on his firearm. I asked him the same questions. Scott didn't answer either, but my bionic eye picked up minor fluctuations of his facial expressions. His scowl lowered a small margin and his eyes narrowed. So he could hear me, unless he just didn't like how my mouth moved.

Was I staring into the face of the council's murderer, as I originally assumed? If so, maybe I could push some buttons, try to manipulate him into giving his true intentions away, but with what? What did I know that he didn't? I stepped closer to him until the edge of my foot barely touched the barrier, and crossed my arms.

"Granak is already on Terra," I told him, but he didn't flinch. I couldn't read his expression, something that time and experience taught him to hide well.

"Scott," I said, losing my composure. "Did you hear me? Granak is already here. You told me you were going to keep surveillance on all the incoming ships. Either he was here before I showed up, or someone on your team allowed him access."

He flinched. My comment about his team, suggesting that someone could betray him, hit a nerve.

"Tell me," he said, his voice blanketed by a rasp, as if he hadn't spoken aloud in hours. "Why are there two dead guards at Damon Derringer's residence, and the third claims you and Autumn attacked them by surprise?"

"Yes, Scott," I said, throwing my arms up over my head. "Autumn ordered the death of her father, and then she teamed up with me to ransack his house and steal all the valuables so I could get rich."

"Mr. Quinn, don't patronize me. I know Autumn would never wish her father harm, but you are a mercenary, and I don't think it would be difficult for you to use her grief to manipulate her."

"Scott," I said, my tone harsh and forced. I stepped back and took a deep breath. I wasn't going to win an argument, nor would I convince him by begging. I needed to use logic, and nothing more. Don't lie, don't try to plead with the man, but use something he can't deny or question.

I dropped my hands to my sides and told him everything I knew. I told him everything about Granak, starting from our meet on Karth up to this point. I told him how I threatened Damon before he got shot. I explained everything that Autumn and I discovered during our trek. The only thing I didn't tell him was the warm feelings I felt towards her. That, at least, deserved secrecy.

Finally, I explained to him why the murders occurred in the manner they did, and why we were attacked.

"Autumn told me about the parade. If the council congregate around it, the killer is going to strike. Each time they're getting more open and public. They're not afraid of being seen or caught. In fact, they want to be seen. They want people to rally and cry for blood against their enemies."

Through my discussion, Scott's resolve faltered minute after minute. His frown grew into a straight line, his shoulders relaxed, and his hand was farther from his gun than it had been. When I mentioned the upcoming event, though, that's when he started to look worried.

"The remembrance," he muttered, more to himself than to me.

"The what?" I asked. Scott walked forward, and his clearance level allowed him to walk through the shield. He grabbed me and shoved me back against it. Its energy sent shocks through my body.

"Why are you doing this, Quinn? What's in it for you? Is it all about money, about getting your ship fixed, and getting the hell out of here? Maybe you just get off on adventure and danger. Tell me why the hell you care what happens to the council."

"Because," I spat out, the irritation of the jolts building into painful spasms. "I know what it's like to be a pawn in someone else's game. People don't deserve to die like that, no matter who they are."

"And this Granak bastard? What's the deal with you two?"

"He was hired by whoever is orchestrating this entire thing. And I get a damn fine paycheck if I can take him down."

Scott pulled me away from the shield. The pain subsided after a few seconds, though my entire body trembled from lingering aftershocks.

"Let's go," he said, pressing a button on his belt, which deactivated the shield. "Autumn is in my office. We don't have much time."

"You mentioned a remembrance. Didn't the council talk about something like that, in honor of Damon?"

"I didn't want the council to go through with the parade, but they felt it would be the perfect staging ground to honor and remember Damon."

"Are they crazy?" I asked, short of breath. The two of us were quickly walking down a long, dull hall. We rounded a couple of corners and walked through two more doors before we reached the main hub of the HQ. "Why would they risk their lives out in the open like that?"

"The council wants to show the killer that they're not afraid, just like Damon. And they want to show the world they're willing to die for peace."

Admirable, if anything.

Then I stopped short, just as Scott reached his door. A recent memory played through my mind, something Autumn had said.

"Commander," I said. "I was under the impression the parade wasn't for another week. If that's the case, why are we rushing like it's happening today?"

"I received the order yesterday afternoon, while you and Autumn were gallivanting around the city."

The order. An order to move the parade up, to speed up the process, and make the council a bunch of sitting ducks. Commander Scott answered to only one man as far as I knew.

"Scott. General Ambrose gave you that order, didn't he?"

He didn't answer, but he didn't deny it, either. I followed him into his office where Autumn sat at his chair, her head buried in her arms. She looked up as we walked in and when she saw me, she stood.

"Daniel! Are you okay?"

I started to answer, but Scott put both his hands up.

"Worry about each other later. We have bigger problems." He reached over his desk and smacked his hand on the table. A green light blinked and a familiar man spoke through the computer.

"Yes, Commander?" Stern, the Sentinel secretary, said.

"Get Trunker in here now, as in five minutes ago." He slammed his hand down again and the desk cracked under his weight. Scott gave no response to the damaged console. When Stern arrived at the door, he pulled another man with him. This man was dressed in the same outfit as Stern and Scott, but his face was stitched in numerous areas. Was this the man who tried to attack Autumn at her father's house? The injuries seemed to confirm that. Stern shoved him into the room, and as the door closed I saw him cover his eyes with his hands.

Scott grabbed the guard—Trunker I guessed—and slammed his head against the table. The impact left a bloodied spot on the table and Trunker fell to the ground, blood trickling from his forehead. He was still conscious enough to scream for help, but Scott drew his gun and shoved it against Trunker's neck.

"That's enough, you bastard," he said. "Tell me Ambrose's endgame. Why is he doing this? How is the Leondren involved?"

I expected Trunker to plead for his life, maybe even deny the allegations, but instead he smiled. His lips and eyes stretched so far it looked, for lack of a better word, evil.

"Death to the Terrans and Gaians," Trunker said, then he pushed off the ground and tackled Scott to the floor. Before I could pull him off, two plasma rounds scorched through

Trunker's body and he fell limp. Scott pushed him off and refused to take my hand when I tried to help him up.

"I hate traitors," he said, then holstered his weapon. He walked outside his office without us, but we followed. He stopped in the middle of the hub, where all eyes turned to him, whether because of rank or the blood on his uniform, I couldn't say.

"Listen to me," he said. "I want every single available Sentinel down at the parade. There is going to be an imminent attack on the council. Arm yourselves well, and spread out along the parade route. I'm going to say this once and leave you to your duty . . . trust absolutely no one. Report to no one but me. Do you all understand?"

A collective shout of "Yes, sir" filled the room as each soldier stood at attention. In that moment, I witnessed greatness. I saw why Scott took betrayal so hard. His honor and pride were more toward his men than himself. He expected each one below him to follow his orders, to do what was necessary for the greater cause. He produced a well-oiled machine in his Sentinels. He didn't care about any other possible traitors. He trusted, maybe to a fault, that his people would do the right thing.

Scott led us back down the hall toward where I was briefly imprisoned, but we took a different turn and stopped at a large, steel door. He input a series of numbers and the door opened to reveal the armory. I couldn't count the different weapons hanging on the walls. Scott pulled down an assault rifle and a handful of battery clips, and then he disappeared between full shelves and counters.

Autumn pulled on a thick vest and grabbed a couple of grenades and a rifle.

"What the hell do you think you're doing?" I asked.

"I'm saving my father's legacy, and seeing that he died for something."

I didn't argue. This was her choice, a way to remember and honor Damon. I wouldn't step in the way of that.

When Scott returned, he brought a few familiar items with him—my revolver and sword.

"I feel like I keep misjudging you, Quinn," he said. "Now you have both Damon and his daughter vouching for you, and they're two of the most important people in my life."

"Don't get all sappy on me, Commander," I said. One corner of my mouth quirked up. "Let's have a heart-to-heart after we save some lives."

"Agreed," he said, and a sense of power and determination reverberated with his words.

An entire convoy of Sentinel vehicles traveled at full speed through the city toward the starting point of the parade. Scott called ahead and learned that the council was minutes away from stepping onto its platform.

Of the three people in the vehicle, only Autumn questioned our intentions.

"What if we're wrong about Ambrose? I mean, he's in charge of all security on Terra. He's been the liaison between the two planets."

"Quinn is right," Scott said. "This parade is the perfect place to stage an attack and drive people into a state of bloodshed. The two of you must have spooked him when you found them trashing Damon's house. They had to move their plans forward and Ambrose was the only man, save the President, to authorize the parade. It's his signature on the confirmation order."

I never met Ambrose and never saw his face. From what I heard, the man was strict and kept himself busy traveling between Terra and Gaia. Somehow during his travels, he managed to orchestrate all of the attacks. He must have been the one who hired Granak to hunt down Damon. What if Damon found out he was behind the attempted murders of the council? He discovered that the account numbers for the Starcade transactions belonged to Ambrose, which led him to flee and find someone outside the system to help. Ambrose had to keep him quiet, so he hired a mercenary to kill him and negated the need for Ambrose to follow himself.

The rest of the ride was a blur—five minutes of discussing plans, but never deciding because we really didn't know what would happen, or how. Scott mentioned that Ambrose would be present to oversee an event of this magnitude. Our first goal was to intercept him and try to reason with him or, if nothing else, take him down and question him later.

When we landed, the parade had already started and Scott's attempts to call ahead and delay the parade were all blocked. There were plenty of soldiers surrounding the floats, though, and my bionic eye picked up multiple weapon signatures in windows and alleys following the parade route. A large contingency of Sentinels surrounded a tall man ahead of us. General Ambrose. Scott rushed forward with us close behind and pushed all of the soldiers out of the way until Scott and Ambrose were face to face.

"Reynold, my friend. This is a pleasant surprise. I thought you were back at—"

The welcome wasn't interrupted by any attack on the parade, or the expression of confusion on Scott's face. Ambrose stopped talking when he looked at me. We stared at each other and in that one second of reality, recollection invaded my mind

I stood on Dawn, in front of the powerful lake of empyreus energy. My friend, a Dawnian I'd bonded with, was murdered. Laraar. No, wait, this wasn't the memory my mind wanted. Something before. Almost like a recording, the memory rewound itself until I looked at a horrible mutation. Jason Hobbes, my best friend, a man I knew since I was a young boy, had been forced to take part in an experiment and was transformed using machinery and technology.

Captain Sarah King used the empyreus to bind the technology of machines into the biology of man, creating the very first cyborgs. But something was different this time when the memory played. At the time, I was focused on Jason. My heart broke and I lost control of my emotions when I saw him, but I never took a good look at the men standing behind him, the other cyborgs King created. Now in my mind, Jason was blurred out, and the images of the other cyborgs were more focused.

Behind Sarah King, toward her left side, stood one of the cyborgs, ready and waiting to kill me. I looked at his face, his nose, and eyes. In my mind and on Terra, these faces were identical.

General Ambrose of Terra was a fluxing cyborg. And if he was a cyborg, then he answered to a higher power—my former commander, Sarah King.

FIFTEEN

I drew my revolver and pointed it at Ambrose, but not before dozens of guards did the same to me. I didn't flinch. I didn't care. The image of the cyborgs emerging from the empyreus lake looped through my mind. The only reason I didn't fire was because Commander Scott threw himself between us.

"Stop! Everyone lower your weapons!"

No one listened to him, though I saw a couple of guards behind Ambrose turn to each other, confused.

The parade continued down the street—a mixture of music and cheers erupting from the crowd. Even now though, in a time of celebration, I heard a soft chorus of boos from people who still supported the war. Somewhere ahead on the floats, the council stood, their lives ticking away like a clock.

"Reynold," Ambrose said, his arms crossed. "Your . . . associate needs to lower his weapon before I order my guards to take him out."

"We're all a little high strung," Scott replied. He stepped toward me and reached out his hand. His fingers wrapped around the barrel of my weapon and pushed it down. At first I fought, but then I told myself Scott was on my side, and he knew the high probability that Ambrose played a part in the murders. I couldn't remember if both his arms were mechanical limbs, but if they were he would have the strength to rip apart the three council members.

"General, this is Daniel Quinn, the advisor to the council. Damon Derringer left him in charge in case of his death."

Ambrose raised an eyebrow and took a long look as if he'd never seen me before. But I knew he recognized me. The second he saw me, he knew who I was. So why was he playing dumb now? He had the advantage, his guards surrounded us, so what was he waiting for?

"General . . . Paul . . . why, with the danger the council faces, did you move the parade up a week?" Scott asked.

"The council wished to mourn their fallen advisor," Ambrose said without hesitation. "And with the recent murders, tensions are at an all-time high. If we waited until next week, the people may have rioted against us and the war would be inevitable."

"Bullshit," I spat, my mouth moving before my mind processed what I said. Ambrose scowled at me and Scott pushed me back from him, away from the guards. No one tried to stop us.

"Quinn," he whispered. "Shut up. Do you want to save the council or wait in a cell while they're murdered?"

Autumn put her hand on my shoulder, gently squeezing and nodding with Scott's words.

"He's right, Daniel. Play along. We have to get to the council. We can't help them from here."

That gave me an idea. I walked past Scott and holstered my weapon. This wasn't the time for rash action, but logical thought. Usually I didn't excel at the latter.

"My apologies, General Ambrose," I said, his name passing through my clenched teeth. "I'm just concerned for the council members, now that I'm in charge of overseeing their well-being. If you would permit, I want to join them in order to personally assure their safety."

Ambrose's scowl slowly morphed into the beginnings of a grin. He liked the idea, as I knew he would. If his intention was to kill the council today, I just offered to stand on ground zero.

"I agree, Mr. Quinn. You belong with the council." Ambrose turned and flicked his hand to one of his guards, who lowered his weapon and walked toward me. He grabbed my arm and pulled me away from the group and my allies. "Ensign Lota will be happy to escort you to their location. Enjoy the parade."

"Wait!" Scott called out as he and Autumn caught up to me. Autumn put her hands on my arms, and for a moment looked like she was about to hug me, but she just smiled and looked down to the ground.

"Please be careful," she said.

I wanted to say something back to her, but the words twisted inside my throat and left me voiceless. Scott interrupted the awkward silence by extending his hand.

"Good luck, Quinn." When I took his grasp, something small and hard pressed against my palm. I kept it lodged in my hand when I pulled back.

"Keep Autumn safe," I said. "And yourself."

"I will."

The guard led me away from the group. I wondered if I would see either of them again. By volunteering to stand with the council, I was risking my life, and Ambrose wouldn't have agreed if he thought I could stop his attack. But Scott and Autumn were right, none of us could help them from far away, let alone a jail cell.

We headed toward the back of the parade, where a number of floats hadn't moved yet. Good. The best chance of enticing the crowd would be if the council's attack came during their procession. Every twenty feet, I passed a guard who stood watch over his section. I couldn't tell if they were men sent here by Scott, or if they belonged to Ambrose. When the attack came, which Sentinels would stand to protect the people, and which would fight against them?

The floats themselves varied in size, shape, and content. Three of them were built identical to each other, but had been painted three different colors. The men and women standing on the first float wore jumpsuits of red with letters on their chests that read, "Unity." The second float, blue, featured the word "Technology," while the gold-colored third float read, "Terra."

When we passed the next float, my heart felt like it stopped. The guard grabbed my forearm hard and pulled me on. We were at the edge of the crowd now, and I couldn't help but stare at the bronze and silver lion float as it passed us. I half expected Granak to be inside, waiting to pounce on me, but nothing happened.

I knew we were close to the council when the next parade group was around fifty or more Sentinel guards, their weapons shouldered and all faces forward. They stepped in perfect unison. I imagined the order given, the guards turning and firing their weapons at the council, killing every one of them, including me. If all of these men were loyal to Ambrose, there may be no way of surviving.

The largest, grandest float of all began to move in front of me. The floor shimmered white and stairs led up to a golden balcony, which rested on a large arch. Men and women, eight of them, stood atop it and smiled with their hands up, waving to the crowds about to welcome them.

The council.

I looked at each of them. What were their names again? If I had more time to be their advisor, I'd make a terrible job of it. The couple of days I'd been on Terra felt like weeks and this was the first time I saw the council face to face. But the more I watched them, I remembered the last names under their profile pictures in Commander Scott's office.

Trent, Burns, Finn, Larson, Smith, Greene, Maxwell, Rider, and Townsend. I'd learn their first names later if we lived through the parade. "No weapons," the guard told me.

"What? I have to protect—"

"Ambrose's orders. No one is permitted within proximity of the council with weaponry of any kind. Now hand them over." To make sure I took him seriously, the guard raised his rifle and pointed it at my head.

Flux.

I pulled my sword off its magnetic strip and removed my revolver. Once the guard took possession of them, I didn't know if I could get them back, but I had little choice. I relinquished them, but took care to make sure I kept the device from Scott between two of my fingers. Once he had possession of my equipment, the ensign knocked on the side of the float and another guard opened from the inside, a rifle hanging from his shoulder.

"Wait a fluxing minute, *he* gets a weapon, but I don't? I'm the damn advisor for stars' sake."

"The previous advisor didn't carry anything and Sentinels have clearance in order to ensure the protection of the council." He sounded like a damn robot. I wanted to punch him, grab my sword and revolver, and haul ass to the council, but the second guard stared at me from inside the float and I needed to get past him.

Maybe these men were true Sentinels, loyal to Scott. I'd be lucky if that happened, but I don't usually get lucky.

I stepped into the float, the undercarriage a narrow hallway. Every step I took felt awkward with the movement of the float underneath me. I walked around in a circle until I reached a set of stairs. The steel steps and a door led me onto the balcony, its floor covered with a red and blue carpet, the colors cut down the middle. The door behind me closed and the latch locked. The council turned toward me, then to each other. Their shoulders shrugged and whispers passed from person to person. Then I realized they never technically saw my face. They only heard my voice.

"Councilmen and women," I said, "I'm Captain Daniel Quinn."

My grand announcement didn't seem to help their memories, until one of the women lifted her eyebrows and pointed at me.

"Quinn . . . Damon's replacement. We talked with you and Commander Reynold Scott?"

"Yes," I said. "Listen to me. All of you." Only now did I feel the nerves creeping inside me, a spreading whirlwind of anxiety and fear. We were all together, and every person in front of me was a target. Any minute—hell any second now—things were going to get bad.

Deep breaths. Don't complicate the situation. Think.

"There is going to be an attempt on your lives," I said, stepping close to them so I didn't have to shout. "We have to find a way to get you to safety."

"Mr. Quinn, Captain Quinn, we've known for weeks that our lives were in danger. You think we didn't know that when we approved of the parade? We told you before, this is a way to show the enemy that we will continue no matter what."

"The enemy is counting on that," I said. "They want you to stand tall and face the public. It just makes it easier to kill you!"

"That's enough," a woman to my right said. I think her name was Burns. "If there is an attempt, the Sentinels are here in force to stop it."

Frustration joined my anxiety and fear, and I wondered how a group so determined to find peace could be so ignorant. I leaned into Burns, my nose almost touching hers.

"The Sentinels are the ones who are going to attack."

Everyone heard me. Their smirks faltered, their arms dropped to their sides. One woman placed her hand on her chest. Maxwell turned his head toward the Sentinels in front of him. That got their attention.

"How could you make an accusation like that?" Burns asked me. "The Sentinels have been protecting our way of life for years."

"Not ours, though," Maxwell said. He must have been a Gaian. "They're your security force, Amanda. What are you playing at?" Burns and Maxwell stared at each other.

"This isn't the time to fight amongst yourselves," I said, my voice loud above their arguments. "You're the peace council for flux sake. The entire reason the parade was moved up a week is because Commander Scott, Autumn Derringer, and I discovered that Ambrose was working against the council to stop the treaty from happening."

"Why would he do such a thing?" another councilwoman asked, one of the only members who currently looked scared.

"That's not important. Listen, you don't know me, and if I were you, I wouldn't trust me either, but trust in Commander Scott. Trust Autumn, Damon's daughter. We are going to do everything we can to keep you safe."

The length of our conversation took us through the first quarter of the parade route. The council talked to each other and tried to determine their next course of action, despite the fact that they didn't really have any choices. We were locked on the balcony, and to jump off would result in severe injuries because the platform was about fifteen meters off the ground.

For the first time, I opened my hand and studied the device Scott gave me—a kind of module, black with transparent lines circling the outside of it. There was a button on the underside, just one. I wish he would have told me what the hell it was for, some kind of whisper or clue. He wouldn't have given it to me if he didn't think I needed it, so I kept my finger close to the button.

The attack was coming. I knew it, but not how or when. I activated every kind of sight with my bionic eye—analysis, infrared, thermal—but didn't see any unusual activity. I looked up, but the buildings were blocked by the large balloons.

I ran through a list of ways Ambrose could pull off the murder of the council, but the options were limited. The easiest method would be snipers from the buildings' windows. Eight shots, nine including me, and the council would be dead, but only the immediate crowd would see it happen.

Enjoy the show, Granak said.

No. Assassination was out of the picture. Whatever was going to happen, it would paint the sky red, raise a flag of blood that screamed war. Something big, like fireworks. The longer our float traveled down the main road, the harder my heart pounded. I itched for my sword and revolver.

I still had one advantage that the soldier couldn't take away—my bionic eye. A scanning grid appeared in my vision, and I walked the perimeter of the float as I looked in every direction. In front of us, the marching soldiers had varying degrees of heart rates and blood pressures. Some of them were highly elevated, which worsened my bad feeling. Above, in the buildings, I detected dozens of soldier silhouettes lined behind the windows, along with various weapon signatures.

"We have to get out of here," I said, the council's half-hearted attempt at waves to the crowd diminished. They stepped away from the edge of the balcony toward me. I tried to open the door; I kicked at it, ran my shoulder into it, but it wouldn't move. I ran past the council towards the balcony and leaned over. Too far.

Our options weren't just limited, they were non-existent. Did I really just back myself into a corner, one that would see the council murdered?

The device Scott gave me—he knew the parade route and how it would work. Just because it moved forward a week didn't mean anything else about it changed. Could a miniscule device help us now? I scanned over the small circular object. My eye picked up a strong energy signature around the button, one that I've seen surrounding two buildings and my prison.

A shield emitter. I pressed the button and a small jolt of energy sparked to life. I dropped the device, and as it landed, a faint shield, one barely noticeable by my human eye, enclosed around us.

I felt the beginning of a smile. The weapons would have trouble penetrating this. I doubt the power supply would last the length of the parade, but it gave us time.

Then I realized that the weapons in the windows weren't meant for us. I kept my eye on them—sniper rifles and the blue fireball shooters—and watched as they aimed forward, high above us, and let out a flurry of discharges.

Each of the balloons in front of us exploded in a burst of red and orange as they were hit, filling the sky with what could only be described as hellfire.

SIXTEEN

Debris rained. As the balloons landed on the floats and crowds around us, flames spread. People screamed in terror and enflamed human shapes ran flailing and falling.

"The Gaians! It has to be them!" people screamed.

"We're all going to die!"

The float in front of us turned into a bonfire, but we were protected. The small module was successful, though it didn't stop the intense heat from pressing against our skin. We dropped to the floor of the balcony as the fire passed over us.

More and more people fled the parade scene, blaming the Gaians for the attack. Ambrose's plan worked perfectly. As much as I wanted to determine the next course of action, the surrounding sickening horror caused me to close my eyes. If it hadn't been for Scott, we would either be dead or dying in agony right now.

Get a grip, I thought. *You have ten seconds to let the fear consume you and then you have to move.*

One . . .

What felt like an asteroid tumbled around in my stomach and tears built up in my eyes.

Three . . .

I let myself relive all the bad experiences I survived. The mutiny on the ESA Echelon, the massacre on the planet Dawn, the death of Damon Derringer, the assassination of the three council members, and more.

Six . . .

I did all I could in each circumstance. Maybe my intentions weren't always honorable and I had more than enough blood on my hands, but I did what I thought was right, what my family would be proud of. Daniel Quinn was one man, but it's possible that all you need is one to make a difference. One more man. One more second.

Ten . . .

I stood tall and looked at the scene around me. Below us, in between our float and the flaming wreck in front of us, were the numerous Sentinel guards I walked by earlier. More than half of them looked up at me, their weapons raised. Others looked confused and didn't know what to do.

"Everyone stay down!" I yelled, and as I did, a majority of the soldiers opened fire at us. Each burst ricocheted off the shield and left behind small ripples.

The confused Sentinels realized what was happening and raised their weapons toward their comrades, but each one was gunned down before defending us.

The weight of their deaths pressed on my shoulders, but at least I knew Ambrose didn't have full control of the Sentinels, which meant help was out there somewhere. Unfortunately, this also meant I had no idea who to trust.

More discharges hit the shield. We couldn't just sit like motionless targets. We had to move. The small size of the module meant that its energy would deplete sooner rather than later. The door behind us was still locked, and I doubted that the guard behind it would open it. My bionic eye searched for anything that could help us.

The floats still moved down the predetermined path of the parade, their structures slowly consumed by fire. How many people still stood on them, helpless? How many shapes did I see fall from them, burning? I tried to shake away my distress and focus instead on myself and the council. Thirty feet ahead of us was a tall glass building, all its windows tinted black. I scanned over the side of the float and the window itself, judging the distance.

Less than ten feet. We could do it.

I looked around the top of the float, trying to find something hard to throw. Nothing. The damn guard took my gun and sword before I got on the float. What the hell were we going to throw at the window to smash it?

As we drew closer, only one option came to mind, but I didn't like it. I scanned down the street as far as I could and tried to see if there were any smaller buildings. That's when I saw the gunmen above us getting closer. If we stayed on the float, we would cross their path. And as if on cue, the shield began to fluctuate.

All choices were void, except one.

"Everyone, get up. We're going to jump."

"Jump?" Burns said, standing. "Are you insane? We're over thirty feet off the ground!"

"We're not jumping to the ground," I replied, backing up to the far side of the float, which was still protected by the shield. My previous fear resurged.

"You're kidding," Maxwell huffed out through short breaths.

"Listen to me. You have two choices. You can all stay here and wait for the shield to fail, in which case the Sentinels will kill you, or you can risk your life by jumping into the building. Two options and only one clear path toward living. Do you seriously need to consider this?"

"But we have nothing," Burns said, her eyes darting back and forth from me to the building. "What are we going to use to break the glass?"

"Me," I said. "So, worst-case scenario, I'll jump and smack into the glass, fall to my death, and you won't have to do anything."

I don't know whether they all realized their options were limited, or if my sacrifice proved my loyalty to them, but one by one the council stood and walked toward me. We all watched the window draw closer. The float in front of us stopped. The fire must have finally damaged the motor.

Flux me.

"Okay, well, at least you won't have to wait to be gunned down. If this doesn't work, you'll all just smack into the float in front of us. At least you might squish a few Sentinels below."

The timing would have to be perfect. If anyone hesitated, the float would crash before they had a chance to jump. I stared at the window and chose my point of entry. Everything blurred, including the council and the screams from the people below.

"Put your whole body into it. Focus on the spot you want to land on." I said to myself so the council would hear it. The window approached. The burning float came closer. Only a few more seconds. The large window passed the front of the float.

I took off at a sprint. I pushed harder than I ever have and used every ounce of energy, but I wasn't a machine. On the Kestrel Belle, I could divert energy where I needed it. Here, I didn't have the ability to transfer more power to my legs, but I imagined it—pictured myself leaping from the platform and clearing the open space to the window. Whether the glass would break, that was out of my control.

Quickly, the floor ended and I pushed off the ground. The time I spent in the air seemed to be an eternity. I saw the Sentinels below, some still firing on us and others reloading. I saw various shapes and sizes of people fleeing the area. Then all I could see was glass. I held my knees up and stuck out my elbows. This was going to hurt.

The glass didn't shatter into a million pieces when I hit it. Instead, the window cracked and large shards broke off. Pain shot through my left arm and leg and I knew one of the shards cut me. But I'd done it—I'd broken through the window. My body fell to the ground and I rolled, ungraceful.

No time, I told myself. *No time to recover. Get up. Help the council.*

I stood and put pressure on my right foot. Every left step I took hurt like hell and I felt blood dripping down my arm and leg. I limped my way back to the window and used my elbow to knock a few more shards out of the way, leaving more room for the council to jump through. The float moved slowly enough, but we only had a minute or two before it crashed.

"Now! Let's go!"

One by one, the council ran from the far end of the platform and jumped into the window. I stood by in case any of them needed help, but so far everyone cleared the window without problems. Burns and Maxwell were the last to jump.

"Ladies first," Maxwell breathed out. I worried about him. The stress from the attack seemed to aggravate him physically. I never took the time to learn their medical histories, but from what I saw, he wasn't in the best of health.

Burns ran as fast as she could and jumped. I saw the fear in her eyes as she stretched her arms toward me. I extended my right hand, ignoring the pain from my left as I held onto the frame. Our hands clasped and I pulled hard. She landed at the edge of the window.

Maxwell leaned over, a coughing fit taking control.

"Maxwell! You have to jump!"

The Sentinels below dispersed as the floats came closer. If Maxwell waited any longer, he wouldn't leap before impact. He spat on the ground and rushed forward. But with his strained look, I knew he wouldn't make it. I reached out to grab him like I did Burns. He gritted his teeth and grunted as he made the best jump he could. I took hold of his wrist, but he wasn't high enough and he swung into the frame below me. The impact jostled both of us and his arm slipped from my fingers. Maxwell grasped the frame and held on for his life. I dropped to the floor to help him, carefully to avoid any glass shards still sticking out of the frame.

The door on the balcony of the float flew open. A Sentinel stepped through and turned toward us.

"No, flux, no," I gasped and tightened my grip on Maxwell.

"Let me go. Save the rest," he said.

"No. No! We're all getting out of this together."

The guard pointed his rifle at me. I couldn't save everyone, but I still held on, not frozen in fear, but determined despite the stacked odds. Maxwell must have seen the look on my face.

"Thank you," was all he said before he released his grip on the window frame. I screamed for him, but he fell to the ground below. I rolled to the side just as plasma bursts flew past me and tore into the opposite wall.

Grinding metal signaled the floats crashing together. In that instant I knew the Sentinel wouldn't wait around. I got to my feet as he landed in the window frame. I felt like I was in slow motion, racing to my feet as he balanced himself and turned his weapon toward me.

I clasped my fingers together, wound my arms back, and thrust them against the weapon. It fired as I diverted the direction of the blast, but the heat that surged from the muzzle burned my hands. I ignored the pain and recoiled, hitting the guard in the chest with my elbow. He fell toward the window opening and I lunged to grab his collar.

"What's your plan of attack?" I asked through gritted teeth. "How many men are trying to kill the council?"

The Sentinel, leaning out the window, his life in my hands, laughed.

"Daniel Quinn, the path of Infinity is endless!" He followed his cryptic words with a push against me. He fell further back and I couldn't hold on without toppling out of the window myself. I let him go, but not before grabbing his rifle.

The path of Infinity is endless?

Solving riddles was an exercise best left for later, if we all survived. I checked the rifle and familiarized myself with the trigger and settings. Its battery had a seventy percent charge. I eased it against my shoulder and assessed the surrounding area.

Grey cubicles filled with boxes and documents lined the area. Above some of the desks, holographic images displayed graphs and statistics. The council had huddled across the room, their gazes shifting back and forth throughout the room, alerted from their fear and adrenaline.

"Can someone tell me where we are?"

Burns stepped forward, wiping her hands on her long skirt. "This is the Sedar building."

"And how far is it from the docking tower?"

"Which one?" the man behind Burns asked. Finn, I think his name was.

Stars above, I couldn't remember the name of the damn tower. The designation started with a letter . . . I think. A? B? Yes, it was B . . . something. I really needed to start remembering these things, or typing them down before I forgot them.

Before . . . B-4! That was it!

"Docking tower B-4," I said.

"That's . . . a little over a mile south of us," Finn said, scratching at his white beard.

That wasn't too far, but with men and women over middle-age, most of them even older than that, our pace would be slower than if I was alone. Still, I didn't trust taking the council anywhere else. And I couldn't trust the Sentinels, even the ones loyal to Terra and the council. Somewhere out there, Commander Scott and Autumn were either running or fighting. I wish I knew if they were okay, but I alone held the council's fate in my hands. No time to waste.

"Alright. We make for B-4 and try to stay off the streets as much as possible. We'll go from building to building until we get there. I want everyone to stay behind me, and keep alert. You're not going to know whether someone is a friend or an enemy. Do you all have communicators?"

Everyone pulled devices from their pockets.

"You'll have to leave them here so the Sentinels can't track us. In fact, if you have any electronic equipment other than that, now is the time to leave it."

The target reticle in my bionic eye flashed toward the other side of a room. The door had opened and movement beyond the entryway flashed in my sight. The guards below the float must have seen us jump in here.

"Everyone find a cubicle and hide under it. We've got company."

The council didn't hesitate. They spread throughout the immediate area. I hid behind a square pillar and peered around it to watch the doorway. My arm and leg burned and blood was still wet against my skin.

My bionic eye counted at least five men beyond the door. The wide area around us, filled with desks and columns, provided good cover, but would also do the same for the soldiers. If I allowed them into the room, they could use the barriers to flank our position. So, my goal was to bottleneck them in the doorway.

As soon as I saw a figure with my normal sight, I opened fire. Green plasma bursts shot out of the barrel and scorched the doorframe. Most of the shots went high because the recoil was hard to control when firing so many rounds at once. The vibration of the weapon numbed my fingers.

"Weapon detected!" one of them shouted. I fired another round, and this time the plasma traveled through the door. I heard cursing, but no grunts of pain.

"Burns," I said. "We need a way out of here."

"That door is the only exit," she said from under the desk beside me.

In other words, we were trapped. Bottlenecking the soldiers wouldn't work forever. The rifle's capacity was already lowered to sixty-five percent. The soldiers just needed to wait until I expended my rounds, and they could come in and have us. There were no other options for escape, so we would have to make one.

"Which way to B-4?" I glanced down at her. She pointed south, toward a wall of windows. Another building with large windows stood across from an alleyway gap, almost the same distance as this building was from our float.

I fired a long round of plasma to force the soldiers to seek cover. Immediately after, I turned and shot the windows of this building and the one across the alley. The glass blew into what looked to be a lobby area of some kind.

"Please tell me we're not jumping," said a council member who must have figured out my plan. Trent, I think his name was.

"It's the only way we're going to get out of this. The distance isn't farther than the last jump. You'll all be fine," I said between peering around the column and firing into the doorway.

The soldiers returned fire and emphasized my point. I heard the blasts a second after feeling the column rumble as plasma bursts pelted it into bits and pieces of concrete.

"We need to move!"

But no one did. The soldiers weren't giving me a chance to fire back. Multiple plasma bursts hit the column and surrounding desks. I fired blindly, hoping to relieve the pressure.

Burns crawled out from under her desk and moved low and quick to the window. She turned to the other council members and gestured for them to follow. Some did, some didn't. I fired another blind round and chanced a peek around the column.

Two soldiers made it into the room—their thermal images displayed in my sight. The other three were still behind the door, and an additional six were advancing up the stairs.

I knelt behind the desk Burns had hidden behind and saw that she and three other council members had already jumped. Brave woman. The rest of the council was still hesitant.

"I'm going to turn around and open fire," I said. "When I do that, you'll have your last chance to jump to that building. Once the chamber empties, I'm jumping. If I go before you, you're left behind. Do you all understand?"

I didn't wait for an answer. The next barrage of fire stopped and I unloaded the rest of the plasma over the desk. When the rifle clicked empty, I didn't sit around to wait, nor did I make sure the council acted. I turned, focused my sights on the far building, and sprinted. When I jumped, I stretched as far as I could, hoping to grab the window frame.

My body smacked against the building in a sudden jolt. I couldn't grab anything and, in that second, expected to fall. My life didn't really flash before my eyes, but I did think about everything that led me up to this moment. After I fell to my death, what would happen? Would the council escape? Or would they be hunted down and slaughtered? In seconds, it wouldn't be my problem anymore.

But I didn't fall. My hands weren't holding anything. Something held on to me. I looked up and saw two of the council members I had yelled at—Trent and Rider. They pulled me up, their faces glistening with sweat.

"Thank you," I breathed. Just then an object, something small and unnoticed, whipped past the top of my head. A second later Rider fell heavily to the ground, his eyes open and a bloodied hole in his forehead.

Must've been the snipers in the buildings.

"Go!" I screamed. Trent took off down the hall to join the rest of the council, those who still lived. I pushed myself up as hard as I could and followed Trent. A bullet struck the ground where my leg used to be. Three more bullets hit the wall as I ran forward. The council turned at an intersection in the hall. I followed into a small, boxed area with two elevator doors.

"Get the elevators up here now," I said. "When they open, pull on the emergency stop so no one can use them."

My voice sounded slurred and distant and I felt exhausted. I collapsed to the floor.

"Mr. Quinn?" Burns asked.

"He's lost too much blood," someone else said. That's right. My wounds. The blood. Everything seemed so much hazier now than a few minutes ago.

"He's not going to make it. We need to leave him here," a female said. Not Burns, though. The voice was higher pitched and younger.

"Samantha Greene, you can't be serious!" Burns said. "This man saved our lives and is losing his own in the process. We are not going to leave him to die. Jack, you have some medical skill, don't you?"

Whoever Jack was didn't answer.

"Jack! We're all scared, but this man needs your help!"

"R-right," Jack said. Someone knelt beside me, though my focus was on the elevator doors. The council did as I asked and stopped them from moving, but that didn't mean someone couldn't override the system.

"I need some kind of bandages. I can't do anything about the blood he lost, but if we can bind his arm and leg, it should stop from him from bleeding out completely."

I heard the tearing of clothes and then felt hands on my arm and leg, holding them up. Jack took the torn pieces of clothing and wrapped them around my wounds.

"That's the best I can do, but I don't know how we're going to survive without weapons. And if he isn't capable of defending us, who is?"

"It looks like they're getting ready to jump across," another man said. "He shouldn't have told us to get rid of our communicators. This is all a waste! The soldiers know where we are anyway!" the woman with the higher-pitched voice cried. Indecipherable whispers spread throughout the group.

"We have to do the best we can in any situation," Burns said. "Mr. Quinn did what he thought was right, but now we have to take control. Ms. Greene, please try to calm yourself. Mr. Trent and Mr. Larson, if you would kindly help Mr. Quinn to his feet?"

Two arms on each side lifted me. My feet felt like goo, but my arms around the other people's shoulders supported me. I knew so little of the council. Hell, I didn't even know most of their first names, but they worked well together. I couldn't tell who belonged to Terra and who belonged to Gaia if my life depended on it. They could have stood around and argued, blamed each other for the chaos outside, but instead they stuck together. If we got out of this alive, there might be hope to end this war if more people thought like them.

"Everyone into the elevator," Burns said.

"But Quinn said—"

"I know what he said, but in his current condition, he's not able to give any more orders is he? We're going to take the elevator up to the 75th floor, take the high ground in a manner of speaking. There's an access hall between this building and the next, if memory serves correctly. We'll make our way there, where we will attempt to call for help."

Burns walked into the elevator and released it. It didn't move. She pressed another button, the 75th floor button I assumed, and held the door for us. We filed in and the elevator moved up at an astounding speed. I thought I might vomit, until I realized I hadn't eaten anything recently.

As we marched through the hallways, my bionic eye started to give me a headache. All the statistics and scans were too much for me to compute, so I forced my right eyelid shut and kept watch with my left. As high as we were, I heard no gunshots, no screaming. If it weren't for the muffled distant sirens, the day might have been calm and normal as any other.

We moved quickly. No one spoke as Burns led us through the building, turning down different hallways as if she knew where she was going. I wanted to warn her to keep an eye out, to peer around corners just in case someone was waiting, but I felt too tired to speak. No one attacked us, but the snipers worried me. Somewhere in some of the buildings, they waited for us. This might have been one of them.

The group stopped in front of another hallway, this one longer and more open than any of the others. This was the bridge leading to the next building. I opened my eyelid and scanned the distance between here and the other side.

Fifty meters. If any soldiers were watching the bridge, we wouldn't make it. There's no way we could cross that fast, especially if Trent and Larson were carrying me.

"Leave me here," I managed to say, the words making me breathless.

"Nonsense, Mr. Quinn. You're just going to have to move quickly."

"You'll die," I said.

Burns walked past the other members and stood close enough for me to see the wrinkles in her gentle face. She was heavy set, but had a gentle face, lightly covered in wrinkles around her mouth and eyes. Her forehead glistened with sweat.

"For once, it's time for you to listen to me," Burns said. "We've had this conversation before, young man, about the necessity of sacrifice and standing up for what you believe in. If our deaths mean these planets will see their folly and unite together, then I'll gladly give mine. You have the benefit of only witnessing the last few days of this war, whereas many of us lived through a majority of it. Some, like myself, even witnessed its birth. Too many people lost their lives, Mr. Quinn, my husband included. Now . . . enough talking. Let's get across this hall and go from there."

I stood there, suspended on the shoulders of Trent and Larson, and wondered what else Burns experienced to become such a strong and admirable woman. Her spirit was as strong and durable as anyone I've ever known. She reminded me of . . . well . . . no one. I've known admirable people in my life, some willing to sacrifice as much as her, but she held the strength and determination of someone who couldn't, and wouldn't, give up.

The council needed her more than anyone. She had to survive this. Some members stood tall, like Smith and Townsend. They said little, but I saw no hesitation in their expressions, while others were worn and tired, their eyes revealing fear and uncertainty.

"Please, listen," I forced myself to say. "If we run scattered, weapon fire will be sure to hit someone. We have to stay together. Burns should lead us forward. Smith and Townsend, stay beside her, and Greene, right behind her. And we'll come up the rear."

"That's a good plan," Burns said, then turned around. "Are we ready?"

We took off at a brisk jog. I used every ounce of energy I had to carry my own weight to lessen the pressure on Larson and Trent. We made it ten meters before the first bullet splintered a window. It missed, but more came. Then there were many more.

Smith was shot down and Greene tripped over his body. She fell, screaming, "We're dead!" I pushed Trent off me and told him to help her up. I almost fell, too, but knew I had to survive. I had to make sure Burns survived.

She thought my plan was good, keeping together in a clump to keep ourselves from spreading out and being hit. But she didn't realize the true reason I suggested it. I did it to protect her. I knew we would be shot at, and possibly killed, but if the council surrounded her, she would be shielded.

The meaning of this rationality suddenly registered. I used a human being as a shield for someone else. I sent them to their deaths. Who the hell was I anymore?

We all made it across the bridge, no other casualties except for Smith. Greene was hysterical, her hands trembling as she stood screaming, looking back at Smith's corpse.

"What was his first name?" I asked.

"What does it matter anymore?" Larson said, his low voice breaking.

"Because I killed him," I said. Everyone turned and looked at me. I figured since I killed the man, it was only respectful to learn his first name, but no one said it.

"Okay," Burns said. "There should be a communication console in the lobby. The enemy has stayed with us this long, so they already have our position. Let's see if we can get some damned help."

I couldn't recall how far up we were, but the main area was built like a massive lobby with a large square table in the center and sectional couches against each corner of the room. Trent and

Larson dragged me over to one and dropped me. I landed on cushions like fluffy clouds. I just wanted to close my eyes and drift to sleep.

"Can anyone hear me?" Burns's loud and determined voice jolted me awake. "This is Amanda Burns and I speak for the peace council."

Oh, her first name was Amanda.

"We have experienced heavy casualties and require immediate medical assistance. Please, can anyone out there hear me? We stand together in the Jericho Communication Building, and we're only a few floors away from the roof. We beg for assistance and an evacuation vessel. Please."

"Every single person trying to kill us just heard that!" Samantha Greene shouted.

"Samantha," Trent said above me. "They're already after us. It doesn't matter."

"I just . . . I don't want to die. Not like this . . ."

No one ever really wanted to die, I wanted to tell her, but couldn't find the strength. Even people who commit suicide do so because they feel there's no alternative, no way to continue living. People know they'll die, sometimes in detail, like Damon Derringer. Sometimes it comes quick and unexpected, like Laraar. Other times, it's placed in front of you, horrible and sad, like Ashley.

"Let's not waste time," Burns said. "We've made our distress call, and now we must follow through with our plan. If we run into the enemy, then I want all of you to know it's been an honor. Mr. Quinn . . ." She knelt beside me. Trent helped me to sit up. "I can only imagine what's going through your head right now, and the pain you must be going through, but we are still alive thanks to you. You are a good man. An honorable one."

She stood and, silent and sure, we made our way to the building's roof. To reach it, we had to walk up seven more flights of stairs. I told Larson to help the others get upstairs while I used my good arm to hold myself up on the railing. Trent still held me on my left. Below us, many floors down, echoes from soldiers could be heard.

"I killed him, Trent," I said softly. "She thanked me for saving her, but I did so using Smith."

Trent said nothing, but he didn't let go and leave me to die. Instead, he took a long breath and let it out.

"His name was Trevor. Trevor Smith."

"In case I die, my name is Frank. I don't know what's running through your head, Mr. Quinn, but I can tell you this much . . . you didn't kill Trevor. A bullet did, one shot from a coward who wouldn't fight his enemy face to face."

"But . . . I knew they would shoot at us. I wanted to protect Burns."

"You did what anyone with the capacity to lead would have done. You knew there would be casualties, and you tried to minimalize the risk."

He talked to me so calmly, so sure of himself. Was it because he thought I was going to die and wanted me to be at peace?

We reached the roof's door long before the soldiers caught up to us, but we had no idea if anything waited on the other side. There was no turning back. Burns put her hands on the door's handle.

"Wait," Trent said. "Larson, you go first, make sure there aren't any soldiers waiting for us."

Larson looked from Trent to Burns, then nodded. Were they thinking the same thing I was—that Burns was too valuable to lose?

He pushed open the door and white light filled the narrow stairwell. No attacks came.

The roof was enormous. Pipelines and platforms had been built into its structure. I heard gunshots again and cries for help below us. Accompanying that were loud engines flying by the buildings, but not high enough for us to see. The fight had evolved to air as well as ground.

"Over there," someone said. "We can hold them off behind those sections of wall."

I looked across the platform, and there were high walls, possibly a housing area for electrical equipment or something of that nature. We stepped toward it and the sound of an engine grew louder from behind us. We turned to see a circular vessel with short wings and turret guns on the dorsal side rise over the building. A ramp lowered to reveal a dozen men holding rifles, their uniform reminiscent of the kind I saw when I landed. Gaian military uniforms.

"Oh . . . oh . . ." Greene panicked.

"Run!" Burns screamed. We ran across the platform as the ship opened fire. Weapon fire exploded on the roof and concrete flew up toward us. Then multiple rounds of plasma burned into Larson's back. He fell. Another shot hit Trent in the leg and he fell, taking me with him. He screamed and I forced my head to turn toward the other council members. They made it safely to the walls. Not that it mattered now. The ship could alter its direction and fire on them at point blank range.

The weapons on the ship stopped and the soldiers on the ramp jumped to the ground. Beside them, from the stairwell door, another dozen men walked onto the roof. The fight was over.

The sound of a second engine roared its way behind us, in front of the council. We were trapped with nowhere to go. The only question was, would they take us as prisoners or kill us here and be done with it?

I saw a moment's hesitation from the soldiers on the roof before multiple plasma rounds shot and destroyed the Gaian vessel. Another round shot toward the ground, taking down a number of soldiers. I turned, expecting to see a Terran ship.

And there was the Kestrel Belle.

How? When? The ship spin on its axis as the cargo bay door opened. Terran soldiers leapt out, led by Commander Reynold Scott. The men hit the ground and opened fire on the enemy who scattered and took shelter in the stairwell and against the platform.

"Advance on the enemy!" Scott ordered, stepping over me. "The two of you get Quinn and the council out of here!"

Arms grabbed me and pulled me up, and I heard a familiar voice.

"Ni ja ti-oh?"

Tress.

Then I heard another voice that warmed my heart, despite my pain and discomfort.

"Daniel," Autumn said. "Daniel, oh my . . . We need to get him out of here now. Take him."

Tress dragged me toward my ship where the council had already jumped onboard. I looked back to see Autumn grab Frank Trent and help him. We all piled in the cargo bay as Scott's men and the enemy exchanged shots.

"Come on!" Autumn screamed.

"Just go! Just go now!" Scott waved violently and turned back to the enemy, covering our retreat. Tress ran to the side of the room and threw up the lever. The doors started to close as he pressed the communicator and said something. Whatever he said, the ship turned and soared away from the firefight.

"Daniel . . . please say something," Autumn pleaded. My vision grew darker.

"Who the flux . . . is flying my ship?"

SEVENTEEN

I awoke in my bed and felt like someone dragged me through muck and grime and filled my head with sludge. Foggy light filled the room, or was my sight blurry? Any attempt to get up failed, as if my body didn't want to continue.

What happened? I tried to drag memories through the thickness inside my mind.

"Captain."

The voice was the last thing I expected to hear. A wave of emotion rolled its way through my body, up my chest, and into my eyes. Tears fell as easily as turning on a tap.

"Al . . . Al, is it really you?" My throat burned as I said the words with a terrible rasp.

"It is agreeable to see that you are well, Captain," Al said. He was okay. I couldn't believe it.

"Al, oh flux, Al. I can't . . . was it the engineers? The engineers repaired you?"

"In a manner of speaking, sir. During the attack by the Leondren vessel, the computer console was damaged, and as such, my database was placed in a secure environment to prevent data loss."

I couldn't describe the relief I felt from hearing his voice again, like an old friend had come home. I never knew his mainframe kept a secure backup storage when the computer was damaged. What else didn't I know about him?

Without thinking, I leaned over to my left and pain shot up my arm. I turned to the other side quickly to relieve the pressure and saw Autumn. I didn't even know she was in the room. She was lying down a couple of feet away from me, not on my bed, but on a stack of mattresses that must have come from the crew quarters. When our eyes met, her lips lifted into a wide grin.

"Hey, you," she said, her voice music to my ears. I returned the smile. I forced my left arm forward, through the pain, to see the damage. A line of binding staples ran down my upper arm. My shirt's sleeve was torn at the shoulder and the fabric was stained ruddy red. Dried blood crusted my skin.

"I don't want to offend you or anything, but you really . . . really need a shower."

I laughed. My arm and leg pulsed with pain as I did, but it felt good. My ship, Al, Tress, and Autumn were all okay. We survived the attack.

"The council?" I asked.

"Amanda Burns, Samantha Greene, Loral Rider, Frank Trent, and Eric Townsend are all that remain," she said and diverted her gaze to the wall.

I sighed. Six dead members. The council had been cut in half.

"How is Trent?"

"Better than you," she replied, looking up at me again. "His leg took a nasty hit, but you had enough medical supplies on the ship to stabilize him. As for you, we didn't know if you were going to make it."

She held up her left arm, which had an IV line hooked into it. Red filled the tubing, which connected her to me.

"You saved me," I whispered.

"Yeah, well, there's still a war going on, and you seem to be doing a good job of keeping people alive," she said with a small smile.

Except for Smith, Larson, and your father, I thought. There was still something I had to admit to her. Despite my feelings when we were together, a small wall of guilt stood between the two of us, only she didn't yet realize it. There was no better time than now to break that wall. "I threatened your father."

Her smile faltered and lifted her head up slightly. "When he found me, I was afraid," I continued before she could stop me, "Afraid of why another human would want to see me. So much happened in my life. When he found me, I pulled out my gun and pointed it at him. When he was shot, his last cognitive thought could have been that I was the one who pulled the trigger."

She looked away toward the bare, steel ceiling of my quarters and pursed her lips. I didn't see any tears or trembles. I couldn't tell if she was upset or sad, but I expected her to pull out the IV and leave, or scold me for being an ignorant, selfish man. Instead, she took a deep breath and looked into my eyes again.

"Would you have killed my father if Granak hadn't?"

"What? No . . . it was a bluff. I just wanted to stay away from everything."

"Thank you for telling me. I wish he died under better circumstances, but he knew the risk he was taking by leaving Terra. Instead of dwelling on what happened between you and my father, try to focus on how you reacted, and what you did for him."

"What do you mean?" I asked.

"What did you do after my father died? Did you leave his body? Escape the planet and go live your life in isolation elsewhere?"

"No, but—"

"There is no but, Daniel. You brought him home, tried to protect the council, looked after me. Stop trying to destroy yourself by focusing on the negative. Don't live in the past. Live in the here and now."

She was right. I did everything I could to honor Damon's memory. It would have cost me my life if the Belle hadn't flown in to save the day . . . which reminded me.

"Who was flying my ship?" I asked. She looked away.

"I don't feel I'm the person to tell you that."

"Why not?"

"Listen, you've been through a lot. I never even realized some of the things you lived through, but you need to take it slow. Let yourself get a little better before we start to unravel this . . . whatever this is."

There were things that frustrated me more than others. For example, being lied to or being betrayed. Another thing was being kept in the dark. I wanted to frown, narrow my eyes and demand to know what was going on, whether Autumn knew the answer or not, but I forced my lips into a pleasant grin.

"Autumn. I want to know who had control of my ship."

She didn't argue.

"Al, is it?" she asked as she looked up at the ceiling. "Could you send him to Daniel's room, please?"

"Acknowledged, Ms. Derringer."

I almost smiled again hearing Al's voice, but I didn't. I wanted answers.

And I got them. With one look to the man who saved me and the council, I got answers to the biggest questions. Who had my ship, and who told Damon Derringer where to find me? I almost didn't recognize him through the thick grey beard and long salt-and-pepper hair. The engineer I met walking off the Belle, the one who awkwardly kept his hand on my shoulder a moment longer than I expected, the one who knew enough about Al to fix him.

In the doorway of my quarters stood the first captain I'd served under, the captain whom Sarah King mutinied.

Gregory Smithson.

He wore a dull gray uniform with black stripes along the collar and down his chest. He held his hands behind his back. The corner of his mouth showed the slightest of smiles.

"C-c-c," I tried to speak, but words failed. The last time I saw Captain Smithson was the first day I flew into space on the Kestrel Belle, after he finished installing Al.

"Hello, Daniel," he said. "It's good to see you."

"C-c-c . . . How?" I finally blurted out.

"We have a little time," he said. "You need to rest, and then we'll talk."

Before I could answer he left, and for a second I was sure the image had been nothing more than a ghost. But Autumn slowly stood and knelt beside my bed, brushing her fingers through my hair.

"Are you okay?" she asked.

"Why is it every time a question gets answered, it just brings up more questions?"

She laughed and reached for a glass of water waiting on a bedside table. She handed it to me and told me to drink slowly, which of course, I didn't. I turned the glass upside down and half of it splashed onto my face. It felt good, both in my mouth and on my skin. I returned the glass and let my arm fall to the ground to press it against the deck. No vibration whatsoever.

"Where are we?"

"Gaia," she said.

"Gaia?"

"A lot's happened. Terra and Gaia are going to declare full-scale war in a matter of days."

EIGHTEEN

Twelve hours passed before I managed to push myself out of bed. Tress took Autumn's place by my side, and when I asked him where she was, he told me the blood transfer made her tired and she was resting in the crew quarters. I tried to stand up by myself, but despite me telling Tress to stay back, he insisted on helping me.

He told me about the day I left him with the engineers. After Autumn and I cleared the docking platform, the men got to work on the ship. Gregory Smithson revealed himself and told Tress who he was and how he fit into the equation. He proved his story by accessing data from the computer's records, and before long, Tress helped Smithson and the other engineers repair the Belle.

I wanted to tell Tress to be more careful, to always have his guard up and watch who he trusted, but it felt like scolding a child who was responsible for saving my life. We walked down the corridor toward the docking bay. I wanted to see Gaia for myself, and find Smithson to ask him questions.

For all the technology Terra had, Gaia compensated in natural economic growth. The Gaians were farmers, first and foremost, and carried only enough technology for defense. What waited for me outside the cargo bay doors?

In short, nothing. I expected to see a field of green, maybe a lush forest or a thriving farming community. Instead, I saw death. Dark clouds covered the sky. The grass and trees in the distance were gray and wasting away. I stepped off the ramp and everything beneath my feet crunched to ash.

"What happened here?" I asked.

"The Gaians would tell you that the Terrans committed this act of terrorism," Smithson said. I turned to find him walking toward me. Behind him stood a small off-white house, bright against all the decay. "Two days ago, the fields and plants all began to die, and soon after, Gaia's rich resources were destroyed."

Stars above. All data on Gaia and its culture told me how much Gaians depended on their economics and harvesting. How many years did it take to build and grow all the vegetables and grain, only to have it reduced to waste in two days?

"Terra was attacked, lives lost . . . and Gaia's ecosystem was destroyed?"

"Doesn't seem fair, does it?" Smithson crossed his arms and stared into the distance. "Each planet was hit where it would hurt the most. Terra was always the boiling pot, ready to overflow if heated too much."

I was still unable to believe that my old commanding officer was here, and had saved my life. The way he talked, so sure of himself and confident, made me feel like a Lieutenant again. I wanted to salute him, shout out, "yes sir!" as he spoke to me, but I reminded myself that years had passed since we were last together. I had changed, and I could only assume at the time that he did, too. I was a captain now and I had to force myself to act like one.

"Why is this happening? What's to gain from Terra and Gaia killing each other?"

Smithson stood there a moment, mulling over my question. He took in a deep breath and turned back toward what I assumed was his home.

"Come with me, Daniel."

Smithson's house appeared to be small on the outside, but it was more than spacious inside. A short hall branched into multiple rooms. The farthest room in the back held the most commotion. I recognized the voices of the council.

"They're all safe?" I asked.

"You saved them, Daniel." He gave me a small smile and led me to an enclosed room on the right. The technology that welcomed me inside was more advanced than any computer I had on the Belle. Except for Al, of course. A touch screen desk, much like the one I saw in Scott's office, sat in the middle. A large video screen hung on the wall behind it. Every corner of the room had some kind of electronic equipment. One looked like a map of Gaia, another showed a tactical display of the surrounding area, and the others I couldn't tell, but their bright lights and countless buttons looked impressive. Smithson walked behind his desk and sat in his chair.

"So, I'm sure you have questions," he said, folding his hands together.

That was an understatement. I had an entire log of questions, though looking at the room, my former superior officer, and reeling from all that happened left me a little speechless. I forced my mind to come up with something to say.

"Are you a native Gaian?"

"No, they would have found me long ago if that was the case. I was born on Earth, grew up there, but I had family on Terra. When Sarah King came looking for me, they went there first."

"I noticed you used the word 'had,'" I said.

His eyes focused on the ground. "Two of my cousins and their families were on the planet. King thought that she could lure me out by threatening their lives. When I refused . . . she followed through with her plan."

By his own admission, his failure to act caused the death of his family. Frozen in the moment, I wondered how anyone could let their family die, no matter the cost.

"What do you know about Sarah King, Daniel?"

The abrupt question pulled me out of my trance and my memories focused on moments of agony and pain. Sarah King imprisoned me and blamed me for the murder of an ESA officer, Ashley. In truth she was behind it all—a plot to take over the ESA's flagship Echelon and take control of the artificial intelligence program. Al.

"Except for the memories . . . I know a little. She is determined, a seasoned strategist, and a cold-hearted bitch."

"And her group? Do you know anything about the people she works with?" I shook my head. "Have you ever heard the term 'Infinity' before?"

My mind flashed to recent moments, the infinity symbol on the mercenaries' outfits, the ones who attacked in the docking tower after I landed, and then later during the parade when a man dressed as a Sentinel muttered the words, "The path to Infinity is endless." At the time, the phrase confused me.

"I've searched hundreds of databases, maybe close to thousands," Smithson continued. "And I only came across the name Infinity five times. They are a rogue faction of humans and one of their top operatives, maybe even their leader, is—"

"Sarah King," I finished.

"Take a look at this." Smithson keyed in commands on his desk and a holographic image appeared above him. Numerous shapes materialized, some larger than others. I recognized them, especially the three battle cruisers in the middle. The Destiny, Triumph, and Echelon—the three most powerful and influential starships in the Earth Star Alliance fleet. Surrounding the flagships were hundreds of smaller cruisers and attack fighters. Smithson pressed another key and a variety of red and white dots glowed within the ships. The Echelon was nearly all red, while Destiny was half-red and white, and Triumph was mostly white. Over half of the smaller ships glowed red.

"What you're seeing here is the progress Infinity has been making within the ESA."

Stars above. The image looked like a virus, spreading out over a large area.

"How? How do you know all this?" My voice broke and I swallowed hard.

"I still have a few friends in the fleet, not enough to prove King's a traitor, but they still provide me with information, star charts, mission logs, things like that. It's taken me over a year to collect and piece all this together."

"What the hell does this Infinity group want? Why are they doing this?"

"You know the answer to that already," Smithson said. I looked at him, confused. I didn't know what King's endgame was. She wanted the Echelon, she wanted AI, and a year ago she tried to take the empyreus energy for her own gain, but beyond that, I didn't have a clue.

My lack of an answer alerted Smithson to my confusion and he pressed another key. A small holographic box appeared in front of all the ships and a wavelength bar rose and fell with a familiar voice recording.

My voice.

Erebos himself used fear to persuade me to take on this mission, threatening my life and my ship in the process. Sarah King was the cause of countless disturbing and horrible nightmares and images that plagued my mind for the last five years. Never did it occur to me that these two powerful people were controlled by fear themselves, fear of the unknown. It all came down to being the dominant race in the galaxy. When you hold all the power, what else is there to fear but losing it? Then something Cessa had recently said about an empire popped into my head, and everything made sense.

"That's what this is all about . . . going back five years to the mutiny . . . the Echelon, the artificial intelligence . . . you are building your own fleet, using one of the flagships of the ESA to jumpstart your ascension and ordering additional sleeper agents to infiltrate other starships."

"My log . . . you heard my log?"

I recorded the log of Dawn while Al and I returned back to human space, shortly after I left the planet. I promised myself and the Dawnians that one day I would share my log with the right kind of people who would be equals and allies. I never knew that my log had already been transmitted off my ship.

"I have access to every log you record, Daniel," he said. "When I installed Al onto your ship, you didn't think I would just let you fly off without any kind of insurance, did you? I needed to know you were safe and kept the artificial intelligence secure."

I couldn't decide which emotion was going to dominate me. Maybe all of them? I felt naked, as if held under a microscope, and confused about Infinity and the log transmissions. Building its way to the top, though, was anger. In the last five years, Smithson always knew where I was and what I was doing.

"Like you said," he continued, as if his reveal was no big issue. "King wants power. She wants control, especially over any alien races. Fear drives people like her and Raymond Erebos to act. Her search for Dawn was relentless. After you sent her back to human space with her star charts scrambled, she went on a rampage, attacking any alien planet she encountered. All attempts at ESA interference were voided, though. She made convincing arguments that the aliens attacked first and were therefore treated as hostile."

"So what do Terra and Gaia have to do with this? What does their war do to benefit her cause?" My voice sounded distant and hollow. I kept asking questions because I wanted answers, but deep down, the fire inside me burned hotter. The man who sat in front of me was my idol, someone I aspired to be when I ascended through the ranks of the Earth Star Alliance. But my friends, Ashley and Benjamin, died while Jason Hobbes became a mutated cyborg, and all of them were a sacrifice to save this man. But instead of the great captain I wanted to be like, all I saw was a man who let his family die rather than protect them, a man who would spy on the officer who saved him.

"Because of you, King didn't get her empyreus. She didn't get her planet to build her fleet and empire. So she looked for ways to expand in the known galaxies."

"General Ambrose . . . he is one of her cyborgs."

"Did you know General Ambrose was one of the founders of the peace council? Paul Ambrose, Damon Derringer, the council, and myself all aspired for peace."

"You?"

"Yes. Together we started to plan for the new era of Terra and Gaia. The council would become the leaders of the planets. While Ambrose would remain in charge of ground security and military, I was to become an admiral for the new joint fleet. Then a year ago, Ambrose went missing."

I thought again about the moment the cyborgs emerged from the empyreus lake, bonded flawlessly with machinery and bionic implants. Jason tried to kill me. He would have succeeded if I didn't use my rifle to overload its EMP field. The blast knocked out all the cyborgs temporarily and, for a moment, brought the real Jason back to me.

"So King ordered Ambrose to come back to add fuel to the fire," I said. Smithson nodded, a small grin playing at the corners of his mouth.

"In fact, she sent all her cyborgs on various missions. So far, they've been too elusive for me to keep tabs on, but I've monitored Ambrose since he returned from Dawn. Daniel . . . King wants Terra and Gaia to destroy each other and remove all obstacles so she can come in and clean up."

An entire solar system, two human planets ripe for control; one with a plethora of organic plants and animal life, and another filled with technological marvels. To control this area of space, Sarah King could begin to build her power.

I rubbed my face with my hands and massaged my temples. By defeating her on Dawn, I thought she would return to human space and regroup, maybe even lose control of her command. Instead, she had contingency plans. They wouldn't be as easy or as powerful as harnessing unlimited energy, but they would cement her rule in the galaxy.

"That's how Damon Derringer found me," I said. "You knew where I was the whole time. So when I traveled to Karth, you sent him to track me down. You sent him to his death."

"He was willing to take the risk. He knew how important the mission was to get you here."

"And now that I'm here, what exactly is your plan?"

Smithson's shoulders dropped and his eyebrows lifted in a sympathetic expression. "Daniel. You aren't the one I wanted. Damon's job was to get you here, but you were merely the means to acquiring what I really needed—the artificial intelligence program."

NINETEEN

"What do you want with Al?" I asked. My heart pounded against my chest like it wanted to break free. After all I'd witnessed and experienced in space and on Terra, I couldn't believe that my visit to Terra and Gaia was solely for the purpose of reuniting Al and Smithson.

"I'm worried about you, Daniel. I admit that I was hesitant to let you fly off in that hunk of junk you call a ship with the A.I., but I felt it necessary that we split up to protect ourselves. Now I regret that decision. You've lived through so much, had so many terrible experiences. Your mind is damaged. Listen to how you talk about it, as if it's a person."

"My . . . mind? What the flux are you talking about? Have you even talked to Al since you repaired him? He's been my companion for the last five years. He was there in times of need. He's more than just a program."

"It's an evolving computer, yes, but his primary goal was never to be "buddies," or your artificial guidance counselor."

"At least he's been there for me," I said, the anger rising into my voice. "Do you know how many Starcade jobs I lost because I couldn't kill someone? Do you know I almost got captured twice by the Echelon since our escape? Do you know anything about the friends I've lost? At least Al's guided me, helped me realize all the good I've done. He's kept me from opening a hatch and getting sucked into space. What the hell have you done? Sit here peacefully and listen to my fluxing logs?"

Smithson raised his hands in surrender. "Okay. I understand you're still tired and hurting from the last couple of days. Why don't you take a walk and try to calm down? When you're ready, we'll continue."

I stormed out of the house and returned to my ship. My head swam with images of shooting the rogue Sentinel at Damon's house, watching council members die in front of me as they carried me to safety. All of it meant nothing, according to Smithson. All he needed was Al. I was the chauffeur and now what would happen if I reunited them? Did Smithson still have administrative access to Al's mainframe? And what was his plan? As much as I wanted to ask, I didn't want my anger clouding the issues at hand.

Sarah King was behind the council murders, that much had been confirmed by Smithson. Once the planets took each other out, the figurative road would be paved for her to take over. What did Autumn tell me? Any day now, the war would begin. Did we still have time to stop it?

I found myself walking past the crew quarters and stepping onto the bridge. Tress was there, still familiarizing himself with the controls of each station. He moved from one to the other, writing notes on a small pad.

"Could I have a moment alone, please?" I asked him. He nodded and left the bridge.

"Al?"

"I'm here, Captain."

"It's really good to hear your voice, old friend."

"Sir, I would not constitute my program as old in any feasible manner."

I laughed out loud. Yes, Al was a computer, and for the most part, he talked like one, too. But his voice, the evolved form of intonations and improvisations, made me believe he was more than just a program. When Smithson first installed him, Al spoke in a monotone, answered only specific questions, and never carried on a conversation. Five years later, he uses sarcasm and attempts to tell jokes.

"Damon Derringer's mission was to find you, Al, not me. I was just the middle man."

"Yes, a wise course of action, sir."

"Wise?"

"Gregory Smithson believes that I can be of use to him."

"In what way?"

"I'm sorry Captain, that information is classified."

"It's . . . classified? Al, I'm the captain of this ship, and I order you to tell me!"

"Smithson's command codes are prioritized over yours, sir."

"Are you joking? What if I ordered you to close the bay door and take off into orbit?"

"Gregory Smithson has grounded the ship. His orders are to remain on Gaia until further notice."

I almost pulled my hair out. In less than a day, Smithson swooped into my life and took control of my ship and Al. I felt trapped, something I've experienced before and hated. In the past, it meant the risk of danger or death. Here I was safe, but that didn't make me feel any better.

For the second time that day I stormed away, off my ship and into the dying field of grass. Ever since I accepted this mission, I felt like I was slowly losing control of everything. All these events—Granak, the council, and the war—happened with me just riding their exhaust streams. I sat down on the dead grass and felt just as trapped as ever.

The crunch of footsteps sounded behind me. I looked over my shoulder with narrowed eyes and a hard scowl.

"What do you want?" My irritated voice startled Autumn. Quickly, my anger turned into embarrassment.

"Is that any way to talk to your blood donor?"

"I-I'm sorry, I didn't know . . ."

"Relax. You've been through a lot."

She sat next to me and wrapped her arms around her knees. For a while, we stared at the decayed landscape. I expected to hear something in our silence—a breeze or birds chirping—but I heard nothing. Soon, two planets would go to war, Terra with its people murdered, and Gaia with its crops and plants reduced to ash.

"She's beautiful," Autumn said, breaking me from my depressing thoughts.

"Huh?"

"Your ship . . . the Kestrel Belle? Did I pronounce that correctly?"

I nodded.

"How did you come up with the name, if you don't mind me asking?"

"The kestrel is a type of falcon back on Earth. When they were designing space cruisers, many models were designed to look like birds. The Belle . . ." I trailed off. Autumn stared at me, her expression somber while she waited for me to speak. "Someone I cared about . . . she enjoyed Earth history, specifically the old west in Old America. One of her favorite historical figures was Belle Starr, who was known as a notorious outlaw of the times. Ashley always liked those stories . . ."

Autumn didn't pursue the information, much to my relief. Over the last year, I grew more accustomed to the memories, but they still hurt. And I couldn't help but realize that both interactions I had with Gregory Smithson followed tragedy.

I felt unable to plot my next course. What should I do? What needed to be done?

The council still lives, I thought. *As long as they are alive, peace is possible.*

I sighed in exasperation and fell back to the ground. The grass crunched under my body and dust rose around me.

"How can we stop this war?" I asked.

"From what I understand, each planet has to make the declaration. There's no doubt that Ambrose convinced the Terran government to do so. Then they'll launch their entire arsenal. The battles and skirmishes we've seen so far are nothing compared to the full might of both militaries."

"But what about Gaia? What if they don't declare and launch?"

"Then the Terrans will probably continue to attack and find ways to force Gaia into declaring. I mean, look at this wasted planet . . . how could they not declare war?"

But if there was a chance, any chance at all . . . . I stood too quickly and it felt like everything in my head crashed from side to side. My arms and legs complained in throbbing discomfort. Autumn must have noticed my unsteadiness. She stood and grabbed my arm to keep me balanced. Goosebumps spread over my skin as our eyes met.

"We need to warn them, or help them, or stop them if necessary," I said. "We can't do anything about the Terrans, but we need to do something while we're here."

"Daniel, stop," Autumn said, pulling on my arm and holding me back as I tried to walk toward the house. "You're still injured. You need to rest."

"Sure, sounds great. I'll rest while billions of people kill each other." I pulled harder at my arm and Autumn let go.

Inside, Smithson was making some kind of alterations to the computer console in his office.

"We need to talk to the Gaian government," I said, "or whoever is in control here. We can't let them declare war."

"Daniel," he said, calm and controlled, "this is a lot bigger than war."

"Yeah, I know that already. Sarah King is going to bring her military into the system and take control."

"You don't get the big picture here, do you, Daniel? Is that why you were never promoted to Tier One Security? Because of your narrow vision?"

His words, dripping with anger and anxiety, were like a smack to my face. He talked more like a bully would to a weaker child than a superior would to his officer. Then again, Smithson wasn't a captain anymore.

"The war isn't going to decimate both militaries," Smithson said. "There will be casualties and losses on both sides. But even if she invaded, there would still be people to resist her."

"So? It's not like she can destroy all military forces on both sides."

Smithson stared at me, one of his eyebrows elevated higher than the other.

"Can she?" I asked.

"The weather device above us is not compatible with Terran technology," he answered. "And I'm sure you've seen the weapons. The blue energy rifles didn't come from Terra or Gaia."

I thought back to the attacks in the docking tower's stairwell and Damon Derringer's house. Those rifles were unbelievably powerful. One blast melted an entire wall and almost burned off a man's arm. Considering the gunmen carried a Starcade contract with them, it didn't surprise me that the weapons were being imported.

"So there is an external weapon supplier," I said.

"More than just a supplier," Smithson said. "I believe there is a weapons manufacturing facility somewhere in this solar system, not only supplying Gaia and Terra with advanced weapons, but preparing for their own attack."

"A facility? Which planet is it on? Have you been able to locate it?"

"I don't think it's on either planet. Something like that would give off enormous power signatures, and as far as I can tell, neither planet has a structure like that."

A weapons facility made perfect sense. But in order to create the appearance that a third party didn't exist, thereby fueling both planets toward war, the factory would have to be close enough to make supply runs and drop-offs without suspicion. Could there have been a space station somewhere close? If there was, I should have detected it when I entered the system, not to mention both planets would have detected it as well.

I tried to put myself in General Ambrose and Sarah King's minds. I wanted these planets to destroy each other, and to do so, I was going to use weapons and technology against them in an attempt to blame each other and launch into war. I needed a facility to manufacture weapons and technology to succeed. But to keep it secret and secure, I would need to put it somewhere Terran and Gaian forces wouldn't look, somewhere isolated, somewhere . . .

The expression "right under your nose" flared in my mind. Did Damon know what had happened when he recruited Tress to find me? His notes made no mention of it, but maybe he created the memory drive prior to meeting up with him. If I was General Ambrose, I could have taken a number of loyal soldiers, plus additional recruits from the Starcade, and invaded a neighboring planet that didn't have defenses or starfleets like Terra or Gaia. I could threaten the leaders of that world to evacuate, and then build my facility and set up defense grids around the planet.

"Tristain," I finally said. "Tress told me his planet went on an evacuation alert. Later, when I flew into the system, I couldn't scan the planet because of a weaponized defense grid."

A hint of a smile played at the corners of Smithson's mouth. He typed furiously on his desk and a holographic screen locked in on planet Tristain. But its image was fuzzy and glowed red.

"It's out of range of my scanners. But that has to be it. All I need to do now is reconfigure my mainframe to merge with the artificial intelligence program."

Al. "What?"

"I told you I needed the program, Daniel. That's why I summoned you here, so you could bring it to me."

"But what's going to happen to Al?" I asked.

Smithson stopped moving his fingers and closed his eyes, taking a deep breath. When he looked up at me, it was with a soft and sympathetic expression.

"Daniel, the artificial intelligence program isn't a person. It doesn't have a name. It's a machine, constructed by engineers. One of those creators was your father, so I understand that you feel an attachment to it. But it's obvious to me now that sending you into space alone was a mistake. You latched on to the program like it was a friend."

Al *was* a friend, no matter what else he was.

"But you need to understand something. With the program installed into my mainframe, I can not only extend my search parameters to Tristain, but it's possible I can use the artificial intelligence to connect to whatever computer they installed in the facility and disable it."

"Meanwhile," I said, trying not to think of Al being ripped out of my ship against my wishes, "what happens to the people and the soldiers who launch the attacks?"

"Daniel." Again, he used my name with a sympathetic tone. "We are only two people. What can we do to change the course of two planets and their people? Even if we told the militaries that Ambrose worked alone, the Gaian people would still label him as a terrorist and launch against Terra."

His words left me speechless. A man I once looked up to was ready to give up and not even attempt to try to stop the onslaught? Autumn stepped in front of me with her arms crossed and spoke louder than either of us.

"Do you know what Daniel did? What he went through up to this point? He risked his life to let me escape from the Sentinels and that Leondren monster. He risked his life and nearly died of blood loss when he surrendered himself to stand with the council . . . so he could save them!"

Not to mention when Granak stranded me in the Karthan solar system, and I flew through the battle between Gaian and Terran starships when I arrived.

"And where did that get him?" Smithson said. "Did it solve anything? We're on the brink of war, General Ambrose and his mercenaries are still out there wreaking havoc, and more council members died."

"*All* council members would be dead if not for him," she said, her voice stern.

Smithson hesitated in his retort, but he was sure and confident in his resolve.

"War is tragic and people die. I want to stop the war as much as anyone, but we have to think of the endgame. If Ambrose is allowed to use his weapons and the fleets are destroyed, Sarah

King and Infinity will have free reign to move into this system and claim it for their empire."

When I first set foot on the Echelon years ago as a security officer, I was proud and honored to serve under my father's friend, Gregory Smithson. I wanted to become him one day. The man who sat in front of me wasn't the man I thought he was.

"What have you done?" I asked. The fear of insubordination was gone, and the thoughts that this man was somehow still in charge of me vanished.

"Excuse me?"

"All this time, the council being murdered and the Gaian economy being destroyed by the atmospheric device, what have you done to stop any of it? What have you done to prevent it?"

"I told you—" he started, but I threw up my hand and spoke over him.

"I heard, you're thinking of the endgame. But while you've been sitting here, tinkering with your computer and luring me to acquire the artificial—no *AI*—people are out there dying. Ambrose is winning. Sarah King is winning. You go ahead and keep thinking about the endgame, Smithson. Meanwhile, I'm going to think about the here and now."

Just like Autumn told me to do.

I walked out of the office, ignoring him as he yelled my name. Down the hall, I could hear the soft conversations of the council. When I walked into the living area, everyone grew silent.

"Mr. Quinn," Burns said.

"Captain, actually," I corrected. Was it Autumn's words that gave me confidence, or maybe the thought of Smithson sitting in his office doing calculations like a coward? Either way, I knew what had to be done now. Tress needed to know about his planet. If there was anything we could do, we would, but this war had to be prevented first and foremost.

"Who among the council is native to Gaia?" I asked.

"I am," Trent said.

"Okay. Everyone else is going to stay here. Trent, you're coming with me."

"Where are we going?" he said as he stood, favoring his left leg.

"We're going to stop this war."

TWENTY

Trent and Autumn followed me out of Smithson's house and into the Belle. We climbed to the first floor corridor and met Tress on the way to the bridge.

"Come with us," I said to him.

Smithson didn't argue against us leaving the house—why would he? With his control of Al's program, he grounded us on Gaia, but that didn't mean we were helpless.

The first thing I did on the Belle was reveal to Tress what happened to his planet, how it was most likely a staging front for outsourcing weapons and technology to Terra and Gaia.

"When I left," he said, his eyes a deep shade of blue, "my parents were still there. I don't know if they ever made it out."

Al translated his words to Autumn and Trent as I spoke to him.

"We will do everything we can for your planet and people, but with the defensive grid surrounding Tristain, we have few options right now."

"And what options are those?" Trent's gritty voice was strained with fatigue. "Terra is about to launch and my planet is nothing but death. What the hell can anyone do now?"

"To fight a war, you need two sides," I said. "You're in a government role of some kind, correct?"

"Yes. I oversee the distribution of sustenance to all the Gaian military and make sure they have adequate food on their ships."

"Then you should have some contacts in the military." I leaned forward and folded my hands together. "We need to get into the Gaian military compound and speak to whoever is in charge. If we can explain the situation to them, maybe we can stop them from launching against Terra."

"Commander Sutton. We could speak to him. Any request or transfer order has to go through him, but even if we convince him to not go to war, what's going to stop Terra from launching an assault on the planet itself?"

"It's a risk," I said. "A damn big risk. But if Gaia lays down its arms and stands against war, then we can use the council to make a plea to any oncoming Terran forces and ask them to disengage. It might work, it might not, but I'm not willing to sit around while Gregory Smithson ignores the here and now."

"I'm going," Autumn said. Tress mirrored her comment, but I shook my head.

"No one else is going with us. Tress, you're the only one besides Smithson who has any idea of how this ship works. I know your training is limited, but it might come to good use. Autumn, I need someone to stand beside Tress. I don't trust Smithson to do what's right for the council."

Both of them nodded, though Autumn crossed her arms and glared at me, obviously unsatisfied with my decision. I needed someone here to watch after my ship and Al. Plus, if things went bad, I didn't want either of them caught in the crossfire.

"Daniel," Autumn said. "Your weapons are in the cargo bay."

"My weapons?"

"After you left to stand with the council, and then the explosion, Reynold and I went looking for you. We found the Sentinel who disarmed you and Reynold took him down and recovered your weapons. I thought you might need them, just in case."

In times of stress, one of the most relieving things is familiarity, and knowing my weapons waited for me lessened my anxiety. Autumn, Tress, and Trent walked down to the cargo bay while I stopped in my quarters. My tactical battle suit was damaged from the parade fight, but it still held the best chance of keeping me alive. Although the left arm and pant leg were sliced up, the rest was in good condition. I eased the shielded breastplate over my head and fastened the shoulder attachments, then attached the knee guards and my reinforced boots.

"Al?" I asked just as I was ready to leave.

"Yes, Captain."

"I know that Smithson has control over you, but I want you to know I'm happy and relieved that you're okay. I wish I could stop him from taking you away."

"Your response is understandable, considering human emotion. I have been installed in your mainframe for five years, eleven months, twenty-two days, three hours, fifteen minutes, and seven seconds. In that time, because you were alone on this ship, you built a psychological connection to me and taught me how to speak more like a human and interact with you and others."

"Right. Well, I just wanted to tell you that you've been an important part of my life."

I exited the room and walked down the corridor, trying my best to fight off tears. I wasn't sure what to expect from Al's answer, but I hoped it wouldn't have been so . . . predictable, so similar to something Smithson would have said. It hurt to think in our years together Al didn't register the difference I noticed in him. He was a computer when it all came down to it, but he truly was one of my closest friends. If the reason was because of my psychological need for something to connect to, then so be it.

"Captain," Al said through the corridor speakers.

"Yes, Al?"

"My programming finds existence would be . . . difficult without your presence, sir."

This time I couldn't hold back the tears.

Just as Autumn said, my weapons were packed into the cargo net in the bay. The door was still open, showing the view of Smithson's home and letting in a warm breeze. I pulled the weapons out and looked them over. The revolver still had the majority of its plasma charge, and the blade looked sharp enough to cut through metal.

I reached back with the sword and the magnetic strip on my back pulled it into position. Smithson emerged from his house. He carried an assault rifle over his shoulder and stared grimly in my direction. Was he coming over to stop me from leaving? Should I aim my revolver at him before he could point his toward me?

"What do you think you're doing?" he asked when he reached the bottom of the ramp. His rifle didn't move from its position, so I didn't move mine either. All the same, I tried to be ready for anything.

"This war doesn't have to happen." I walked toward him. "I understand you're concerned about this weapons facility, but there's little use for distributing them if we can convince everyone to stop pulling the triggers."

"So, you think you're going to march into Gaian HQ and demand that they lay down their arms?"

"We're going to try. Have you ever stopped scanning and analyzing to take a look at the worlds around you? Do you even know everything that's happened? How three of the council were horrifically murdered? How thousands of people were probably killed in the parade bombing? Do you realize what the atmospheric device that's killing Gaia's plants means for its economy? Stop looking at just the facts and look past them, see what it's going to mean for the people in the future. "

He glanced back at his house and lowered his rifle.

"The computer will take another hour or two to stabilize and backup the data before I attempt to install the artificial intelligence. Despite what you think of me, Daniel, I want these people saved just as much as you do. And if you're going to talk to the Gaian government, you're going to need a ride there. So, let's go."

Smithson returned to his house without any response from us. I didn't know what to think. Was this his way of supporting my opinions, or was it his way of keeping an eye on me to make sure I didn't make a bad situation worse?

Either way, he said he had a ride, so I had little choice but to accept his offer, if you could call it that. A small wooden garage sat past his house. My bionic eye detected decay and rot in the wood. I didn't notice the same abnormalities from his house, but at the time, I wasn't focused on that. I didn't even stop to think about the atmospheric device's ramifications on buildings.

A robust open-ended hover vehicle waited for us inside the garage. After we climbed in, Smithson activated its engines and sped into the open field. The closer we got to the surrounding forest, the more I saw just how bad the damage was. Leaves abandoned the numerous trees, and even their branches were wilting into nothing.

"If this device is killing plants and trees, how is it not affecting living creatures?" I asked.

"It is affecting us. Slowly, but many people have already suffered in health from unknown ailments," Smithson said in a neutral tone. "In the last twenty-four hours, patient counts for the hospitals in the region nearly doubled. Whether the device is affecting us directly or through the water supply, we're all going to start dying off one by one."

The thought of the tainted air I breathed made my skin crawl.

"Why hasn't the military shot the damn thing down yet?"

"It has some kind of cloaking device. You can trace it and narrow its location, but the radius is still too wide to see it or disable it."

I couldn't help but wonder what kind of facility could create devices so destructive and deadly. It seemed to me that Ambrose and King weren't just trying to fuel the fire between the Terrans and Gaians; they were also trying to accelerate the process.

What was Infinity? And how did King fit into it? Was she its leader or another pawn being controlled by someone even more dangerous? A radical group seemed the perfect place for Raymond Erebos, what with his fear of alien races and aspirations for control. But when he showed up on Dawn with King, he claimed he held no allegiance to her whatsoever. If he told the truth, that meant humanity had two groups of dangerous people ready and willing to destroy or enslave alien life for the greater good of humanity.

How ironic that in her quest to strengthen her own species, she was willing to murder millions to attain her goal. It disgusted me.

The trip was quiet. Neither Smithson nor Trent muttered a single word. With the infected wind whipping at our faces, whistling as we drove past, my thoughts traveled to Granak. The last time I saw him was at Damon Derringer's home, trashing it to make a statement. How did he fit into all this? And why would an alien hater like King hire him? Unless she didn't hire him, in which case Ambrose did. So, did the cyborgs still retain some kind of individuality, or were they controlled completely by King? Somewhere out there in the galaxy, my best friend Jason Hobbes stood by her side, a mutated cybernetic freak all because of her.

Multiple structures appeared down the road. Each structure was dome-shaped with glass roofs and walls of a warm off-white. The buildings were spread out more than the Terran ones, which made this look less like a city and more like a rural town. As we drove closer, I scanned them to find that their walls suffered from the same degradation as the wood and grass around Smithson's home.

Trent's breath caught as he witnessed the desolate roads and buildings with no person in sight. Every now and then, my eye picked up movement past some of the windows, but Smithson quickly drove us beyond them.

"Last I heard, the emergency system requested everyone to get indoors and under a secure shield. Some mobile units were distributed as safe houses."

And here we were outside, cruising. Smithson turned left at an intersection and drove another mile before we slowed in front of a five-story rectangular building. A steel fence surrounded it and camouflaged assault vehicles littered the parking lot. We drove up to a security access tower and stopped.

"That's odd," Trent said. "Someone should be here."

"Maybe they just took shelter like everyone else?"

"Maybe, but each building has its own filtered air unit for protection from gasses."

Smithson opened the door and eased out, aiming his rifle. My eye didn't scan anything threatening in the vicinity, but it's never a bad thing to be prepared. He climbed the stairs into the tower and opened the security gate.

"No sign of anyone being stationed there for a few days," he said after he got back into the vehicle. We moved forward and stopped in front of the main entrance, where we got out. That's when the hair on the back of my neck stood erect and a cold tingle traveled through my body. On instinct, I drew my revolver with my left hand and reached for the sword with my right. I turned in a slow circle and made sure my eye scanned over every detail within my line of sight. Again, nothing appeared out of the ordinary, but when I focused on the entrance door, I saw that the locking mechanism was disengaged. I walked up to it and eased the door open. The room beyond was dark.

"Daniel," Smithson said while walking past me, "you take the rear. Trent, you stay between us. I'll take point."

Smithson marched into the dark hallway and while Trent followed, I held back and switched my bionic eye to night vision mode. A scanner line highlighted all the corners and textures of the room. The hallway led into an open, circular room with a round steel desk at the center. Target reticles in my vision highlighted dozens of splotches and scorch marks on the floor and walls.

"Blood ahead," I whispered. Smithson froze and turned back to me. I pointed at my eye to indicate how I knew. He nodded and continued down the corridor.

Seconds later, I heard numerous footsteps closing in around us. My gut told me they weren't friendly.

TWENTY ONE

A discharge of hot, blue rifle fire passed my face. The heat smacked into me as if I'd opened a furnace. I dropped to the ground, aimed my weapon toward the point of origin, and fired. The green plasma didn't hit the target, but it illuminated him. I modified my direction and fired again, but he already took cover behind the corner of the wall.

Smithson fired in a different direction, down the middle toward the main desk. I tried to lock on to any movement ahead of us, but was too late. One of the enemy weapons fired and the discharge narrowly missed Trent, but burned his arm. He backed to the closest wall, grasping his arm and crying out.

We had to fall back, but when I turned toward the door, I saw a handful more soldiers advancing on us from the street.

They were waiting for us and we walked right into it. I figured I could smack my head against a wall later. Now we had to get out of the line of fire. The long hallway pinned us from the entrance to the lobby, but there were a couple of doors on each side. I aimed the revolver toward the closest door and fired at its handle. The lock melted after a few hits, and I stood and grabbed Trent's shirt.

"This way," I said, pulling the wounded council member to safety. Smithson opened a barrage of fire and spun to prevent the soldiers at the entrance from shooting.

The good news was that every office in the area had the same design—two chairs, a desk, and walls that turned into windows four feet off the ground. That meant we were able to smash the glass and move from office to office. The bad news was that the windows led right out to the lobby area, four office rooms down, where the soldiers caught sight of us. I dropped Trent as gently as I could and hustled to take cover behind the lower wall. Glass shattered.

"This doesn't really help much," Smithson spat as he took position beside me.

"It's a flux of a lot better than staying in the narrow hall where they could pick us off one by one."

A crackling noise came from above me, something similar to static. A communication speaker was attached to the ceiling. The static fluctuated for a couple of seconds before a voice spoke that made my heart skip a beat.

"Daniel Quinn and party," Granak purred over the intercom. "Welcome."

I had little difficulty determining who caused all the bloodshed now. If Granak was here, it meant everyone was most likely dead.

"Daniel," he continued. "Your honor is respectable and your determination admirable. However, do you see where they lead you? You are trapped, your vehicle is under our control, and as I speak my operatives are determining the vehicle's point of origin."

Stars above . . . the council, Tress, and Autumn . . .

We had to do something. But what? The soldiers' assault stopped the moment Granak spoke, which meant they followed him. I thought back to my previous encounter with him at Damon's estate.

"*Your* operatives?" I shouted. I wasn't sure if he could hear me over the intercom or not, but I didn't stop. "If I recall, Granak, you don't care for humans, even the ones who obey you. You threw one of your men to the side just to get a piece of me. Well, here I am. Let's finish this."

I aimed my revolver in the general direction of the lobby and released a barrage of plasma.

"What the hell was that all about?" Smithson asked.

"Granak is the threat here, not the soldiers." I whispered and pulled Trent close. "Where are the closest communication stations?"

He winced and his eyes darted from entrance to lobby. He looked terrified. I grabbed his good arm hard and shook him.

"Trent, we're in a shitty situation, but if we don't contact Smithson's home and warn the council, Granak is going to kill them. Where are the comm stations?"

He squinted and took deep breaths. Smithson leaned out the office door and fired a few rounds toward the entrance.

"There are two, I think . . . third floor about a dozen doors down from the southeast stairwell . . . and then on the fifth floor, but I can't remember where that is."

"Good enough. You and Smithson are going to the third floor, and I'll try to make it to the fifth. Contact the council and get them the hell out of there."

Smithson grabbed me as I advanced toward the door.

"How the hell is splitting up going to help anything?"

"Granak will come after me. Our rivalry is like a game to him. He has my scent. And if I can draw some of the soldiers' fire, then you and Trent can get up to the third floor and warn the council."

I worried that Smithson would grab me or try to hold me back, but instead he unloaded another round toward the entrance and pushed me out. I sprinted as fast as I could toward the northwest stairs, opposite of where Trent and Smithson would go. When I entered the hallway, I aimed toward the soldiers hiding behind the lobby wall and fired. They didn't expect me and both plasma blasts found their marks. I didn't wait to see if the soldiers went down. Besides, my focus was on Granak. He was somewhere in the building.

I reached the stairwell door and slammed my boot against it. It burst open and I aimed at the opening in case Granak waited there. Empty. I moved up the stairs with my bionic eye scanning for movement.

While I concentrated on upper floors, a crash and multiple footsteps clanged against the metal stairs beneath me. Two soldiers aimed and shot. Their blue discharges missed, but I felt their heat and didn't wait for another attack.

At that point, I reached the fifth floor and broke into a sprint down the carpeted hallway, ducking behind the first corner. Sweat burned my eye and I violently thrust my finger into it to wipe the pain away. All the while, I aimed down the hall at the stairwell door, which remained open.

Anxiety crept over my body, as if millions of tiny bugs crawled on my skin. The soldiers would be coming through the stairwell doors any moment, and Granak was here, somewhere, waiting to attack.

Where the hell was he? Fear escalated when I realized that he might have gone after Trent and Smithson. My confidence in his games allowed me to ignore any other outlet, but how well did I really know him? Smithson wouldn't be able to save both of them, especially with Trent's injuries, if it came to a fight with the Leondren mercenary.

My worries were both relieved and intensified when the soldiers emerged from the stairwell and shot at me. I leaned over to retaliate, but plaster and wood exploded from the stairs and the hulking form of Granak grabbed the two soldiers by their heads and charged toward the opposite wall, using their bodies as battering rams to break through the wall.

I fired off a round of plasma, but it only scorched the wall at the end of the hall. I switched my bionic eye to theoretical analysis mode to predict his next move, all the while breathing hard from exhaustion.

The problem was the mode wasn't designed to anticipate Granak smashing through walls.

I heard the crack of glass and plaster a second before the Leondren pounced. I could only register fear, but fortunately, the fear of death motivated me to survive, and I rolled under him. I grabbed my sword's hilt and pulled it off the magnetic lock. Granak liked to play things close, so my best bet to hurt him would be with the blade, like last time.

I just needed an opportune moment, so I ran away from him and he gave chase. I aimed over my shoulder and unleashed two plasma rounds. Both found their mark, judging by his painful grunts, but our pace never lessened. I dodged into an open doorway before Granak's large claws could take off my head. Flashes of pain lanced across my back. I landed on a large metal desk and tumbled off its side. Somehow, I'd managed to keep the sword and revolver in my hands as I went down.

When Granak stormed into the room, I scrambled to a glass window that led to open air, five stories above a small courtyard of dead grass and gray cement. I raised both weapons toward him.

"There is a thrill when chasing you, young one," Granak said, his grin revealing sharp teeth. "So many others give up and die. They scream as I tear into them and break them. But you are one of a few who manage to evade me."

"Give up and die? Or you just kill them because they're in your way?" I asked, thinking of the officers he killed.

"We are all that matter, you and I," he said with a hint of a purr.

Leaning against the window only worsened the pain in my back, but I didn't feel any blood seeping from the wounds.

"Why do you pursue me? What's this all worth? How much is Ambrose paying you?"

He laughed throatily. I just needed to keep him distracted long enough to provide Trent and Smithson enough time to warn the others. If my death meant that a handful of people would live, including Tress and Autumn, my conscience would be clear.

"Money is involved, yes, but there's so much more to it. If only you knew the scope of events."

"Then tell me," I said. *Keep him talking, keep his focus on me.*

"The general wants you captured, you know, but I have a proposal for you. Let me end your life here. Now. I will give you a glorious death, one you will be remembered for."

He seemed . . . serious. Even, dare I say it, sympathetic.

"Um, that's kind of you," I said, unable to think of another response, "but I'd prefer to take my chances living."

"You say that now, but these humans want you for something. The money they paid me to find you, it is no secret that they want you contained for their amusement. After fighting with you, I feel it is a disgraceful way to live—one you do not deserve."

The bastard had a damn good point. In less than ten years, I'd been captured and imprisoned on more than one occasion. Both times, I wished for death before Sarah King and her people could have their way with me. But what if there was still a sliver of a chance I could save the council and prevent the war from happening?

"I won't give up," I said, hardening my grip on the sword's hilt. "I'll stop you, Ambrose, and this fluxing war from happening."

"Ha! You think you can stop events already set in motion? Why do you think I'm here? The orders have been given. The commander of this station is dead, the declaration of war signed with his blood. As you speak of being a savior, the Terrans and Gaians launch their ships to destroy each other."

No. If that was true, it meant I failed. Through the pain and fatigue, anger and frustration rose over all the blood spilled and lives lost. I glared and bared my teeth, despite their lack of sharp points.

"Go to hell!"

I threw my sword swift and straight, the sharp edge going for its second hit in Granak's midsection. He growled furiously and jumped over it with his claws extended. By focusing on me and nothing else, he missed an important fact: when you're airborne, you can't adjust your movement.

All he saw was a beaten, tired man. He didn't see me shoot the glass behind me. Strong gusts of wind flew into the room. I leaned hard to the side and he landed atop me. I pushed off the ground and rolled toward the new opening. He flipped and fell out the window. His continuous roar deepened as he dropped. Until he landed.

I stood and grabbed my sword, knowing full well Granak was still alive. If he could survive plasma blasts and sword stabs, a five-story fall wouldn't be much for him. Exhausted, I loped toward the southeast stairs and Smithson and Trent.

I stumbled down two flights of stairs to the third floor, opened the door, and heard the shouting. I assumed they were under attack, and held my weapons up as I advanced.

Twelve doors down, just like Trent said, the two of them stood behind a large, rectangular desk with a computerized glass top like I'd seen on Terra. A green wavelength bar grew and softened as people spoke. I recognized Tress in the background; he was the only one speaking his native Restran language. Trent and Smithson were staring daggers at each other.

"What's going on?" I asked. Neither had seen me come in. Moving at the same time, Trent jumped back, almost falling from his leg injury, while Smithson pointed his rifle at me.

"Daniel, where's the Leondren?"

"He'll be back soon. Did you tell them what's going on?"

"Oh, we told them," Trent said. "But *he* isn't letting them leave!"

I looked to where Trent pointed. At Smithson.

"What the flux are you doing?"

"Daniel, if we lose the Belle, we lose the artificial intelligence program. I can't find a way to Tristain or a way to deactivate the weapons without it."

"Are you kidding me?" I said and walked into the room. "Capt . . . Smithson . . . it's too late. Terra and Gaia have lost. Our best option now is to get the remaining council to safety, get them clear. If we can regroup, we might be able to plan some—"

"Plan?" Smithson spat. "Your plans don't seem to work very well, Daniel."

When I didn't answer, Smithson lowered his rifle. That's when I aimed my weapon at his head.

"It's not a plan anymore," I said. "Now it's a threat. Give Al permission to take off with the council, Tress, and Autumn Derringer."

"Or what? You'll shoot me? Your former commanding officer, the man who helped you get your ship, who gave you the A.I. in the first place?"

"Smithson . . . Greg," I said, putting in all the hurt and stress I could muster. "In minutes, Granak will come in here and kill us all, if the soldiers aren't on their way already. We lost, but don't let the council lose. Let them live. Let Damon's daughter live."

Smithson eyes shifted from mine to my revolver. Then, he looked down at the whispering computer.

Smithson keyed a command on the desk and read aloud a line of computer code.

"Authorization Smithson, Gregory. The Kestrel Belle is clear for departure."

Al's voice came over the speaker.

"Access is granted to set course off planet. Orders, Captain?" He was speaking to me, possibly for the last time.

"Al, as soon as Autumn, Tress, and the council are onboard, take off and set course away from the planets. Give Autumn and Tress access to set course controls."

"Acknowledged, sir. Good luck."

Al didn't believe in luck, a human concept, which meant all the more coming from him. Autumn's soft voice was the next to speak.

"Daniel? We're coming for you."

"Do not!" I yelled. "There's no time left for us. Get the council to safety. Promise me!"

She didn't argue, but the silence for the next few seconds felt like it lasted a lifetime.

"I promise," she whispered.

"Take care of the council and Tress."

The communication desk exploded in sparks and flames. I fell back and hit my head against the wall, while Smithson ducked before he was hit from debris flying around the room. A handful of soldiers charged in, followed by General Ambrose. Granak strode in moments later, his eyes wide and hateful toward me. I smiled in satisfaction at his limp.

"Grab them and bind their hands," Ambrose ordered. Granak took the pleasure of grabbing my neck and lifting me off the ground. My vision blackened as my airway became tighter and tighter.

"Granak, release him now."

He did and I breathed in refreshing air. I didn't care whether it was tainted. But as I watched Granak's hand pull away, I saw my necklace around his fingers. Before I could reach for it, he crushed Ashley's ring and Al's microdrive with it.

"You are clever," he said. "But I've studied you, Daniel Quinn. There will be no escape now."

Few people knew about the teleportation module inside the drive, but I used it twice against Sarah King. If she knew about it, then her cyborgs probably knew, although Ambrose didn't seem to care. He looked to the soldier on his left as my eyes glazed over with tears.

"Did we secure the location for the remaining council?" Ambrose asked.

"Yes, sir. We analyzed the communication signal and determined where it was sent. Our forces will be there in minutes."

Stars above, would that be enough time for the Belle to take off without being detected? And if it was, would Ambrose's men pursue it into space with their own ships? All I could do was stand there, still devastated over the loss of Ashley's engagement ring, and wonder about the fate of my friends as our hands were bound. Ambrose, Granak, and their men marched us out of the building toward our fate, and I had no idea if my ship escaped. I didn't know whether Autumn, Tress, and the council were safe or dead.

TWENTY TWO

The starship's movements made my stomach complain with strong waves of nausea. That, coupled with the pounding headache volleying behind my forehead, meant a possible concussion. When Ambrose and Granak marched us out of the Gaian compound, we boarded a small ship and took off towards space. They placed us in some kind of storage room that contained four metal walls with shelves on two sides. Smithson sat against a bare side across from the door, his eyes locked on the ground.

No one told us where we were going, but I had a good idea.

"I almost didn't join the council," Trent said, more to himself than anyone else. "I first thought the idea was ludicrous and a waste of time."

"What changed your mind?" I asked.

He didn't turn his head or look at me. Instead, he stared at the wall, but his eyes looked out of focus, as if dazed or zoned out of the moment.

After a couple of minutes, he answered. "There was a particular day when I toured some of the schools. News broke out that another space battle occurred with heavy losses on both sides. Standard protocol dictated that we go about our business unless called back to the Randout . . . that's where all the government leaders convene to discuss political necessities on

Gaia. I think it was the third or fourth classroom I visited. My job was to educate the students on how our system worked, how they could become involved when they grew up. Anyway, in that one class, three children lost their fathers. The looks on their faces, the shock and depression, it ignited something inside me. If the war could end, then children like that would never have to grow up without their fathers again. I was one man, but together with the other members of the council, we made something special, something that could make a difference." The passion in his speech diminished as he took stock of our location. "Not that it matters anymore."

"Don't give up just yet," I said.

At my words, Smithson's head lifted. His eyes focused not on mine, but right below them, as if he was ashamed of looking at me.

"How can you say something like that? What kind of false hope is that? We've lost. The fleets are moving against each other and Ambrose has the three of us. If the Belle isn't already in their hands, then it's probably been destroyed."

"There's always a chance as long as you don't give up," I said. "You lose when you won't stand up for what you believe in."

"And what the hell is it that you believe in?" he asked and then spat. The globule landed inches from my foot. I had no idea where my optimism came from in that moment, except that I knew we couldn't give up. Despite what we lost, it could be worse if we allowed Ambrose and Granak to win. I thought about my answer, choosing my words carefully. Getting out of this mess would work a lot easier if all three of us were working together rather than against each other.

"I believe that as long as you keep your eyes open, an opportunity will present itself."

Neither of them responded. We sat in silence for what felt like hours when the hull trembled.

"We're entering an atmosphere," I said. On the Belle I could describe in detail what each sound and vibration meant. This ship wasn't her, but it felt so similar that it made me teary at the thought that she might have been destroyed.

No, I couldn't believe that. Because if she was destroyed, that meant Autumn and Tress were dead, as well as the rest of the council. Instead of allowing my mind to dwell on it, I closed my eyes and tried to work through the situation. When faced with a dire situation, what's the one thing that can save you? What can make the difference between life or death?

My first thought was choice. Our lives are dictated by the choices we make, but right now, we didn't really have a choice about where we were going or what would happen. So what's more basic than a choice?

Details. Sometimes the smallest detail can cause change and leave you open to make that choice. So what details did I know already? Tristain had some kind of weapon's facility where Ambrose prepared to destroy the Terran and Gaian star fleets.

The planet was outfitted with a defense grid, which would prevent any ship from entering the atmosphere unless it had a code clearance.

Somehow, we had to deactivate the grid. That would allow the star fleets to advance on Tristain. But I had to contact them first, somehow.

What else did I know? Granak was hired by Ambrose to kill Damon Derringer and be a huge thorn in my side, but Granak had his own loathing for the human race, made apparent by the three soldiers he killed during our encounters. If he didn't care for humans, was there a reason for it and, if so, could I use that to my advantage?

The defense grid. The weapons. Granak and Ambrose. Within these thoughts was an answer somewhere. I just had to pay close attention to everything that happened next. My chances of survival were still slim, but something Granak said stuck with me—I wanted to die with honor, defending my beliefs.

The ship jostled us and then settled, and I knew we had landed. On the other side of the door, steel grinded against steel and the door opened. Three soldiers stood in front of us with their rifles aimed at our heads. Apprehension exploded throughout my body, the kind that feared to die, the kind that feared to fight to the last breath.

"Move it," the lead man said. One by one, we filed out of the room. Wires and jagged edges of steel protruded from the ceiling and walls of the corridor. I stepped over a couple of sharp brackets on the floor. Whoever designed this ship used no consideration in how they put her together.

When I stepped onto the ground of Tress's home planet, I noticed three things—the sky was green; the air felt similar to human planets, except for a light, sweet taste as it passed into your lungs; and how massive the weapons facility was.

The intimidating structure of shimmering metal was big enough to fit ten Kestrel-class star cruisers. Far down the roof, some type of telescope pointed into the sky. Four soldiers guarded the two giant doors that made up the front entrance.

"Stars above," I whispered and Trent and Smithson similarly cursed.

Guns poked us in our backs and we walked. As we neared the building, I saw the guards' uniforms in detail. Navy blue pants and jackets with dark red stripes on the shoulders. Each arm carried the Infinity symbol.

Everything I learned about this group seemed to confirm they were the antithesis of the Earth Star Alliance. The ESA was built and designed to explore space and make contact with alien races. They were a peacekeeping group, but Infinity seemed bent on control by any means necessary. Humans were the dominant species in the universe, even if they had to act against others to ensure it.

A mix of weapon crates, computer terminals, and staging areas—where holographic diagrams were drawn—filled the warehouse's interior. I saw starship drawings and space stations, enough designs to outfit this solar system with an Infinity fleet. A giant screen separated into three separate video feeds on the right wall. One showed camera angles of the warehouse itself, another was blank, and the third was a tactical layout of the space between Terra and Gaia. Hundreds of red blips on each side moved toward each other—the planets' fleets advancing to war. In a little less than an hour—judging by a clock that ticked down time—the fleets would reach firing range.

Ambrose led us to the middle of the facility while Granak kept to our backs. I focused on him over my shoulder, expecting him to stare at me. After beating him at his own game, I thought he'd be fueled with anger to attack me, but instead he gazed at Ambrose.

There's something there . . . something more to this story. Not only did Granak loathe humans, but in comparison, King and her Infinity group hated anything that wasn't human. So why did they hire Granak and not a human mercenary, like me? Unless they didn't. What if Granak offered his services to them, all the while holding his own agenda secret?

"What do you think, Mr. Quinn?" Ambrose's voice echoed and jolted me from my thoughts.

He stood in front of the telescope. Here, it stood on a round platform separated from the rest of the room. I peered over the edge and saw nothing but vents and grids covering the walls of a pit. A computer console connected to the base of the telescope on the platform, and when my bionic eye scanned the screen, I had a terrible realization.

It wasn't a telescope at all.

"This is the pride of Infinity, Mr. Quinn. The Infinity Cannon." Ambrose smiled and spread his arms wide. "And we have you to thank for it!"

"Me?"

"I remember you from that miserable planet with the golden lake of energy, the one that made me what I am today." He removed his coat and hat and revealed his monstrous parts. Half of his head was covered in metal, as was his entire right arm. "Sarah King hoped to strengthen our faction with the golden empyreus, but you got in our way, hacked into our ship, and sent us back home. She was furious. It took an entire week for her to calm down. But when she did, she realized that using the empyreus was simply the easy way to do things.

"When I told her about my world and the brewing war with the Gaians, her eyes lit up, her resolve refocused, and she had a new goal. Two worlds and their resources were all for the taking. All we had to do was help them destroy themselves."

"You horrifically murdered three members of the council," I spat. "Why the flux would you do this? Why destroy your own people?"

In response, Ambrose pulled the sleeve back on his left arm and revealed an infinity symbol tattoo. "These are my people. Now that you're all caught up, let's give you a demonstration.

I'm locking coordinates onto an asteroid belt on the other side of the solar system."

The other side? My surroundings hazed over as I focused on the cannon and realized the power it contained. If it could travel that far . . . if it could destroy an entire asteroid belt . . .

"The fleets. You're going to use the cannon to destroy the fleets."

He smiled at me then nodded to two soldiers standing behind us. They jammed the butts of their rifles against Smithson and Trent. They fell into the cannon's pit.

"No!" Despite my arms being locked behind my back, I lurched forward and tried to save them. Granak grabbed my neck and lifted me. "No! Granak! Stop!"

"I care not for pathetic, weak humans," he growled. Ambrose ambled across the catwalk to reach the cannon's computer console. In that time, I peered over the side as much as Granak's grip would let me. Both men were alive. Smithson pushed himself up and Trent grasped at his injured leg, screaming in pain.

"You may or may not know this," Ambrose said while typing on the control screen, "but this planet has abundant minerals and metals. I sent a dozen survey teams here to study the planet and determine the prime location to build our facility. All the weapons you see were built using this planet's resources."

I wanted to demand to know how he convinced the Restran government to evacuate its people. But I knew the answer—he forced them, threatened them. Leave or be exterminated. After all, they were only aliens to him.

I feared for Smithson and Trent, but I couldn't ignore the look on Granak's face. His eyes narrowed at Ambrose, his mouth twisted in a deep scowl. Then the two men at the bottom of the pit started coughing. And I felt the heat.

"What's happening?" I asked. Ambrose smiled. "Trent! Smithson! Are you okay?"

The heat grew more intense, and Trent lay on the floor. Smithson tried to stand up and grab the wall, but he snatched his hand back with a scream and fell to the floor. Our eyes met.

"I'm so sorry, Daniel," Smithson said, his voice soft and raspy. Ambrose pressed a button and the cannon fired. A thick beam of pure energy erupted into the Tristain atmosphere and its booming sound smacked against my eardrums. The power behind it was so immense that the aftershock needed an escape. The pit was designed as an exhaust. Flames spewed from the vents and engulfed Smithson and Trent.

TWENTY THREE

I screamed as the energy of the cannon dissipated and the smoke of the exhaust cleared. Sarah King finally accomplished her task. I saved Gregory Smithson once, so long ago. The worst part of it was how meaningless his death seemed to be. And Trent. Their bodies were burnt to smoking, blackened figures. Now that I was alone in this place, my only hope was the very alien that hunted and tried to kill me.

"They died without honor," I said.

"They had no honor to begin with," Granak answered.

"Well said." Ambrose walked back to us. "In less than an hour, there will be millions of deaths without honor."

Even Granak blinked.

"You're going to wait until the fleets are fighting each other, close enough to shoot them down," I said, barely above a whisper. This time instead of a smile, Ambrose confirmed my fear.

"One blast will eradicate them all and the stage will be set for Sarah King and Infinity to make their grand entrances," Ambrose said.

"And once you have your fleet of ships, you will hunt down every non-human in the galaxy and force them to recognize humanity as the dominant species."

Ambrose didn't respond. Up until now he had played around the topic of aliens, never mentioning them in Granak's presence, but what could he say with a non-human standing with us?

With Granak's hand still on the back of my neck, I felt the rumble building in his chest. My words had lit the fuel inside him. He released me and took a step toward Ambrose.

"Humans think of themselves as invincible," Granak said. "Yet, I've slain many of them."

"Granak," Ambrose said. "We have to stay focused. We have almost won."

"No, there is no *we* in this. You humans are low and pitiful. Your bodies break so easily. Yet you claim that you are in control."

"What happened, Granak?" I asked him, wheedling his anger. "You were attacked, weren't you?"

I took a shot in the dark and hit on target.

"The giant ship of silver came to our planet. Attacked my people."

The Echelon. Smithson had told me that Sarah King took out her frustrations on non-humans.

Ambrose knew what was happening. He tried to take control of the situation by moving to attack Granak. He punched with his bionic arm, but Granak caught it. His claws extended and his teeth barred. He growled at Ambrose. He dug his claws into the metal arm. Ambrose thrust his right foot into Granak's stomach. His leg must have been bionic, too, because the hit made Granak release his hold and tumble to the ground. But even after a hit like that, he stood up without nursing his wound.

The two guards who had pushed Smithson and Trent advanced and aimed their weapons at Granak, but their leader was in the way. I used the opportunity to throw my shoulder into them. One fell to the ground and the other into the pit. I stuck my foot out to catch myself from falling, and turned to see the guard get up. I kicked him multiple times until he stopped struggling. At his belt was a small, straight dagger. I knelt down with my back to him and grabbed it, then cut the strap around my wrists.

There were more guards, and Ambrose and Granak wouldn't ignore me forever. I grabbed the unconscious guard's rifle and took cover behind the closest box. If I peeked over the top, I could see them. Granak punched Ambrose, trying to cut with his claws, but Ambrose deflected with his bionic arm. None of the scratches or damage seemed to hurt him.

They reminded me of the fight against my friend, Jason Hobbes, when he had become a cyborg. They were strong, but Granak proved himself to have more strength than humans. His downfall was his hotheadedness and arrogance. To the right, a handful of warehouse workers fled toward a rear gate. Four soldiers passed them on their way in. I aimed the rifle at them and let out a flurry of blue discharges. Two went down and the others returned fire. I jumped to the side as the box behind me burst into flames. Most of these packages were flammable, so if I wanted to prevent the facility from going boom while I was still inside, the fight had to be close enough for hand-to-hand combat. I didn't have my sword or my revolver, but I'd kept the dagger. I leapt as the fiery box exploded. Fortunately, none of the flames passed to other containers, but if we continued the fight, it would only be a matter of time.

I quickly crawled behind containers and workstations as the soldiers yelled and searched for me. There had to be weapons I could use somewhere in this facility. Risking my position, I opened a large container. The moment a soldier spotted movement, he shot a blue hole through the lid.

"You're going to blow us all up!" I yelled, hoping he would hold his fire and advance closer. Inside the container were, of all things, grenades. Nothing I could use.

No, wait.

Multiple varieties were placed inside the container. I ducked as another discharge almost vaporized my head. A crash from across the facility drew my attention. Whether it was Granak or Ambrose, I didn't know and didn't care. If it drew my attention, maybe it drew the soldiers' attentions, too. In fact, as both men turned toward the commotion, I grabbed one of every grenade and moved to behind a nearby computer station.

Two of the four grenades wouldn't work. They were explosive and would take out this entire installation. That being said, I attached one to my belt. If things escalated to the point where I couldn't stop Ambrose and Granak, I would activate the grenades and blow up the whole fluxing place. It wouldn't be the first time I acted drastically.

The other two grenades were smoke and EMP. The last time I fought against the cyborgs, an EMP disabled their bionic bodies. It could also disable the cannon, and the smoke could provide the cover I needed. I just had to get close enough.

The guards resumed their search, except now there were four instead of two. Flux. Each moved in a different direction. Using my bionic eye, I scanned the surrounding area. No flammable material was detected by the soldier on the far right, so I sidestepped from cover and fired the rifle. The first shot missed, but the second hit him square in the chest.

"There he is!" one shouted and they all turned toward me.

I moved farther back into the facility and barely avoided their blue fireballs. Fifteen meters ahead I found a narrow corridor that gave me a chance to turn the advantage in my favor, assuming no other guards waited for me on the other side.

I shot a few rounds above the soldiers, careful not to hit anything that could explode. They took cover and gave me a chance to run to the corridor. The other side was an extension of the warehouse—boxes and crates of what I could only assume were weapons. The split second I took to survey the area proved to be a mistake, because in that moment a soldier crashed into me.

His weapon clattered to the ground. As he reached out for it, I brought my boot down on his hand. He yelled as I rolled over, and kicked the weapon away from him. Both of us stood at the same time and exchanged blows. He threw his right fist at me, but I blocked it with my forearm. He reached in and grappled with me. We still stood at the end of the open corridor, vulnerable to attack. The three soldiers advanced and shot at us with no regard for their comrade. I twisted quickly to put the soldier in between me and the blast. He went limp when it hit. I dodged the second and third blasts and reached for the smoke grenade at my belt.

I pulled the pin, counted to three, and threw it back into the corridor. The soldiers yelled, the grenade popped, and smoke poured out. They coughed violently and I returned to the corridor. My bionic eye scanned over each of their hunched figures. I inhaled deeply, held my breath, and ran toward them knowing full well that the more actively I fought, the shorter I could hold it in and the weaker I'd be.

I grabbed the first soldier and rammed his head against the wall. Soldier number two turned. I punched him in the face and heard his nose crack. He fell. The third guard swung his arms wildly in an attempt to hit me. My vision blurred and my lungs burned for air. I had to get out of the smoke, so I chose the quickest method of disabling the soldier. The next swing he took, I ducked and threw a hard punch at his groin, then ran out of the smoke as my lungs forced my mouth open to suck in oxygen. With the smoke close behind me, I still inhaled it and coughed, but the three soldiers were down . . . for now.

Back in the main room, I saw Ambrose once again at the cannon's control pad. Where was Granak? A loud roar from the far side of the facility gave me the answer. Three Infinity soldiers flanked him and released a barrage of firepower. This was my chance. I ran to the edge of the pit and grabbed the EMP grenade from my belt. If I threw it at the perfect moment, it would blow just as it landed next to Ambrose and the computer station.

I judged what I thought would be the best time to throw. I pulled out the pin, waited a few seconds, and threw the EMP.

"Catch that, you bastard," I muttered.

And he did just that. Ambrose turned, apparently knowing I was there, and caught the grenade. His mechanical hand crushed and disabled it. I had only grabbed the one.

"Nice try, Quinn," he said and threw the debris back at me. The pieces hit my armor and fell to the floor. As he stared me down, I noticed he'd taken a lot of damage. His uniform was slashed across the chest and arms, absorbing blood from various wounds. His metal arm was scratched and punctured in multiple places.

"Ambrose. Please. These are human beings you're going to murder." I didn't expect pleading with him to work, but I was running out of options.

"More than you realize, I'm afraid," he said with a sadistic smile. "Collateral damage. And it seems there's an additional ship I'll get to destroy." He pointed to the side wall where the large display screen showed three videos. The tactical screen counted down to less than thirty minutes. But what stopped my heart, or felt like it at least, was the small blip in between two fleets. The ship's designation was mine. What the hell were they doing?

The decision had been made. Not only was my ship in the path of the cannon, but everyone onboard. Tress, Al, and Autumn would all die. I wouldn't let that happen. I pulled out my last two grenades, the kind that would make this entire place go boom.

But I underestimated Ambrose's speed. I thought I had enough time to pull the pins and make peace with myself. Ambrose, even from the other side of the platform, leapt across the pit in a second, grabbed my wrists, and squeezed. My hands, growing numb under his pressure, dropped the grenades. Ambrose kicked them away and, with his metal hand, crushed my left wrist.

I screamed in pain and grabbed my arm when he let go of me. But he used the opportunity to kick me in the stomach, which sent a surge of agony through my chest. I fell to the ground as Ambrose laughed.

"Sarah King will be pleased to see you again, Daniel. I won't kill you, you know. That's her job. I do feel bad that I'll be destroying the artificial intelligence she's long sought, but it was just an unfortunate accident your ship got caught in the crossfire."

I could barely register his words through the pain. I looked around, gasping and trying to find one of the grenades. I pressed against the floor with my right hand and rose to my knees, but Ambrose kicked me again and I nearly rolled into the pit. The catwalk to the platform saved me from falling. Ambrose put his metal foot on my chest, pinning me.

"It's over. We've won," he said.

The growl from across the pit seemed to contradict his statement. I watched Ambrose's eyes grow wide and his mouth gape. I craned my neck to see Granak holding two of the Infinity soldiers, their bodies clawed and bloody. He threw them into the pit and they landed with a dull clunk.

"You overestimate yourself, Ambrose," Granak said. "Someone is going to win today, but that will not be you."

Although Ambrose had thrown the first punch, he looked genuinely frightened at the sight of Granak's advance.

"We had a deal! I paid you for your service!"

"Our business deal was merely a way to facilitate getting close to you and your organization. Now, I will end you and demonstrate to your master who is truly the dominant species."

TWENTY FOUR

Granak pounced on Ambrose and swiped at him, creating a shower of sparks when his claws scratched against his metal forearm. Ambrose retaliated and backhanded Granak, who recovered in seconds. All this time, their hatred and focus was on each other. For the second time they ignored me completely. Why shouldn't they? My wrist was broken, possibly a few ribs, and I thought my teeth might shatter from gritting them together so hard to keep from screaming.

But if I could move . . . if I moved back toward the weapon crates, I would be right in the thick of their fight. My only choice was to turn and move toward the cannon control. I would have little time. Once they saw me, they'd stop fighting and come after me. I had no weapon and my body wanted to give up, but I crawled across the catwalk to the cannon platform. Granak snarled and Ambrose screamed, but I dared not check what happened. I couldn't waste any more seconds.

Once I reached the computer screen, I knelt and looked at the controls. There were various menus and options, but I couldn't find one that would deactivate the cannon. Power built inside it, readying to fire into space and destroy the two fleets. There was no fluxing off switch; what the hell was I going to do? Could I just unplug the damn thing?

There didn't seem to be any cords or electric outlets, which meant they might have been built into the structure itself. I quickly scanned the menu options and stopped when I saw a link to the targeting system. I tapped the button and brought up a display map similar to the one on the facility's large screen. I couldn't deactivate the cannon, but I could reposition it! I searched over the map, trying to find a point where the blast wouldn't hit the fleet or any surrounding planets.

The defense grid. If I destroyed the defense grid surrounding Tristain, then the fleet, whichever one survived, could investigate without being blown to pieces. I also hoped that the cannon blast acted as a kind of flare. If the fleets saw the blast and scanned it, they would detect the high energy level and have no choice but to come. All I needed to do was change the cannon's course.

I touched my right hand to the map and zoomed in to see a computerized simulation of Tristain's orbit. The square-shaped grid markers, similar to satellites, were evenly placed around orbit. Half of them were equipped with plasma technology and the other with missiles. I chose a course that would incinerate two of the markers, which should, in theory, deactivate the connected grid. I hit execute and the cannon grinded against its mechanical parts, turning slightly to the south.

When Ambrose heard its sound, he turned and screamed when he saw me. I smiled and gave him a half-assed Terran salute—one I saw Scott and his men use. The gesture held his attention long enough for Granak to stab him with his claws.

Four sharp points went through Ambrose's back and came out his front, accompanied by a small trickle of blood seeping from the wounds. Granak growled and pulled his hand out, crunching bone along the way.

General Ambrose of Terra fell dead. Granak panted, covered in blood, though I didn't know whose it was. He looked beaten and bruised and scarred. Blood dripped from his nose as he approached me.

"How many of your people did they kill?" I asked. We weren't friends, and he was most likely coming to kill me, but I felt enough sympathy to learn what happened to his people. Sarah King didn't realize that she kicked a beehive when she attacked the Leondren.

"Far too many," he said. "My people are angry, and they demand that blood be spilled. They deserve blood to be spilled!"

"Blood has been spilled," I told him, too tired to even look up. "So much blood . . . this needs to end."

"I agree," he said, reaching me. He grabbed my collar and hoisted me off the ground. "It's time I finish the General's work!"

"What? I don't understand," I said, gasping.

"The humans do not deserve to live. They are small, weak, and die easily. Ambrose had a good plan. Destroy the fleets. Open the way for invasion, but it will not be King's invasion that comes."

"You're going to bring the Leondren here . . ."

"I will contact our planet and tell them to prepare for a glorious war. We will invade your planets and cities and show you how weak and fragile you are. You do not deserve to travel the stars."

He stopped a moment, peering into my eyes.

"I will admit this," Granak snarled. "You have been a worthy opponent, unlike the rest of your pathetic species. But now is the time to obliterate humans. You may watch it happen before you die."

He threw me across the catwalk and I screamed when I landed hard on my wrist, which probably broke the rest of my arm. Tears and sweat burned my eyes.

Is this how it would end? Granak wins and humanity loses? Instead of Sarah King building her empire here, we would have millions of Leondren invading and killing people? I had few options. I might be able to crawl and reach a grenade, but my mind focused solely on Granak. He set it all up, got himself involved with Ambrose, just to get close to humanity so he could attack. He started it all with the death of Damon Derringer.

He may have started it, but I wouldn't lie around and wait to die. I was going to fluxing finish it. I pushed myself up with my good arm and grimaced. Granak had already turned to study the console. He only needed seconds to key in the sequence that would return the cannon to its original firing position. He didn't consider me to be a threat anymore and, therefore, ignored me. That's where I had him.

In his time with humanity, Granak learned that we can die easily and that we cower and flee in the face of fear. The entire Leondren race may have the same outlook toward us, but they weren't considering the big picture—the power of survival and sacrifice.

Damon Derringer worried so much that he was a target that he hid his information with Tress. Granak blamed fear as the reason Damon fled to Karth, but that wasn't the reason at all. He fled to Karth so he would reach me. All that mattered to him was the mission.

I didn't want to die, but I couldn't live knowing that my sacrifice could have saved millions of people. I summoned the rest of my strength; adrenaline quenched my pain and fatigue. Neither of them would matter soon enough.

I charged. My chest and arm protested with every step. I nearly collapsed twice, but my footing held and I continued toward my fate.

Granak turned as my feet clanged loudly against the catwalk. When our eyes met, I released a primal roar filled with my pain, exhaustion, and rage. The noise that echoed throughout the facility sounded inhuman. I threw my arms wide and drove my shoulder into his midsection.

The impact was like hitting a metal bulkhead. I wasn't sure if I broke my collarbone or dislocated my shoulder, but it hurt. The sound of screaming changed from anger to agony; all other cognitive thought was lost in the pain.

Granak was tough, his physique built to endure, but when he pivoted to look at me, he didn't fully turn his body, which caused his footing to be awkward. We fell off the command pedestal into the exhaust chamber. The cannon would fire in minutes and kill us both.

When we hit the ground, I forced myself to think only three words.

Don't let go.

I had landed atop Granak, but it still stole the air from my lungs. I grabbed his clothing. Intense heat emanated from the exhaust vents. In mere seconds, I felt the sweat beading all over my body. My senses were overloaded. All I could smell was blood and body odor. My bionic eye fluctuated between various readings: heart rate, blood pressure, and oxygen levels, combined with static. I heard and felt the energy levels of the cannon rising to optimal levels. The ground trembled, ready to let loose its power. Thick, suffocating heat poured into the chamber.

Granak tried to push me off, but I held on firmly. His fist, denser than a sledgehammer, came down on my right arm. I cried out and let go of him. But for every time he hit my arm, I grabbed him again, and would continue to do so as long as I could. He growled in frustration, hitting me harder and faster. My arm demanded to let go, but I knew if I held on for just another minute, everything would end.

The next time I reached to grab him, I missed. I tried to grab at anything to stop him, but when I touched something firm, I looked up to see one of the dead soldiers. This couldn't be happening. I couldn't fail. Granak moved slowly, reaching to grab the ladder's first rung. If I could crawl toward him, maybe I could pull him back down.

My hand passed over the soldier's uniform and felt something solid. I grabbed the object and hope returned to me— possibly the last time I would feel it. I pointed the soldier's rifle as straight as I could and aimed for Granak's back.

The blue discharge hit him squarely and he stumbled forward with a scorch wound on his back. But it wasn't enough. He stood his ground and continued to climb the ladder. I pulled the trigger again and again, pushing my finger harder each time as if it could add force to the discharge. I shot until the battery had well worn out.

"Fall! You fluxing bastard, fall!"

I clicked the weapon countless times, straining my neck to look up at Granak, who no longer climbed the ladder. Black burn marks covered his back. With a deep groan, the Leondren finally fell to the ground.

I dropped the rifle and sighed. The cannon would fire at any second, and all I had to do was lie here and wait for the exhaust flames to overtake me. But then I remembered Autumn's face, Tress's enthusiastic attitude, and Al's voice. There were still things I wanted to do, people I wanted to live for.

I crawled with only one arm to pull me forward. I knew that I might still die, but dying while attempting to live gave me a sense of pride. Granak's back was hot when I reached him. Somehow he still breathed, but otherwise didn't move. His body had astounding durability. If a war really did break out between humanity and the Leondren, it would be brutal and terrifying. After all, look how much chaos just one of them caused.

I grabbed the first rung of the ladder. Slowly and painfully, I pulled myself up. My body begged me to stop, to let go and wait for the inevitable. I cringed at every sound and froze, sure that the cannon was about to fire. Rung after rung, I jumped with my good foot and held tightly to the next. I was going to see Autumn again, and Tress, and Al. I was going to live. All I needed to do was move a dozen more rungs up.

I reached the top of the chamber and pulled myself onto the platform. I swung my right leg over, but as I followed with the left, a sharp object pierced my calf. I screamed and found Granak's claw in my leg. He was right below me, his eyes wide and terrible, his teeth barred. He pulled hard and I nearly fell back into the chamber, but I managed to grab a conduit connected to the main computer console.

That's when the cannon fired. I pulled hard as the blast released a resounding boom. My leg didn't come with me. Hot, white, blinding pain overloaded my senses. With it came darkness I was sure meant the end of my life.

TWENTY FIVE

My eyes opened; a simple movement that held a complex revelation—I was alive. Whatever damage I sustained was either healed or numbed, or paralyzed because I couldn't move my head to see what the rest of me looked like. The ceiling was white and there were too many odors to describe. I heard beeping.

"You have a ridiculous will to live, my friend." A man's voice spoke to me from where my feet should have been. I recognized it, but my thoughts and memories swam in a thick haze.

The man leaned in so his head was above mine.

Commander Reynold Scott. The last time I saw him, we had fled Terra. He and his men held off the Sentinel forces so we could escape. He survived.

I tried to speak, but only rasped a gurgle. I winced from the dry irritation. Scott placed a small, sealed cup with a straw in front of my lips. I sipped cold, refreshing water.

"Don't try to speak. Let me do the talking. You, young man, are stubborn, ignorant, and the bravest man I've ever had the honor of meeting."

There was little feeling in anything below my neck, but I raised my eyebrows.

"I have someone who wants to see you, but I need to know you understand what I'm saying." I nodded. He returned the gesture and waved his hand for that someone to come in. I waited to see Autumn's face, or even Tress, but the woman who appeared was older. For the first time, I saw a genuine smile cross her face.

"Mr. Daniel Quinn, I wanted to personally thank you for all you've done," Samantha Burns said. "You risked your life and your ship to protect us and show us all what matters most. Because of you and your associates, Terra and Gaia have called for a ceasefire."

A ceasefire? How the hell long was I out? That couldn't have happened overnight.

"Daniel," Scott chimed in. "You're now looking at the Terran delegate who will run for President of the Genesis system."

Genesis. Creating a new way of life. Appropriate. Less than a handful of council members survived, and I thought back to Trent and his pointless death. Both he and Smithson deserved better. Burns told me that in the last week, which is apparently the time I had been unconscious, dozens of men and women from both planets pledged their interest in creating a new council. This one would help maintain control under the Genesis President.

"This is a lot of information, but I needed you to know how grateful I was as soon as you woke up. You honored the memories of all the council who lost their lives." Burns kissed my forehead before she left the room.

I passed out minutes later. When I opened my eyes again, Scott was gone. I made some sounds with my throat and managed to form a couple of words, namely "help" and "water." I felt more now, which meant I wasn't paralyzed. My left arm throbbed, but medication must have been drowning out the pain. When a smaller, much softer hand touched my right one, I turned my head to see Autumn. She gave me a teary grin.

"Hi," she said.

"Hey."

She held a cup of water as I sipped. I choked on some of it and coughed. The sensation ignited pain in my chest.

"Easy, Daniel," she said, caressing my chest with her hand.

In slow, sluggish words, I asked her to explain what happened in space after I last talked to her.

Autumn, the defiant woman she was, took my ship straight into the middle of the two fleets. Tress and Al worked together to send an open message to every ship, and the council made their final plea to end the war. Commander Scott corresponded with them and sent his own message, detailing all events about General Ambrose working for an outside faction and pitting the two planets against one another for mutual destruction. Al communicated reports, graphs, and plans that proved the council's words.

"And then," she said as she wiped another tear from her eye, "we saw the cannon blast. Al pinpointed its location and detected that the defense grid around Tristain was destroyed. Daniel, it was like a beacon of hope. The Terrans and Gaians halted their advances and each sent a handful of ships to investigate Tristain. When they found the warehouse and the weapons, things changed. Many were hesitant. Gaia had lost its military commander so they had no one to lead them, but the council stood up for the people, told them the time for war was over, and peace and prosperity were required to usher in a new era."

She finished the story by describing how a common enemy can be the greatest motivation for change. After seizing Ambrose's records and interrogating captured soldiers, the two planets learned about Infinity.

"Any rational person knows that survival is more important than conquest," I muttered. Now that Terra and Gaia knew what they could lose compared to what they could gain, did that mean the peace treaty would be signed? Technically, all they had now was a ceasefire—an agreement to leave each other alone while a thorough investigation was conducted about Infinity, Ambrose, and the Sentinels.

"What about the atmospheric distortion device above Gaia?"

"When the warehouse was assaulted, all computer systems were shut down. The wireless control for the device failed and it fell from the sky. All conditions on the planet have stabilized, but it's going to take years to regrow all the plants and crops on the planet."

But they would grow back. Gaia and Terra would grow and evolve with their people. As long as both planets agreed to share their resources, the healing process would begin.

Two weeks passed before I could move my upper body. I wore a brace from my wrist to my bicep. Granak shattered the bone and I was told that the doctors had a lot of trouble setting it.

Granak. I often thought about him. When they found me, they also found him. One of my first requests was to see his body.

"Daniel," Autumn said as she looked away from me. "Granak is alive."

At those words, my breath caught in my throat. He lived. She must have seen my anxiety because she held her hands up.

"He's in a coma! It's okay! He's in bad shape and his vitals are low. He hasn't woken up since we found him." The Leondren son of a bitch lived through the cannon's exhaust, but his condition was apparently far worse than mine. Still, I wanted to see him, whether for closure or just to confirm his status. When I tried to move my legs, my left one responded, but not my right. Under the bedcovers, I saw the leg move, but something kept it from lifting up.

"Autumn, what's wrong with my leg?"

She hesitated, but placed a gentle hand on my chest and gave me a soft, reassuring smile.

"Autumn?"

"You're okay, Daniel. You're alive. Let me go get the doctor and we'll talk about everything that happened." she said, then walked out before I could say another word. That's when I remembered the searing pain I felt when the exhaust went off, killing . . . no, rendering Granak comatose. I pressed my hands on the mattress and tried my best to ignore the pain. Soon, I was sitting. My stomach roiled and I wanted to lie back down, but I didn't listen. I grabbed the sheet covering my leg and threw it off the bed.

Stars above.

My leg . . . ended right above the knee, or at least, where my knee used to be. A crude contraption of metal gears and piping composed the rest of my leg.

"You would have bled out if the cannon's exhaustion blast hadn't cauterized your wound," the doctor said as he walked into the room. He studied the charts and bleeps from the computer station. My nausea increased.

"Where did this leg come from?" I asked.

"Mr. Quinn, in order to provide you with the best motion—"

"Tell me where this leg came from!" I screamed, the pressure in my head exploding into spots in my vision.

"Daniel," Autumn whispered as she held my hand.

Tears escaped down my cheeks. The doctor released a sigh.

"Mr. Quinn, this leg came from General Ambrose."

I had a bad feeling that would be the answer—that I now carried a monstrous device used by Sarah King. After hearing it out loud, I leaned over the side of the bed and vomited. Nothing came out but water. Autumn let go and backed up as I convulsed. Three nurses had to force me down while the doctor gave me some kind of sedative.

I succumbed to sleep, and in my dreams I saw the cyborgs being created. Their grotesque bodies outfitted with the bionic machines dropped into the empyreus lake, emerging reborn. Now one of those bionic parts was a part of me.

TWENTY SIX

I spent almost every waking hour staring at the leg, watching it as if it would come alive at the command of Sarah King. In the back of my head I knew that was ridiculous, but in my mind, I felt that every memory and every encounter now housed themselves within the leg, like some kind of permanent disease. Unless I did something about it. When the nurse came in to check on me, she ran to the wall and smacked her hand against the alarm button. Three other nurses came in to see me attempting to tear into my flesh to remove the leg myself. For the second time in a day, or maybe two—I wasn't really keeping track of the hours here—they had to sedate me.

There were no nightmares this time, but a soft, awkward voice woke me from my sleep a while later. I opened my eyes and turned my head to find Tress sitting in the chair beside me, reading a book out loud to himself. My bionic eye, a device I chose and accepted to install into my retinal socket, scanned over the book and read the title: *Even An Alien Can Learn English*.

Tress saw me and closed the book, giving me a nod and soft smile. "Morning," he said in English, though it sounded more like "Mooing." which made me laugh. It felt good to laugh.

"How is your planet doing?" I asked him, and to answer he switched to his native language.

"They are sending out sweeps of messages throughout the surrounding solar systems, beckoning our people to come back. I last heard that 200,000 Restrans returned."

"Your parents?" He looked down and shook his head.

"There's still time," I said, and then looked around the room, careful not to make eye contact with the monstrosity attached to my leg. "Have you seen Autumn?"

"She is taking care of her father's estate, and meeting with the council."

Now that the war had ended, it looked like she took the mantle of her father's job. I wondered if she came back to visit me at all while I slept, or if I scared her when I lost control over my new leg.

I didn't get an answer for another three days. In fact, in that time, no one came to visit me, except for another doctor who claimed to be a therapist. He wanted to talk about my leg, tell me how it was okay, that now the technology could be used for good. I wanted to tell him he could shove it, but I held my tongue. He did speak a certain truth with some of his words. Since the leg had been coated with empyreus, it was the most compatible device for me. But I still felt tainted wearing the damn thing.

On that third day, Commander . . . no, General Scott walked into my room wearing his Sentinel gear, weapon at the ready.

"Let's go, Captain," he said.

"Where?"

"The doctor told me that your injuries are no longer life threatening, nor do you require any critical medical attention. You're free to leave."

My eyes shifted to the leg. In order to leave, I would have to stand on it and use it.

"Captain Daniel Quinn. By order of the Sentinel Guard of Terra, on behalf of the Genesis council, I hereby order you to stand up, walk on that leg, and move your ass."

I blinked and my eyebrows shot up, creating ridges in my forehead. Scott moved to me and grabbed my arm. I protested, but he pulled hard and I fell off the bed onto the cold, tiled floor. My left leg, back, and chest all throbbed in pain.

"Up on your feet, soldier. You have an appointment to keep."

"An appointment? What the flux are you talking about?"

"Let's go," is all he said as he knelt down and wrapped his arm around my chest. I watched him struggle trying to lift me.

This is ridiculous, I thought, but it wasn't Scott's actions that led me to think that—it was my lack of them. People are always going to fall, lose themselves to despair, but a pit like that isn't infinite. There's always a stopping point, and most of the time, we fail to realize that we control it.

I pushed Scott away, turned over on my knees—or knee and metal—and reached up to the bed, pulling myself up into a standing position. Even standing still, my balance failed me and I fell backwards, but Scott stepped behind and caught me. After I managed to keep myself balanced, Scott picked up a pile of clothes from the chair in the corner of the room. He helped me get dressed in a long sleeve blue shirt and black combat trousers. I felt pathetic as he knelt down to lace up a pair of boots. The lack of feeling in my new leg made me sick.

"This will take time, but remember that the first step is always the most important," he said. He threw my arm over his shoulder and we began a slow trek down the hall. I had no idea where we were going, but in truth, it felt incredible to be up and walking, even if the bionic leg wasn't responding to me, or maybe it was I who didn't respond to it? Like Scott said, this would take time.

Nurses and doctors, some I vaguely recognized, applauded as we passed them. I rolled my eyes.

"Seriously, all this just because I'm up and walking?"

"Or maybe it's because you saved their planet," he said. I turned to look at him, and he met my blank stare with a warm grin. "Believe it or not, Captain Quinn, but to a lot of these people, you're a hero."

I didn't respond. Not out of ignorance, but a lack of anything clever to say. I just kept pushing forward, using Scott as a crutch while I tried to get used to the leg. At the same time, a part of my mind still wanted to rip the damn thing off.

He led us to the elevator, and once we hobbled in, he hit the arrow pointing up.

"Why are we going up? Aren't we leaving?"

Again, a warm grin. "No Daniel, *we* are not leaving."

The doors cracked open and a radiant line of sunshine welcomed us. We took a step out and I saw a massive form in front of me, but the sun was too bright, even for my bionic eye. When my eyes adjusted, I saw the Kestrel Belle. She never looked more beautiful to me than in that moment. I took her all in—the dull colors, the elegant falcon shape, and even a dent on one of the wings, which reminded me of an old friend.

Two rows of men and women dressed in Sentinel uniforms lined the way to the cargo bay. A number of people stood in front of the ship, waiting for us. Tress, Samantha Burns, and Autumn Derringer. My eyes glistened and I couldn't hold back the tears.

Burns was the first to walk up to me.

"Captain," she said, extending her hand. I took it and held it firm. "You have the thanks of both Terra and Gaia. Your actions prevented a terrible war from being unleashed on billions of people."

"I can't take credit for that, Ms. Burns," I said, and she directed me to use her first name. "Samantha. Everyone on this roof right now is a hero, all acting together to stop the war. You yourself helped save my life."

She seemed pleased by my answer, but leaned in to me and placed her other hand over our joined ones. "Yes. General Scott, Ms. Derringer, and this wonderful Restran, Tress, all played their parts, but are you familiar with the Earth game called dominos?" I nodded.

"The pieces all fall together only when the first domino is pushed forward. You were the first domino, Captain Quinn. Damon Derringer was the finger that pushed you into action, causing the cascade that saved our worlds."

Samantha Burns left me speechless. Her words were . . . beautiful. I wished I could think up something just as clever and wonderful, but all I could do was kiss her check, and say two words.

"Thank you."

She gave me one more smile, then nodded to General Scott and walked back toward the elevator. I waited for Tress or Autumn to step forward, expecting this to be a line of goodbyes, but they held their ground at the base of the cargo bay door. Scott helped me approach them. For the first time, I saw the object they stood in front of—a large container with a thick oval window at the top.

"Is that?" I asked, but my voice cut out.

"Granak."

Tress and Autumn stepped to the side so I could get my first look at Granak since we fought on Tristain. His hair, the thick mane that covered his head, had been singed to nothing. Over half of his skin had been scorched black by burns, but in all the horror and goose bumps that crawled on my skin, I couldn't help but think of how peaceful he looked.

Granak was my enemy, but his course was charted the day Sarah King launched an attack on his people. His thirst for vengeance reminded me of the feelings I had toward the woman, and now those feelings spread out to her faction. The alien asleep in front of me wanted justice for his race, but his answer for that was the extinction of ours. Granak scared me, and he had to be stopped, but that didn't mean I couldn't feel sympathy for him now. And I did.

"We collect bounty," Tress said in broken English. His words broke me from my trance.

"We?" I said.

"My people back. Family back. All well on Tristain." He smiled wide, I assumed because of his family, but a silver glimmer in his eyes also told me he felt proud. "You want to come with me?" he asked, but Autumn was the one who answered.

"Yes, *we* do."

"I don't understand," I said. "I mean, I don't exactly live a calm life. In the last two years—"

"In the last two years you helped save three planets," Autumn said, resting one hand on my shoulder, the other taking my right hand. "Daniel, you don't have to be alone anymore."

"What about your father's work? What about the council?"

"I've been meeting with them all week. I gave them all of my father's data. It's in good hands."

I looked at her and Tress, searching in their eyes for something that would convince me they were hesitant in joining me, but both looked eager and ready.

"And you," I said to Tress, just to be sure. "You are willing to leave your home and family now that they're back on your planet?"

He nodded. "I want be like you, Captain. I want make difference."

Behind me, General Scott laughed. "If that's not the sign of a good officer, I don't know what is."

From the inside of the Belle, the speaker crackled in static for a moment, then it cleared and a voice spoke.

"Captain, I feel it appropriate to mention that by having two additional people on board, it will give you a chance at social interaction, not to mention the body language you and Ms. Derringer emanate toward each other shows that there is some se—"

"Al, do not finish that sentence!" I yelled before he could embarrass me anymore. Tress, Scott, and Autumn laughed, but her face turned red. I felt the heat in my own as well.

"Shall we board our ship, Captain? Like Mr. Tress said, we have a bounty to collect."

General Scott ordered two of his soldiers to push the containment case onto the ship and lock it into the cargo bay. Coincidentally, they placed him close to where the Karthans put Damon when I brought him home.

The first time I traveled to Karth, I was alone. I had Al, but otherwise I just tried my damnedest to stay under everyone's radar. Now I had an actual crew, and the thoughts of isolation were at their lowest. This began change, and the more I thought about it, the more other things needed to change as well, not just the number of people on my ship.

With Granak secured in the cargo bay, we all stood in front of General Scott and his men. He gave an order and the dozen soldiers saluted us. I nodded at them and extended my hand.

"It's been an honor, General."

"The honor is mine," he said. "Are you sure you don't want to stay? We're going to need a Space Fleet Administrator once the treaty is signed."

"I'll have to pass. I'm just a lowly mercenary."

He looked at Autumn and Tress. "I thought mercenaries worked alone?"

"We not merc then," Tress said, unable to pronounce the full word. "We be . . . pirates!"

Where the flux did he learn the term "pirate"? I suppose I'd have enough time to find out now.

Autumn laughed and gave Scott a tight embrace. "Thank you for everything you've done for me and my family."

Scott stared at me as they stepped apart. "Quinn, now that her father is gone, I have to look out for her. You harm her in any way and I'll be coming after you."

I knew he was joking, but that didn't stop my eyes from widening. The three of us boarded the Belle.

"Captain," Scott called. I turned to look at him and he threw a small device at me. I caught it and looked over the miniscule hard drive. "When the doctors studied Ambrose for the transplant, they discovered this inside his cranium, or the cyborg part of it anyway. It looks like there's a lot of data and memories stored on it. I figured you could use a copy, just in case you decide to investigate this Infinity group."

I closed my hand around the device, and gave Scott a deep nod. We kept our eyes locked on each other until the doors closed.

"Al," I said. "Prepare the ship for departure back to Karth."

"Aye, sir."

"Mr. Tress, take position at the tactical station. Ms. Derringer, you will be stationed at communications."

"Aye-aye," they said together as if they'd practiced, and they climbed toward the bridge.

I kept still for a few minutes, watching the case where Granak slept. Despite the cease-fire and treaty between Terra and Gaia, a larger fight was brewing. Sarah King had been dealt yet another serious blow. Now that she had lost both the empyreus and this sector of space, Infinity would be even more dangerous as they grew more desperate for control.

Granak threatened me with the revelation that his race wanted the same vengeance he craved, and they would one day launch an attack on humanity. How truthful were his words? By stopping him, did we prevent another war, or just postpone it? Either way, humanity needed to stand together and Infinity stood in the way of that.

I couldn't feel Ambrose's leg, its cybernetic wires and mechanisms attached to my biology, but I still felt infected as if King and her faction were a disease. For over five years, I spent my time fleeing from King, but no matter where I traveled, I couldn't escape. If I chose to run again, would she find me?

Maybe it was time to start fighting back. In Smithson's last few hours alive, he told me the cyborgs had been mobilized in different parts of the galaxy, searching for the next great discovery that would turn the tide in Infinity's favor. I knew what I had to do—get the word out, spread the news that humanity was in terrible danger, not only from hostile alien worlds, but from within itself. If Infinity, namely King and her cyborgs, succeeded in their goals, there's no telling how powerful they could become.

But I was going to stop them. I would study the data on Ambrose's hard drive, learn all I could . . . no, all *we* could. With my crew, my ship, and Al, Captain Daniel Quinn would no longer be the hunted. Now I would become the hunter.

The adventures of Daniel Quinn continue in

MECHANIZE

FROM THE LOGS OF DANIEL QUINN

Coming winter 2015!

ACKNOWLEDGEMENTS

During the year I took to write Antagonize, I knew it had to be bigger and better than its predecessor. Did I succeed? Only you can tell me that. But I did everything I could to expand and evolve, and that included bringing in more people to help me accomplish my task.

First I have to thank Robert Jackson-Lawrence. His correspondence and guidance has been invaluable to me. Thank you Rob for the countless days of bouncing ideas, exchanging notes, and sharing our creativity with one another.

Nicole Bartley provided many of the critique notes and edits for Antagonize. Nicole, you were the blacksmith who crafted my book into a steel broadsword. You were the engineer who reinforced the weapons, shields, and engines. This book would not be what it is today without your incredible assistance. I will never be able to thank you enough.

One year ago I helped to create a writing group, Literary Fusion, and I have to thank everyone in that group for all the amazing feedback I received concerning my writing style and craft. Thank you for helping me sharpen my blade and reinforce my shields.

Lauren and Patrick were my first beta readers for the Daniel Quinn series, reading and providing feedback for both Energize and Antagonize. Thank you for helping me launch into this amazing journey.

When I first set out to become a writer, one of the first people I told was my best friend, Jorge. Together, we decided we would become writers, and throughout the last few years we've helped to keep each other motivated. Jorge, you will always be one of the key players in helping me become an author.

Feedback, critiques, beta readers, editors, and so much more are paramount when publishing a book. But there was one person who provided invaluable support in other areas, such as letting me sit at the computer for hours on end, writing. This person kept our children away from the computer while I worked hard to finish my story. Every time I wavered in my confidence and wanted to stop, this person pushed me forward and kept me standing. Cecelia, you are the most unbelievable person in the world. Thank you for everything you've done for me. Thank you for believing in me on this literary journey. I know you'll always be there to support my writing, but my favorite story, above all others, is our story.

Thomas R. Manning is the author of
Energize and Antagonize: From the Logs of Daniel Quinn. Born
just outside the city of Pittsburgh, Pennsylvania, Thomas spent his
life in the worlds of creativity and imagination, whether through
drawing comic books, performing in school musicals,
or writing stories.

His love of science fiction inspired the Daniel Quinn series, but
Thomas is excited to share many other stories in various genres in
the near future. For more information, visit
www.thomasrmanning.com

"Like" Thomas R. Manning on Facebook:
www.facebook.com/authorthomasraymann

"Follow" Thomas R. Manning on Twitter:
www.twitter.com/thomasrmanning